Salted With Fire

George MacDonald

1st WORLD
LIBRARY
Literary Society

Salted With Fire

George MacDonald

© 1st World Library – Literary Society, 2004
PO Box 2211
Fairfield, IA 52556
www.1stworldlibrary.org
First Edition

LCCN: 2004195299

Softcover ISBN: 1-4218-0130-2
Hardcover ISBN: 1-4218-0030-6
eBook ISBN: 1-4218-0230-9

Purchase *"Salted With Fire"*
as a traditional bound book at:
www.1stWorldLibrary.org/purchase.asp?ISBN=1-4218-0130-2

1st World Library Literary Society is a nonprofit
organization dedicated to promoting literacy by:

- Creating a free internet library accessible from any
  computer worldwide.
- Hosting writing competitions and offering book
  publishing scholarships.

Readers interested in supporting literacy
through sponsorship, donations or
membership please contact:
literacy@1stworldlibrary.org
Check us out at: www.1stworldlibrary.ORG
and start downloading free ebooks today.

Salted With Fire
contributed by Tim, Ed & Rodney
in support of
1st World Library Literary Society

CHAPTER I

"Whaur are ye aff til this bonny mornin', Maggie, my doo?" said the soutar, looking up from his work, and addressing his daughter as she stood in the doorway with her shoes in her hand.

"Jist ower to Stanecross, wi' yer leave, father, to speir the mistress for a goupin or twa o' chaff: yer bed aneth ye's grown unco hungry-like."

"Hoot, the bed's weel eneuch, lassie!"

"Na, it's onything but weel eneuch! It's my pairt to luik efter my ain father, and see there be nae k-nots aither in his bed or his parritch."

"Ye're jist yer mither owre again, my lass! - Weel, I winna miss ye that sair, for the minister 'ill be in this mornin'."

"Hoo ken ye that, father?"

"We didna gree vera weel last nicht."

"I canna bide the minister - argle-barglin body!"

" Toots, bairn ! I dinna like to hear ye speyk sae scorn-fulike o' the gude man that has the care o' oor sowls!"

"It wad be mair to the purpose ye had the care o' his!"

"Sae I hae: hasna ilkabody the care o' ilk ither's?"

"Ay; but he preshumes upo' 't - and ye dinna; there's the differ!"

"Weel, but ye see, lassie, the man has nae insicht - nane to speak o', that is; and it's pleased God to mak him a wee stoopid, and some thrawn (*twisted*). He has nae notion even o' the wark I put intil thae wee bit sheenie (*little shoes*) o' his - that I'm this moment labourin ower!"

"It's sair wastit upo' him 'at caana see the thoucht intil't!"

"Is God's wark wastit upo' you and me excep' we see intil't, and un'erstan't, Maggie?"

The girl was silent. Her father resumed.

"There's three concernt i' the matter o' the wark I may be at: first, my ain duty to the wark - that's me; syne him I'm working for - that's the minister; and syne him 'at sets me to the wark - ye ken wha that is: whilk o' the three wad ye hae me lea' oot o' the consideration?"

For another moment the girl continued silent; then she said -

"Ye maun be i' the richt, father! I believe 't, though I canna jist *see* 't. A body canna like a'body, and the minister's jist the ae man I canna bide."

"Ay could ye, gi'en ye lo'ed the *ane* as he oucht to be

George MacDonald

lo'ed, and as ye maun learn to lo'e him."

"Weel I'm no come to that wi' the minister yet!"

"It's a trowth - but a sair pity, my dautie *(daughter - darling)*."

"He provokes me the w'y that he speaks to ye, father - him 'at's no fit to tie the thong o' your shee!"

"The Maister would lat him tie his, and say *thank ye*!"

"It aye seems to me he has sic a scrimpit way o' believin'! It's no like believin' at a'! He winna trust him for naething that he hasna his ain word, or some ither body's for! Ca' ye that lippenin' til him?"

It was now the father's turn to be silent for a moment. Then he said, -

"Lea' the judgin' o' him to his ain maister, lassie. I ha'e seen him whiles sair concernt for ither fowk."

"'At they wouldna hand wi' *him,* and war condemnt in consequence - wasna that it?"

"I canna answer ye that, bairn."

"Weel, I ken he doesna like you - no ae wee bit. He's aye girdin at ye to ither fowk!"

"May be: the mair's the need I sud lo'e him."

"But noo *can* ye, father?"

"There's naething, o' late, I ha'e to be sae gratefu' for to

Him as that I can. But I confess I had lang to try sair!"

"The mair I was to try, the mair I jist couldna."

"But ye could try; and He could help ye!"

"I dinna ken; I only ken that sae ye say, and I maun believe ye. Nane the mair can I see hoo it's ever to be broucht aboot."

"No more can I, though I ken it can be. But just think, my ain Maggie, hoo would onybody ken that ever ane o' 's was his disciple, gien we war aye argle-barglin aboot the holiest things - at least what the minister coonts the holiest, though may be I think I ken better? It's whan twa o' 's strive that what's ca'd a schism begins, and I jist winna, please God - and it does please him! He never said, Ye maun a' think the same gait, but he did say, Ye man a' loe are anither, and no strive!"

"Ye dinna aye gang to his kirk, father!"

"Na, for I'm jist feared sometimes lest I should stop loein him. It matters little about gaein to the kirk ilka Sunday, but it matters a heap aboot aye loein are anither; and whiles he says things aboot the mind o' God, sic that it's a' I can dee to sit still."

"Weel, father, I dinna believe that I can lo'e him ony the day; sae, wi' yer leave, I s' be awa to Stanecross afore he comes."

"Gang yer wa's, lassie, and the Lord gang wi' ye, as ance he did wi' them that gaed to Emmaus."

With her shoes in her hand, the girl was leaving the house when her father called after her -

"Hoo's folk to ken that I provide for my ain, whan my bairn gangs unshod? Tak aff yer shune gin ye like when ye're oot o' the toon."

"Are ye sure there's nae hypocrisy aboot sic a fause show, father?" asked Maggie, laughing, "I maun hide them better!"

As she spoke she put the shoes in the empty bag she carried for the chaff. "There's a hidin' o' what I hae - no a pretendin' to hae what I haena! - Is' be hame in guid time for yer tay, father. - I can gang a heap better withoot them!" she added, as she threw the bag over her shoulder. "I'll put them on whan I come to the heather," she concluded.

"Ay, ay; gang yer wa's, and lea' me to the wark ye haena the grace to adverteeze by weirin' o' 't."

Maggie looked in at the window as she passed it on her way, to get a last sight of her father. The sun was shining into the little bare room, and her shadow fell upon him as she passed him; but his form lingered clear in the close chamber of her mind after she had left him far. And it was not her shadow she had seen, but the shadow, rather, of a great peace that rested concentred upon him as he bowed over his last, his mind fixed indeed upon his work, but far more occupied with the affairs of quite another region. Mind and soul were each so absorbed in its accustomed labour that never did either interfere with that of the other. His shoemaking lost nothing when he was deepest sunk in some one or other of the words of his

Lord, which he sought eagerly to understand - nay, I imagine his shoemaking gained thereby. In his leisure hours, not a great, he was yet an intense reader; but it was nothing in any book that now occupied him; it was the live good news, the man Jesus Christ himself. In thought, in love, in imagination, that man dwelt in him, was alive in him, and made him alive. This moment He was with him, had come to visit him - yet was never far from him - was present always with an individuality that never quenched but was continually developing his own. For the soutar absolutely believed in the Lord of Life, was always trying to do the things he said, and to keep his words abiding in him. Therefore was he what the parson called a mystic, and was the most practical man in the neighbourhood; therefore did he make the best shoes, because the Word of the Lord abode in him.

The door opened, and the minister came into the kitchen. The soutar always worked in the kitchen, to be near his daughter, whose presence never interrupted either his work or his thought, or even his prayers - which often seemed as involuntary as a vital automatic impulse.

"It's a grand day!" said the minister. "It aye seems to me that just on such a day will the Lord come, nobody expecting him, and the folk all following their various callings - as when the flood came and astonished them."

The man was but reflecting, without knowing it, what the soutar had been saying the last time they encountered; neither did he think, at the moment, that the Lord himself had said something like it first.

"And I was thinkin, this vera meenute," returned the soutar, "sic a bonny day as it was for the Lord to gang aboot amang his ain fowk. I was thinkin maybe he was come upon Maggie, and was walkin wi' her up the hill to Stanecross - nearer til her, maybe, nor she could hear or see or think!"

"Ye're a deal taen up wi' vain imaiginins, MacLear!" rejoined the minister, tartly. "What scriptur hae ye for sic a wanderin' invention, o' no practical value?"

"'Deed, sir, what scriptur hed I for takin my brakwast this mornin, or ony mornin? Yet I never luik for a judgment to fa' upon me for that! I'm thinkin we dee mair things in faith than we ken - but no eneuch! no eneuch! I was thankfu' for't, though, I min' that, and maybe that'll stan' for faith. But gien I gang on this gait, we'll be beginnin as we left aff last nicht, and maybe fa' to strife! And we hae to loe ane anither, not accordin to what the ane thinks, or what the ither thinks, but accordin as each kens the Maister loes the ither, for he loes the twa o' us thegither."

"But hoo ken ye that he's pleased wi' ye?"

"I said naething aboot that: I said he loes you and me!"

"For that, he maun be pleast wi' ye!"

"I dinna think nane aboot that; I jist tak my life i' my han', and awa' wi' 't til *Him*; - and he's never turned his face frae me yet. - Eh, sir! Think what it would be gien ever he did!"

"But we maunna think o' him ither than he would hae us think."

"That's hoo I'm aye hingin aboot his door, luikin for him."

"Weel, I kenna what to mak o' ye! I maun jist lea' ye to him!"

"Ye couldna dee a kinder thing! I desire naething better frae man or minister than be left to Him."

"Weel, weel, see til yersel."

"I'll see to *him*, and try to loe my neebour - that's you, Mr. Pethrie. I'll hae yer shune ready by Setterday, sir. I trust they'll be worthy o' the feet that God made, and that hae to be shod by me. I trust and believe they'll nowise distress ye, sir, or interfere wi' yer comfort in preachin. I'll fess them hame mysel, gien the Lord wull, and that without fail."

"Na, na; dinna dee that; lat Maggie come wi' them. Ye wad only be puttin me oot o' humour for the Lord's wark wi' yer havers!"

"Weel, I'll sen' Maggie - only ye wad obleege me by no seein her, for ye micht put *her* oot o' humour, sir, and she michtna gie yer sermon fair play the morn!"

The minister closed the door with some sharpness.

CHAPTER II

In the meantime, Maggie was walking shoeless and bonnetless up the hill to the farm she sought. It was a hot morning in June, tempered by a wind from the north-west. The land was green with the slow-rising tide of the young corn, among which the cool wind made little waves, showing the brown earth between them on the somewhat arid face of the hill. A few fleecy clouds shared the high blue realm with the keen sun. As she rose to the top of the road, the gable of the house came suddenly in sight, and near it a sleepy old gray horse, treading his ceaseless round at the end of a long lever, too listless to feel the weariness of a labour that to him must have seemed unprogressive, and, to anything young, heart-breaking. Nor did it appear to give him any consolation to be aware of the commotion he was causing on the other side of the wall, where a threshing machine of an antiquated sort responded with multiform movement to the monotony of his round-and-round.

Near by, a peacock, as conscious of his glorious plumage as indifferent to the ugliness of his feet, kept time with undulating neck to the motion of those same feet, as he strode with stagey gait across the cornyard, now and then stooping to pick up a stray grain spitefully, and occasionally erecting his superb neck to give utterance to a hideous cry of satisfaction at his own beauty - a cry as unlike the beauty as ever was discord to harmony. His glory, his legs and his voice, perplexed Maggie with an unanalyzed sense of contradiction and unfitness.

Radiant with age and light, the old horse stood still just as the sun touched the meridian; the hour of repose and food was come, and he knew it; and at the same moment the girl, passing one of the green-painted doors of the farm house, stopped at the other, the kitchen one. It stood open, and in answer to her modest knock, a ruddy maid appeared, with a question in her eyes, and a smile on her lips at sight of the shoemaker's Maggie, whom she knew well. Maggie asked if She might see the mistress.

"Here's soutar's Maggie wanting ye, mem!" said the maid and Mistress Blatherwick who was close at hand, came; to which Maggie humbly but confidently making her request had it as kindly granted, and followed her to the barn to fill her pock with the light plumy covering of the husk of the oats, the mistress of Stonecross helping her the while and talking to her as she did so - for the soutar and his daughter were favourites with her and her husband, and they had not seen either of them for some while.

"Ye used to ken oor Maister Jeames I' the auld land-syne, Maggie!" for the two has played together as children in the same school although growth and difference in station had gradually put and end to their intimacy so that it became the mother to refer to him with circumspection, seeing that, in her eyes at least, Maister Jeames was now far on the way to becoming a great man, being a divinity student; for in the Scotch church, although it sets small store on apostolitic descent, every Minister, until he has shown himself eccentic or incapable of interesting a congregation, is regarded with quite as much respect as in England is accorded to the claimant of a phantom-priesthood; and therefore, prospectively, Jeames was to his mother a man of no little note. Maggie remembered how, when a boy, he had liked to talk with her father; and how her father would listen to him with a curious look on his rugged face, while the boy set forth the commonplaces of a lifeless theology with an occasional freshness of logical presentation that at least interested himself. But she remembered also that she had never heard the soutar on his side make any attempt to lay open to the boy his stores of what one or two in the place, one or two only, counted wisdom and knowledge.

"He's a gey clever laddie," he had said once to Maggie, "and gien he gets his een open i' the coorse o' the life he's hardly yet ta'en hand o', he'll doobtless see something; but he disna ken yet that there's onything rael to be seen, ootside or inside o' him!" When he heard that he was going to study divinity, he shook his head, and was silent.

"I'm jist hame frae peyin him a short veesit," Mrs. Blatherwick went on. "I cam hame but twa nichts ago. He's lodged wi' a dacent widow in Arthur Street, in a flat up a lang stane stair that gangs roun and roun till ye come there, and syne gangs past the door and up again. She taks in han' to luik efter his claes, and sees to the washin o' them, and does her best to hand him tidy; but Jeamie was aye that partic'lar aboot his appearance! And that's a guid thing, special in a minister, wha has to set an example! I was sair pleased wi' the auld body."

There was one in the Edinburgh lodging, however, of whom Mrs. Blatherwick had but a glimpse, and of whom, therefore, she had made no mention to her husband any more than now to Maggie MacLear; indeed, she had taken so little notice of her that she could hardly be said to have seen her at all - a girl of about sixteen, who did far more for the comfort of her aunt's two lodgers than she who reaped all the advantage. If Mrs. Blatherwick had let her eyes rest upon her but for a moment, she would probably have looked again; and might have discovered that she was both a good-looking and graceful little creature, with blue eyes, and hair as nearly black as that kind of hair, both fine and plentiful, ever is. She might then have discovered as well a certain look of earnestness and service that would at first have attracted her for its own sake, and then repelled her for James's; for she would assuredly have read in it what she would have counted dangerous for him; but seeing her poorly dressed, and looking untidy, which at the moment she could not help, the mother took her for an ordinary maid-of-all-work, and never for a moment doubted that her son must see her just as she did. He was her only son; her heart was full of ambition for him; and she brooded on the honour he was destined to bring her and his father. The latter, however, caring less for his good looks, had neither the same satisfaction in him nor an equal expectation from him. Neither of his parents, indeed, had as yet reaped much pleasure from his existence, however much one of them might hope for in the time to come. There were two things indeed against such satisfaction or pleasure - that James had never been open-hearted toward them, never communicative as to his feelings, or even his doings; and - which was worse - that he had long made them feel in him a certain unexpressed claim to superiority. Nor would it

George MacDonald

have lessened their uneasiness at this to have noted that the existence of such an implicit claim was more or less evident in relation to every one with whom he came in contact, manifested mainly by a stiff, incommunicative reluctance, taking the form now of a pretended absorption in his books, now of contempt for any sort of manual labour, even to the saddling of the pony he was about to ride; and now and always by an affectation of proper English, which, while successful as to grammar and accentuation, did not escape the ludicrous in a certain stiltedness of tone and inflection, from which intrusion of the would-be gentleman, his father, a simple, old-fashioned man, shrank with more of dislike than he was willing to be conscious of.

Quite content that, having a better education than himself, his son should both be and show himself superior, he could not help feeling that these his ways of asserting himself were signs of mere foolishness, and especially as conjoined with his wish to be a minister - in regard to which Peter but feebly sympathized with the general ambition of Scots parents. Full of simple paternal affection, whose utterance was quenched by the behaviour of his son, he was continuously aware of something that took the shape of an impassable gulf between James and his father and mother. Profoundly religious, and readily appreciative of what was new in the perception of truth, he was, above all, of a great and simple righteousness - full, that is, of a loving sense of fairplay - a very different thing indeed from that which most of those who count themselves religious mean when they talk of the righteousness of God! Little, however, was James able to see of this, or of certain other great qualities in his father. I would not have my reader think that he was consciously disrespectful to either of his parents, or knew that his behaviour was unloving. He honoured their character, indeed, but shrank from the simplicity of their manners; he thought of them with no lively affection, though not without some kindly feeling and much confidence - at the same time regarding himself with still greater confidence. He had never been an idler, or disobedient; and had made such efforts after theological righteousness as served to bolster rather than buttress his conviction that he was a righteous youth, and nourished his ignorance of the fact that he was far from being the person of moral strength and value that he imagined himself. The person he saw in the mirror of his self-consciousness was a very fine and altogether trustworthy personage; the reality so twisted in its reflection was but a decent lad, as lads go, with high but untrue notions of personal honour, and an altogether unwarranted conviction that such as he admiringly imagined himself, such he actually was: he had never discovered his true and unworthy self! There were many things in his life and ways upon which had he but fixed eyes of question, he would at once have perceived that they were both judged and condemned; but so far, nevertheless, his father and mother might have good hope of his future.

It is folly to suppose that such as follow most the fashions of this world are more enslaved by them than multitudes who follow them only afar off. These reverence the judgments of society in things of far greater importance than the colour or cut of a gown; often without knowing it, they judge life, and truth itself, by the falsest of all measures, namely, the judgment of others falser than themselves; they do not ask what is true or right, but what folk think and say about this or that. James, for instance, altogether missed being a gentleman by his habit of asking himself how, in such or such circumstances, a gentleman would behave. As the man of honour he would fain know himself, he would never tell a lie or break a promise; but he had not come to perceive that there are other things as binding as the promise which alone he regarded as obligatory. He did not, for instance, mind raising expectations which he had not the least intention of fulfilling.

Being a Scotch lad, it is not to be wondered at that he should turn to Theology as a means of livelihood; neither is it surprising that he should do so without any conscious love to God, seeing it is not in Scotland alone that untrue men take refuge in the Church, and turn the highest of professions into the meanest, laziest, poorest, and most unworthy, by following it without any genuine call to the same. In any profession, the man must be a poor common creature who follows it without some real interest in it; but he who without a spark of enthusiasm for it turns to the Church, is either a "blind mouth," as Milton calls him - scornfullest of epithets, or an "old wife" ambitious of telling her fables well; and James's ambition was of the same contemptible sort - that, namely, of distingui-shing himself in the pulpit. This, if he had the natural gift of eloquence, he might well do by its misuse to his own glory; or if he had it not, he might acquire a spurious facility resembling it, and so be every way a mere windbag.

Mr. Petrie, whom it cost the soutar so much care and effort to love, and who, although intellectually small, was yet a good man, and by no means a coward where he judged people's souls in danger, thought to save the world by preaching a God, eminently respectable to those who could believe in such a God, but to those who could not, a God far from lovely because far from righteous. His life, nevertheless, showed him in many ways a believer in Him who revealed a very different God indeed from the God he set forth. His faith, therefore, did not prevent him from looking upon the soutar, who believed only in the God he saw in Jesus Christ, as one in a state of rebellion against him whom Jesus claimed as his father.

Young Blatherwick had already begun to turn his back upon several of the special tenets of Calvinism, without, however, being either a better or a worse man because of the change in his opinions. He had cast aside, for instance, the doctrine of an everlasting hell for the unbeliever; but in doing so he became aware that he was thus leaving fallow a great field for the cultivation of eloquence; and not having yet discovered any other equally productive of the precious crop, without which so little was to be gained for the end he desired - namely, the praise of men, he therefore kept on, "for the meantime," sowing and preparing to reap that same field. Mr. Petrie, on the other hand, held the doctrine as absolutely fundamental to Christianity, and preached it with power; while the soutar, who had discarded it from his childhood, positively refused, jealous of strife, to enter into any argument upon it with the disputatious little man.

As yet, then, James was reading Scotch metaphysics, and reconciling himself to the concealment of his freer opinions, upon which concealment depended the success of his probation, and his license. But the close of his studies in divinity was now near at hand.

CHAPTER III

Upon a certain stormy day in the great northern city, preparing for what he regarded as his career, James sat in the same large, shabbily furnished room where his mother had once visited him - half-way up the hideously long spiral stair of an ancient house, whose entrance was in a narrow close. The great clock of a church in the neighbouring street had just begun to strike five of a wintry afternoon, dark with snow, falling and yet to fall: how often in after years was he not to hear the ghostly call of that clock, and see that falling snow! - when a gentle tap came to his door, and the girl I have already mentioned came in with a tray and the materials for his most welcomed meal, coffee with bread and butter. She set it down in a silence which was plainly that of deepest respect, gave him one glance of devotion, and was turning to leave the room, when he looked up from the paper he was writing, and said -

"Don't be in such a hurry, Isy. Haven't you time to pour out my coffee for me?"

Isy was a small, dark, neat little thing, with finely formed features, and a look of child-like simplicity, not altogether removed from childishness. She answered him first with her very blue eyes full of love and trust, then said -

"Plenty o' time, sir. What other have I to do than see that you be at your ease?"

He shoved aside his work, and looking up with some concentration in his regard, pushed his chair back a little from the table, and rejoined -

"What's the matter with you this last day or two, Isy? You're not altogether like yourself!"

She hesitated a moment, then answered -

"It can be naething, I suppose, sir, but just that I'm growin older and beginnin to think aboot things."

She stood near him. He put his arm round her little waist, and would have drawn her down upon his knees, but she resisted.

"I don't see what difference that can make in you all at once, Isy! We've known each other so long that there can be no misunderstanding of any sort between us. You have always behaved like the good and modest girl you are; and I'm sure you have been most attentive to me all the time I have been in your aunt's house."

He spoke in a tone of superior approval.

"It was my bare duty, and ye hae aye been kinder to me than I could hae had ony richt to expec'. But it's nearhan' ower noo!" she concluded with a sigh that indicated approaching tears, as she yielded a little to the increased pressure of his arm.

"What makes you say that?" he returned, giving her a warm kiss, plainly neither unwelcome nor the first.

"Dinna ye think it would be better to drop that kin' o' thing the noo, sir?" she said, and would have stood erect, but he held her fast.

"Why now, more than any time - I don't know for how long? Where does a difference come in? What puts the notion in your pretty little head?"

"It maun come some day, and the langer the harder it'll be!"

"But tell me what has set you thinking about it all at once?"

She burst into tears. He tried to soothe and comfort her, but in struggling not to cry she only sobbed the worse. At last, however, she succeeded in faltering out an explanation.

"Auntie's been tellin me that I maun luik to my hert, so as no to tyne't to ye a'thegither! But it's awa a'ready," she went on, with a fresh outburst, "and it's no manner o' use cryin til't to come back to me. I micht as weel cry upo' the win' as it blaws by me! I canna understan' 't! I ken weel ye'll soon be a great man, and a' the toon crushin to hear ye; and I ken jist as weel that I'll hae to sit still in my seat and luik up to ye whaur ye stan', no daurin to say a word - no daurin even to think a thoucht lest somebody sittin aside me should hear't ohn me spoken. For what would it be but clean impidence o' me to think 'at there was a time when I was sittin whaur I'm sittin the noo - and thinkin 't i' the vera kirk! I would be nearhan' deein for shame!"

"Didn't you ever think, Isy, that maybe I might marry you some day?" said James jokingly, confident in the gulf between them.

"Na, no ance. I kenned better nor that! I never even wusst it, for that would be nae freen's wuss: ye would never get ony farther gien ye did! I'm nane fit for a minister's wife - nor worthy o' bein ane! I micht do no that ill, and pass middlin weel, in a sma' clachan wi' a wee bit kirkie - but amang gran' fowk, in a muckle toon - for that's whaur ye're sure to be! Eh me, me! A' the last week or twa I hae seen ye driftin awa frae me, oot and oot to the great sea, whaur never a thoucht o' Isy would come nigh ye again; - and what for should there? Ye camna into the warl' to think aboot me or the likes o' me, but to be a great preacher, and lea' me ahin ye, like a sheaf o' corn ye had jist cuttit and left unbun'!"

Here came another burst of bitter weeping, followed by words whose very articulation was a succession of sobs.

"Eh, me, me! I doobt I hae clean disgraced mysel!" she cried at last, and ended, wiping her eyes - in vain, for the tears would keep flowing.

As to young Blatherwick, I venture to assert that nothing vulgar or low, still less of evil intent, was passing through his mind during this confession; and yet what but evil was his unpitying, selfish exultation in the fact that this simple-hearted and very pretty girl should love him unsought, and had told him so unasked? A true-hearted man would at once have perceived and shrunk from what he was bringing upon her: James's vanity only made him think it very natural, and more than excusable in her; and while his ambition made him imagine himself so much her superior as to exclude the least thought of marrying her, it did not prevent him from yielding to the delight her confession caused him, or from persuading her that there was no harm in loving one to whom she must always be dear, whatever his future might bring with it. Isy left the room not a little consoled, and with a new hope in possession of her innocent imagination; leaving James exultant over his conquest, and indulging a more definite pleasure than hitherto in the person and devotion of the girl. As to any conscious-ness in him of danger to either of them, it was no more than, on the shore, the uneasy stir of a storm far out at sea. Had the least thought of wronging her invaded his mind, he would have turned from it with abhorrence; yet was he endangering all her peace without giving it one reasonable thought. He was acting with a selfishness too much ingrained to manifest its own unlovely shape; while in his mind lay all the time a half-conscious care to avoid making the girl any promise.

As to her fitness for a minister's wife, he had never asked himself a question concerning it; but in truth she might very soon have grown far fitter for the position than he was for that of a minister. In character she was much beyond him; and in breeding and consciousness far more of a lady than he of a gentleman - fine gentleman as he would fain know himself. Her manners were immeasurably better than his, because they were simple and aimed at nothing. Instinctively she avoided whatever, had she done it, she would at once have recognized as uncomely. She did not know that simplicity was the purest breeding, yet from mere truth of nature practised it unknowing. If her words were older-fashioned, that is more provincial than his, at least her tone was less so, and her utterance was prettier than if, like him, she had aped an Anglicized mode of speech. James would, I am sure, have admired her more if she had been dressed on Sundays in something more showy than a simple cotton gown; and I fear that her poverty had its influence in the freedoms he allowed himself with her.

Her aunt was a weak as well as unsuspicious woman, who had known better days, and pitied herself because they were past and gone. She gave herself no anxiety as to her niece's prudence, but continued well assured of it even while her very goodness was conspiring against her safety. It would have required a man, not merely of greater goodness than James, but of greater insight into the realities of life as well, to perceive the worth and superiority of the girl who waited upon him with a devotion far more angelic than servile; for whatever might have seemed to savour of the latter, had love, hopeless of personal advantage, at the root of it.

Thus things went on for a while, with a continuous strengthening of the pleasant yet not altogether easy bonds in which Isobel walked, and a constant increase of the attraction that drew the student to the self-yielding girl; until the appearance of another lodger in the house was the means of opening Blatherwick's eyes to the state of his own feelings, by occasioning the birth and recognition of a not unnatural jealousy, which "gave him pause." On Isy's side there was not the least occasion for this jealousy, and he knew it; but not the less he saw that, if he did not mean to go further, here he must stop - the immediate result of which was that he began to change a little in his behaviour toward her, when at any time she had to enter his room in ministration to his wants.

George MacDonald

Of this change the poor girl was at once aware, but she attributed it to a temporary absorption in his studies. Soon, however, she could not doubt that not merely was his voice or his countenance changed toward her, but that his heart had grown cold, and that he was no longer "friends with her." For there was another and viler element than mere jealousy concerned in his alteration: he had become aware of a more real danger into which he was rapidly drifting - that of irrecoverably blasting the very dawn of his prospects by an imprudent marriage. "To saddle himself with a wife," as he vulgarily expressed it, before he had gained his license - before even he had had the poorest opportunity of distinguishing himself in that wherein lay his every hope and ambition of proving his excellence, was a thing not for a moment to be contemplated! And now, when Isobel asked him in sorrowful mood some indifferent question, the uneasy knowledge that he was about to increase her sadness made him answer her roughly - a form not unnatural to incipient compunction: white as a ghost she stood a moment silently staring at him, then sank on the floor senseless.

Seized with an overmastering repentance that brought back with a rush all his tenderness, James sprang to her, lifted her in his arms, laid her on the sofa, and lavished caresses upon her, until at length she recovered sufficiently to know where she lay - in the false paradise of his arms, with him kneeling over her in a passion of regret, the first passion he had ever felt or manifested toward her, pouring into her ear words of incoherent dismay - which, taking shape as she revived, soon became promises and vows. Thereupon the knowledge that he had committed himself, and the conviction that he was henceforth bound to one course in regard to her, wherein he seemed to himself incapable of falsehood, unhappily freed him from the self-restraint then most imperative upon him, and his trust in his own honour became the last loop of the snare about to entangle his and her very life. At the moment when a genuine love would have hastened to surround the woman with bulwarks of safety, he ceased to regard himself as his sister's keeper. Even thus did Cain cease to be his brother's keeper, and so slew him.

But the vengeance on his unpremeditated treachery, for treachery, although unpremeditated, it was none the less, came close upon its heels. The moment that Isy left the room, weeping and pallid, conscious that a miserable shame but waited the entrance of a reflection even now importunate, he threw himself on the floor, writhing as in the claws of a hundred demons. The next day but one he was to preach his first sermon before his class, in the presence of his professor of divinity! His immediate impulse was to rush from the house, and home hot-foot to his mother; and it would have been well for him to have done so indeed, confessed all, and turned his back on the church and his paltry ambition together! But he had never been open with his mother, and he feared his father, not knowing the tender righteousness of that father's heart, or the springs of love which would at once have burst open to meet the sorrowful tale of his wretched son; and instead of fleeing at once to his one city of refuge, he fell but to pacing the room in hopeless bewilderment; and before long he was searching every corner of his reviving consciousness, not indeed as yet for any justification, but for what palliation of his "fault" might there be found; for it was the first necessity of this self-lover to think well, or at least endurably, of himself.

George MacDonald

Nor was it long before a multitude of sneaking arguments, imps of Satan, began to assemble at the agonized cry of his self-dissatisfaction - for it was nothing more.

For, in that agony of his, there was no detestation of himself because of his humiliation of the trusting Isobel; he did not loathe his abuse of her confidence, or his having wrapt her in the foul fire-damp of his miserable weakness: the hour of a true and good repentance was for him not yet come; shame only as yet possessed him, because of the failure of his own fancied strength. If it should ever come to be known, what contempt would not clothe him, instead of the garments of praise of which he had dreamed all these years! The pulpit, that goal of his ambition, that field of his imagined triumphs - the very thought of it now for a time made him feel sick. Still, there at least lay yet a possibility of recovery - not indeed by repentance, of which he did not seek to lay hold, but in the chance that no one might hear a word of what had happened! Sure he felt, that Isy would never reveal it, and least of all to her aunt! His promise to marry Isy he would of course keep! Neither would that be any great hardship, if only it had no consequences. As an immediate thing, however, it was not to be thought of! there could be at the moment no necessity for such an extreme measure! He would wait and see! he would be guided by events! As to the sin of the thing - how many had not fallen like him, and no one the wiser! Never would he so offend again! and in the meantime he would let it go, and try to forget it - in the hope that providence now, and at length time, would bury it from all men's sight! He would go on the same as if the untoward thing had not so cruelly happened, had cast no such cloud over the fair future before him! Nor were his selfish regrets unmingled with annoyance that Isy should have yielded so easily: why had she not aided him to resist the weakness that had wrought his undoing? She was as much to blame as he; and for her unworthiness was he to be left to suffer? Within an hour he had returned to the sermon under his hand, and was revising it for the twentieth time, to perfect it before finally committing it to memory; for so should the lie of his life be crowned with success, and seem the thing it was not - an outcome of extemporaneous feeling! During what remained of the two days following he spared no labour, and at last delivered it with considerable unction, and the feeling that he had achieved his end.

Neither of those days did Isy make her appearance in his room, her aunt excusing her apparent neglect with the information that she was in bed with a bad headache, while herself she supplied her place.

The next day Isy went about her work as usual, but never once looked up. James imagined reproach in her silence, and did not venture to address her, having, indeed, no wish to speak to her, for what was there to be said? A cloud was between them; a great gulf seemed to divide them! He wondered at himself, no longer conscious of her attraction, or of his former delight in her proximity. His resolve to marry her was not yet wavering; he fully intended to keep his promise; but he must wait the proper time, the right opportunity for revealing to his parents the fact of his engagement! After a few days, however, during which there had been no return to their former familiarity, it was with a fearful kind of relief that he learned she was gone to pay a visit to a relation in the country. He did not care that she had gone without taking leave of him, only wondered if she could have said anything to incriminate him.

The session came to an end while she was still absent; he took a formal leave of her aunt, and went home to Stonecross.

His father at once felt a wider division between them than before, and his mother was now compelled, much against her will, to acknowledge to herself its existence. At the same time he carried himself with less arrogance, and seemed humbled rather than uplifted by his success.

During the year that followed, he made several visits to Edinburgh, and before long received the presentation to a living in the gift of his father's landlord, a certain duke who had always been friendly to the well-to-do and unassuming tenant of one of his largest farms in the north. But during none of these visits did he inquire or hear anything about Isy; neither now, when, without blame he might have taken steps toward the fulfilment of the promise which he had never ceased to regard as binding, could he persuade himself that the right time had come for revealing it to his parents: he knew it would be a great blow to his mother to learn that he had so handicapped his future, and he feared the silent face of his father at the announcement of it.

It is hardly necessary to say that he had made no attempt to establish any correspondence with the poor girl. Indeed by this time he found himself not unwilling to forget her, and cherished a hope that she had, if not forgotten, at least dismissed from her mind all that had taken place between them. Now and then in the night he would wake to a few tender thoughts of her, but before the morning they would vanish, and during the day he would drown any chance reminiscence of her in a careful polishing and repolishing of his sentences, aping the style of Chalmers or of Robert Hall, and occasionally inserting some fine-sounding quotation; for apparent richness of composition was his principal aim, not truth of meaning, or lucidity of utterance.

I can hardly be presumptuous in adding that, although growing in a certain popularity with men, he was not thus growing in favour with God. And as he continued to hear nothing about Isy, the hope at length, bringing with it a keen shoot of pleasure, awoke in him that he was never to hear of her more. For the praise of men, and the love of that praise, having now restored him to his own good graces, he regarded himself with more interest and approbation than ever; and his continued omission of inquiry after Isy, heedless of the predicament in which he might have placed her, was a far worse sin against her, because deliberate, than his primary wrong to her, and it now recoiled upon him in increased hardness of heart and self-satisfaction.

Thus in love with himself, and thereby shut out from the salvation of love to another, he was specially in danger of falling in love with the admiration of any woman; and thence now occurred a little episode in his history not insignificant in its results.

He had not been more than a month or two in his parish when he was attracted by a certain young woman in his congregation of some inborn refinement and distinction of position, to whom he speedily became anxious to recommend himself: he must have her approval, and, if possible, her admiration!

Therefore in his preaching, if the word used for the lofty, simple utterance of divine messengers, may without offence be misapplied to his paltry memorizations, his main thought was always whether the said lady was justly appreciating the eloquence and wisdom with which he meant to impress her - while in fact he remained incapable of understanding how deep her natural insight penetrated both him and his pretensions. Her probing attention, however, he so entirely misunderstood that it gave him no small encouragement; and thus becoming only the more eager after her good opinion, he came at length to imagine himself heartily in love with her - a thing impossible to him with any woman - and at last, emboldened by the fancied importance of his position, and his own fancied distinction in it, he ventured an offer of his feeble hand and feebler heart; - but only to have them, to his surprise, definitely and absolutely refused. He turned from the lady's door a good deal disappointed, but severely mortified; and, judging it impossible for any woman to keep silence concerning such a refusal, and unable to endure the thought of the gossip to ensue, he began at once to look about him for a refuge, and frankly told his patron the whole story. It happened to suit his grace's plans, and he came speedily to his assistance with the offer of his native parish - whence the soutar's argumentative antagonist had just been removed to a place, probably not a very distinguished one, in the kingdom of heaven; and it seemed to all but a natural piety when James Blatherwick exchanged his parish for that where he was born, and where his father and mother continued to occupy the old farm.

CHAPTER IV

The soutar was still meditating on things spiritual, still reading the gospel of St. John, still making and mending shoes, and still watching the development of his daughter, who had begun to unfold what not a few of the neighbours, with most of whom she was in favour, counted beauty. The farm labourers in the vicinity were nearly all more or less her admirers, and many a pair of shoes was carried to her father for the sake of a possible smile from Maggie; but because of a certain awe that seemed to pervade her presence, no one had as yet dared a word to her beyond that of greeting or farewell: each that looked upon her became at once aware of a certain inferiority. Her beauty seemed to suggest behind it a beauty it was unable to reveal.

She was rather short in stature, but altogether well proportioned, with a face wonderfully calm and clear, and quiet but keen dark eyes. Her complexion owed its white-rose tinge to a strong, gentle life, and its few freckles to the pale sun of Scotland, for she courted every breeze bonnetless on the hills, when she accompanied her father in his walks, or carried home the work he had finished. He rejoiced especially that she should delight in feeling the wind about her, for he held it to indicate sympathy with that spirit whose symbol it was, and which he loved to think of as folding her about, closer and more lovingly than his own cherishing soul.

Of her own impulse, and almost from the moment of her mother's death, she had given herself to his service, first in doing all the little duties of the house, and then, as her strength and faculty grew, in helping him more and more in his trade. As soon as she had cleared away the few things necessary for a breakfast of porridge and milk, Maggie would hasten to join her father where he stooped over his last, for he was a little shortsighted.

When he lifted his head you might see that, notwithstanding the ruggedness of his face, he was a good looking man, with strong, well-proportioned features, in which, even on Sundays, when he scrubbed his face unmercifully, there would still remain lines suggestive of ingrained rosin and heelball. On week days he was not so careful to remove every sign of the labour by which he earned his bread; but when his work was over till the morning, and he was free to sit down to a book, he would never even touch one without first carefully washing his hands and face. In the workshop, Maggie's place was a leather-seated stool like her father's, a yard or so away from his, to leave room for his elbows in drawing out the lingels (*rosined threads*): there she would at once resume the work she had left unfinished the night before; for it was a curious trait in the father, early inherited by the daughter, that he would never rise from a finished job, however near might be the hour for dropping work, without having begun another to go on with in the morning. It was wonderful how much cleaner Maggie managed to keep her hands; but then to her fell naturally the lighter work for women and children. She declared herself ambitious, however, of one day making with her own hands a perfect pair of top-boots.

The advantages she gained from this constant intercourse with her father were incalculable. Without the least loss to her freedom of thought, nay, on the contrary, to the far more rapid development of her truest liberty, the soutar seemed to avoid no subject as unsuitable for the girl's consideration, but to insist only on its being regarded from the highest attainable point of view. Matters of indifferent import they seldom, if ever, discussed at all; and nothing she knew her father cared about did Maggie ever allude to with indifference. Full of an honest hilarity ever ready to break out when occasion occurred, she was at the same time incapable of a light word upon a sacred subject. Such jokes as, more than elsewhere, one is in danger of hearing among the clergy of every church, very seldom came out in her father's company; and she very early became aware of the kind of joke he would take or refuse. The light use, especially, of any word of the Lord would sink him in a profound silence. If it were an ordinary man who thus offended, he might rebuke him by asking if he remembered who said those words; once, when it was a man specially regarded who gave the offence, I heard him say something to this effect, "The maister doesna forget whaur and whan he spak thae words: I houp ye do forget!" Indeed the most powerful force in the education of Maggie was the evident attitude of her father toward that Son of Man who was even now bringing the children of God to the knowledge of that Father of whom the whole family in heaven and earth is named. Mingling with her delights in the inanimate powers of Nature, in the sun and the wind, in the rain and the growth, in the running waters and the darkness sown with stars, was such a sense of

His presence that she felt like him, He might at any moment appear to her father, or, should it so please Him, even to herself.

Two or three miles away, in the heart of the hills, on the outskirts of the farm of Stonecross, lived an old cottar and his wife, who paid a few shillings of rent to Mr. Blatherwick for the acre or two their ancestors had redeemed from the heather and bog, and gave, with their one son who remained at home, occasional service on the farm. They were much respected by the farmer and his wife, as well as the small circle to which they were known in the neighbouring village - better known, and more respected still in that kingdom called of heaven; for they were such as he to whom the promise was given, that he should yet see the angels of God ascending and descending on the Son of Man. They had long and heartily loved and honoured the soutar, whom they had known before the death of his wife, and for his sake and hers, both had always befriended the motherless Maggie. They could not greatly pity her, seeing she had such a father, yet old Eppie had her occasional moments of anxiety as to how the bairn would grow up without a mother's care. No sooner, however, did the little one begin to show character, than Eppie's doubt began to abate; and long before the time to which my narrative has now come, the child and the child like old woman were fast friends. Maggie was often invited to spend a day at Bogsheuch - oftener indeed than she felt at liberty to leave her father and their common work, though not oftener than she would have liked to go.

One morning, early in summer, when first the hillsides had begun to look attractive, a small agricultural cart, such as is now but seldom seen, with little paint except on its two red wheels, and drawn by a thin, long-haired little horse, stopped at the door of the soutar's house, clay-floored and straw-thatched, in a back-lane of the village. It was a cart the cottar used in the cultivation of his little holding, and his son who drove it, now nearly middle-aged, was likely to succeed to the hut and acres of Bogsheuch. Man and equipage, both well known to the soutar, had come with an invitation, more pressing than usual, that Maggie would pay them a visit of a few days.

Father and daughter, consulting together in the presence of Andrew Cormack, arrived at the conclusion that, work being rather slacker than usual, and nobody in need of any promised job which the soutar could not finish by himself in good time, Maggie was quite at liberty to go. She sprang up joyfully - not without a little pang at the thought of leaving her father alone, although she knew him quite equal to anything that could be required in the house before her return - and set about preparing their dinner, while Andrew went to execute a few commissions that the mistress at Stonecross and his mother at Bogsheuch had given him. By the time he returned, Maggie was in her Sunday gown, with her week-day wrapper and winsey petticoat in a bundle - for she reckoned on being of some use to Eppie during her visit When they had eaten their humble dinner, Andrew brought the cart to the door, and Maggie scrambled into it.

"Tak a piece wi' ye," said her father, following her to the cart: "ye hadna muckle to yer denner, and ye may be hungry again or ye hae the lang road ahint ye!"

He put several pieces of oatcake in her hand, which she received with a loving smile; and they set out at a walking pace, which Andrew made no attempt to quicken.

It was far from a comfortable carriage, neither was her wisp of straw in the bottom of it altogether comfortable to sit upon; but the change from her stool and the close attention her work required, to the open air and the free rush of the thoughts that came crowding to her out of the wilderness, put her at once in a blissful mood. Even the few dull remarks that the slow-thinking Andrew made at intervals from his perch on the front of the cart, seemed to come to her from the realm of Faerie, the mysterious world that lay in the folds of the huddled hills. Everything Maggie saw or heard that afternoon seemed to wear the glamour of God's imagination, which is at once the birth and the very truth of everything. Selfishness alone can rub away that divine gilding, without which gold itself is poor indeed.

Suddenly the little horse stood still. Andrew, waking up from a snooze, jumped to the ground, and began, still half asleep, to search into the cause of the arrest; for Jess, although she could not make haste, never of her own accord stood still while able to keep on walking. Maggie, on her part, had for some time noted that they were making very slow progress.

"She's deid cripple!" said Andrew at length, straightening his long back from an examination of Jess's fore feet, and coming to Maggie's side of the cart with a serious face. "I dinna believe the crater's fit to gang ae step furder! Yet I canna see what's happent her."

Maggie was on the road before he had done speaking.

Andrew tried once to lead Jess, but immediately desisted. "It would be fell cruelty!" he said. "We maun jist lowse her, and tak her gien we can to the How o' the Mains. They'll gie her a nicht's quarters there, puir thing! And we'll see gien they can tak you in as weel, Maggie. The maister, I mak nae doobt, 'ill len' me a horse to come for ye i' the morning."

"I winna hear o' 't!" answered Maggie. "I can tramp the lave o' the ro'd as weel's you, Andrew!"

"But I hae a' thae things to cairry, and that'll no lea' me a ban' to help ye ower the burn!" objected Andrew.

"What o' that?" she returned. "I was sae fell tired o' sittin that my legs are jist like to rin awa wi' me. Lat me jist dook mysel i' the bonny win'!" she added, turning herself round and round. " - Isna it jist like awfu' thin watter, An'rew? - Here, gie me a haud o' that loaf. I s' cairry that, and my ain bit bundle as weel; syne, I fancy, ye can manage the lave yersel!"

Andrew never had much to say, and this time he had nothing. But her readiness relieved him of some anxiety; for his mother would be very uncomfortable if he went home without her!

Maggie's spirits rose to lark-pitch as the darkness came on and deepened; and the wind became to her a live gloom, in which, with no eye-bound to the space enclosing her, she could go on imagining after the freedom of her own wild will. As the world and everything in it gradually disappeared, it grew easy to imagine Jesus making the darkness light about him, and stepping from it plain before her sight. That could be no trouble to him, she argued, as, being everywhere, he must be there. He could appear in any form, who had created every shape on the face of the whole world! If she were but fit to see him, then surely he would come to her! For thus often had her father spoken to her, talking of the varied appearances of the Lord after his resurrection, and his promise that he would be with his disciples always to the end of the world. Even after he had gone back to his father, had he not appeared to the apostle Paul? and might it not be that he had shown himself to many another through the long ages? In any case he was everywhere, and always about them, although now, perhaps from lack of faith in the earth, he had not been seen for a long time. And she remembered her father once saying that nobody could even *think* a thing if there was no possible truth in it. The Lord went away that they might believe in him when out of the sight of him, and so be in him, and he in them!

"I dinna think," said Maggie aloud to herself, as she trudged along beside the delightfully silent Andrew, "that my father would be the least astonished - only filled wi' an awfu' glaidness - if at ony moment, walkin at his side, the Lord was to call him by his name, and appear til him. He would but think he had just steppit oot upon him frae some secret door, and would say, - 'I thoucht, Lord, I would see you some day! I was aye greedy efter a sicht o' ye, Lord, and here ye are!'"

CHAPTER V

The same moment to her ears came the cry of an infant. Her first thought was, "Can that be Himsel, come ance again as he cam ance afore?"

She stopped in the dusky starlight, and listened with her very soul.

"Andrew!" she cried, for she heard the sound of his steps as he plodded on in front of her, and could vaguely see him, "Andrew, what was yon?"

"I h'ard naething," answered Andrew, stopping at her cry and listening.

There came a second cry, a feeble, sad wail, and both of them heard it.

Maggie darted off in the direction whence it seemed to come; nor had she far to run, for it was not one to reach any distance.

They were at the moment climbing a dreary, desolate ridge, where the road was a mere stony hollow, in winter a path for the rain rather than the feet of men. On each side of it lay a wild moor, covered with heather and low berry-bearing shrubs. Under a big bush Maggie saw something glimmer, and, flying to it,

George MacDonald

found a child. It might be a year old, but was so small and poorly nourished that its age was hard to guess. "With the instinct of a mother, she caught it up, and clasping it close to her panting bosom, was delighted to find it cease wailing the moment it felt her arm. Andrew, who had dropped the things he carried, and started at once after her, met her half-way, so absorbed in her treasure trove, and so blind to aught else, that he had to catch them both in his arms to break the imminent shock; but she slipped from them, and, to his amazement, went on down the hill, back the way they had come: clearly she thought of nothing but carrying the infant home to her father; and here even the slow perception of her companion understood her.

"Maggie, Maggie," he cried, "ye'll baith be deid afore ye win hame wi' 't! Come on to my mither. There never was wuman like her for bairns! She'll ken a hantle better nor ony father what to dee wi' 't!"

Maggie at once recovered her senses, and knew he was right - but not before she had received an instantaneous insight that never after left her: now she understood the heart of the Son of Man, come to find and carry back the stray children to their Father and His. When afterward she told her father what she had then felt, he answered her with just the four words and no more -

"Lassie, ye hae 't!"

Happily the moon was now up, so that Andrew was soon able to find the things they had both dropped in their haste, and Maggie had soon wrapped the baby in the winsey petticoat she had been carrying. Andrew took up his loaf and his other packages, and they set out again for Bogsheuch, Maggie's heart all but overwhelmed with its exultation. Had the precious thing been twice the weight, so exuberant was her feeling of wealth in it that she could have carried it twice the distance with ease, although the road was so rough that she went in constant terror of stumbling. Andrew gave now and then a queer chuckle at the ludicrousness of their home-coming, and every second minute had to stop and pick up one or other of his many parcels; but Maggie strode on in front, full of possession, and with the feeling of having now at last entered upon her heavenly inheritance; so that she was quite startled when suddenly they came in sight of the turf cottage, and the little window in which a small cresset-lamp was burning. Before they reached it the door opened, and Eppie appeared with an overflow of question and anxious welcome.

"What on earth - " she began.

"Naething but a bonny wee bairnie, whause mither has tint it!" at once interrupted and answered Maggie, flying up to her, and laying the child in her arms.

Mrs. Cormack stood and stared, now at Maggie, and now at the bundle that lay in her own arms. Tenderly searching in the petticoat, she found at last the little one's face, and uncovered the sleeping child.

"Eh the puir mither!" she said, and hurriedly covered again the tiny countenance.

"It's mine!" cried Maggie. "I faund it honest!"

"Its mither may ha' lost it honest, Maggie!" said Eppie.

"Weel, its mither can come for't gien she want it! It's

mine till she dis, ony gait!" rejoined the girl.

"Nae doobt o' that!" replied the old woman, scarcely questioning that the infant had been left to perish by some worthless tramp. "Ye'll maybe hae't langer nor ye'll care to keep it!"

"That's no vera likly," answered Maggie with a smile, as she stood in the doorway, in the wakeful night of the northern summer: "it's ane o' the Lord's ain lammies 'at he cam to the hills to seek. He's fund this ane!"

"Weel, weel, my bonnie doo, it sanna be for me to contradick ye! - But wae's upo' me for a menseless auld wife! come in; come in: the mair welcome 'at ye're lang expeckit! - But bless me, An'rew, what hae ye dune wi' the cairt and the beastie?"

In a few words, for brevity was easy to him, Andrew told the story of their disaster.

"It maun hae been the Lord's mercy! The puir beastie bude to suffer for the sake o' the bairnie!"

She got them their supper, which was keeping hot by the fire; and then sent Maggie to her bed in the ben-end, where she laid the baby beside her, after washing him and wrapping him in a soft well-worn shift of her own. But Maggie scarcely slept for listening lest the baby's breath should stop; and Eppie sat in the kitchen with Andrew until the light, slowly travelling round the north, deepened in the east, and at last climbed the sky, leading up the sun himself; when Andrew rose, and set his face toward Stonecross, in full but not very anxious expectation of a stormy reception from his mistress before he should have time to explain. When he reached home, however, he found the house not yet astir; and had time to feed and groom his horses before any one was about, so that, to his relief, no rendering of reasons was necessary.

All the next day Maggie was ill at ease, in much dread of the appearance of a mother. The baby seemed nothing the worse for his exposure, and although thin and pale, appeared a healthy child, taking heartily the food offered him. He was decently though poorly clad, and very clean. The Cormacks making inquiry at every farmhouse and cottage within range of the moor, the tale of his finding was speedily known throughout the neighbourhood; but to the satisfaction of Maggie at least, who fretted to carry home her treasure, without any result; so that by the time the period of her visit arrived, she was feeling tolerably secure in her possession, and returned with it in triumph to her father.

The long-haired horse not yet proving equal to the journey, she had to walk home; but Eppie herself accompanied her, bent on taking her share in the burden of the child, which Maggie was with difficulty persuaded to yield. Eppie indeed carried him up to the soutar's door, but Maggie insisted on herself laying him in her father's arms. The soutar rose from his stool, received him like Simeon taking the infant Jesus from the arms of his mother, and held him high like a heave-offering to him that had sent him forth from the hidden Holiest of Holies. One moment in silence he held him, then restoring him to his daughter, sat down again, and took up his last and shoe. Then suddenly becoming aware of a breach in his manners, he rose again at once, saying -

George MacDonald

"I crave yer pardon, Mistress Cormack: I was clean forgettin ony breedin I ever had! - Maggie, tak oor freen ben the hoose, and gar her rest her a bit, while ye get something for her efter her lang walk. I'll be ben mysel' in a meenute or twa to hae a crack wi' her. I hae but a feow stitches mair to put intil this same sole! The three o' 's maun tak some sarious coonsel thegither anent the upbringin o' this God-sent bairn! I doobtna but he's come wi' a blessin to this hoose! Eh, but it was a mercifu fittin o' things that the puir bairn and Maggie sud that nicht come thegither! Verily, He shall give his angels chairge over thee! They maun hae been aboot the muir a' that day, that nane but Maggie sud get a haud o' 'im - aiven as they maun hae been aboot the field and the flock and the shepherds and the inn-stable a' that gran' nicht!"

The same moment entered a neighbour who, having previously heard and misinterpreted the story, had now caught sight of their arrival.

"Eh, soutar, but ye *ir* a man by Providence sair oppressed!" she cried. "Wha think ye's been i' the faut here?"

The wrath of the soutar sprang up flaming.

"Gang oot o' my hoose, ye ill-thouchtit wuman!" he shouted. "Gang oot o' 't this verra meenit - and comena intil 't again 'cep it be to beg my pardon and that o' this gude wuman and my bonny lass here! The Lord God bless her frae ill tongues! - Gang oot, I tell ye!"

The outraged father stood towering, whom all the town knew for a man of gentlest temper and great courtesy. The woman stood one moment dazed and uncertain, then turned and fled. Maggie retired with Mistress Cormack; and when the soutar joined them, he said never a word about the discomfited gossip. Eppie having taken her tea, rose and bade them good-night, nor crossed another threshold in the village.

CHAPTER VI

As soon as the baby was asleep, Maggie went back to the kitchen where her father still sat at work.

"Ye're late the night, father!" she said.

"I am that, lassie; but ye see I canna luik for muckle help frae you for some time: ye'll hae eneuch to dee wi' that bairn o' yours; and we hae him to fen for noo as weel's oorsels! No 'at I hae the least concern aboot the bonny white raven, only we maun consider *him* like the lave!" "It's little he'll want for a whilie, father!" answered Maggie. " - But noo," she went on, in a tone of seriousness that was almost awe, "lat me hear what ye're thinkin: - what kin' o' a mither could she be that left her bairn theroot i' the wide, eerie nicht? and what for could she hae dene 't?"

"She maun hae been some puir lassie that hadna learnt to think first o' His wull! She had believt the man whan he promised to merry her, no kennin he was a leear, and no heedin the v'ice inside her that said *ye maunna*; and sae she loot him dee what he likit wi' her, and mak himsel the father o' a bairnie that wasna meant for him. Sic leeberties as he took wi' her, and she ouchtna to hae permittit, made a mither o' her afore ever she was married. Sic fules hae an awfu' time o' 't; for fowk hardly ever forgies them, and aye luiks doon upo' them. Doobtless the rascal ran awa and left her to fen for hersel; naebody would help her; and she had to beg the breid for hersel, and the drap milk for the bairnie; sae that at last she lost hert and left it, jist as Hagar left hers aneath the buss i' the wilderness afore God shawed her the bonny wall o' watter."

"I kenna whilk o' them was the warst - father or mither!" cried Maggie.

"Nae mair do I!" said the soutar; "but I doobt the ane that lee'd to the ither, maun hae to be coontit the warst!"

"There canna be mony sic men!" said Maggie.

"'Deed there's a heap o' them no a hair better!" rejoined her father; "but wae's me for the puir lassie that believes them!"

"She kenned what was richt a' the time, father!"

"That's true, my dauty; but to ken is no aye to un'erstan'; and even to un'erstan' is no aye to see richt intil't! No wuman's safe that hasna the love o' God, the great Love, in her hert a' the time! What's best in her, whan the vera best's awa, may turn to be her greatest danger. And the higher ye rise ye come into the waur danger, till ance ye're fairly intil the ae safe place, the hert o' the Father. There, and there only, ye're safe! - safe frae earth, frae hell, and frae yer ain hert! A' the temptations, even sic as ance made the haivenly hosts themsels fa' frae haiven to hell, canna touch ye there! But whan man or wuman repents and heumbles himsel, there is He to lift them up, and that higher than ever they stede afore!"

"Syne they're no to be despised that fa'!"

"Nane despises them, lassie, but them that haena yet learnt the danger they're in o' that same fa' themsels. Mony ane, I'm thinking, is keepit frae fa'in, jist because she's no far eneuch on to get the guid o' the shame, but would jist sink farther and farther!"

"But Eppie tells me that maist o' them 'at trips gangs on fa'in, and never wins up again."

"Ou, ay; that's true as far as we, short-lived and short-sichtit craturs, see o' them! but this warl's but the beginnin; and the glory o' Christ, wha's the vera Love o' the Father, spreads a heap further nor that. It's no for naething we're tellt hoo the sinner-women cam til him frae a' sides! They needit him sair, and cam. Never ane o' them was ower black to be latten gang close up til him; and some o' sic women un'erstede things he said 'at mony a respectable wuman cudna get a glimp o'! There's aye rain eneuch, as Maister Shaksper says, i' the sweet haivens to wash the vera han' o' murder as white as snow. The creatin hert is fu' o' sic rain. Loe *him*, lassie, and ye'll never glaur the bonny goon ye broucht white frae his hert!"

The soutar's face was solemn and white, and tears were running down the furrows of his cheeks. Maggie too was weeping. At length she said -

Supposin the mither o' my bairnie a wuman like that, can ye think it fair that *her* disgrace should stick til *him?*"

"It sticks til him only in sic minds as never saw the lovely greatness o' God."

"But sic bairns come na intil the warl as God wad hae them come!"

"But your bairnie *is* come, and that he couldna withoot the creatin wull o' the Father! Doobtless sic bairnies hae to suffer frae the prood jeedgment o' their fellow-men and women, but they may get muckle guid and little ill frae that - a guid naebody can reive them o'. It's no a mere veesitin o' the sins o' the fathers upo' the bairns, but a provision to haud the bairns aff o' the like, and to shame the fathers o' them. Eh, but sic maun be sair affrontit wi' themsels, that disgrace at ance the wife that should hae been and the bairn that shouldna! Eh, the puir bairnie that has sic a father! But he has anither as weel - a richt gran' father to rin til! - The ae thing," the soutar went on, "that you and me, Maggie, has to do, is never to lat the bairn ken the miss o' father or mother, and sae lead him to the ae Father, the only real and true ane. - There he's wailin, the bonny wee man!"

Maggie ran to quiet her little one, but soon returned, and sitting down again beside her father, asked him for a piece of work.

All this time, through his own cowardly indifference, the would-be-grand preacher, James Blatherwick, knew nothing of the fact that, somewhere in the world, without father or mother, lived a silent witness against him.

CHAPTER VII

Isy had contrived to postpone her return to her aunt until James was gone; for she dreaded being in the house with him lest anything should lead to the discovery of the relation between them. Soon after his departure, however, she had to encounter the appalling fact that the dread moment was on its way when she would no longer be able to conceal the change in her condition. Her first and last thought was then, how to protect the good name of her lover, and avoid involving him in the approaching ruin of her reputation. With this in view she vowed to God and to her own soul absolute silence with regard to the past: James's name even should never pass her lips! Nor did she find the vow hard to keep, even when her aunt took measures to draw her secret from her; but the dread lest in her pains she should cry out for the comfort which James alone could give her, almost drove her to poison, from which only the thought of his coming child restrained her. Enabled at length only by the pure inexorability of her hour, she passed through her sorrow and found herself still alive, with her lips locked tight on her secret. The poor girl who was weak enough to imperil her good name for love of a worthless man, was by that love made strong to shield him from the consequences of her weakness. Whether in this she did well for the world, for the truth, or for her own soul, she never wasted a thought. In vain did her aunt ply her with questions; she felt that to answer one of them would be to wrong him, and lose her last righteous hold upon the man who had at least once loved her a little. Without a gleam, without even a shadow of hope for herself, she clung, through shame and blame, to his scathlessness as the only joy left her. He had most likely, she thought, all but forgotten her very existence, for he had never written to her, or made any effort to discover what had become of her. She clung to the conviction that he could never have heard of what had befallen her.

By and by she grew able to reflect that to remain where she was would be the ruin of her aunt; for who would lodge in the same house with *her*? She must go at once! and her longing to go, with the impossibility of even thinking where she could go, brought her to the very verge of despair, and it was only the thought of her child that still gave her strength enough to live on. And to add immeasurably to her misery, she was now suddenly possessed by the idea, which for a long time remained immovably fixed, that, agonizing as had been her effort after silence, she had failed in her resolve, and broken the promise she imagined she had given to James; that she had been false to him, brought him to shame, and for ever ruined his prospects; that she had betrayed him into the power of her aunt, and through her to the authorities of the church! That was why she had never heard a word from him, she thought, and she was never to see him any more! The conviction, the seeming consciousness of all this, so grew upon her that, one morning, when her infant was not yet a month old, she crept from the house, and wandered out into the world, with just one shilling in a purse forgotten in the pocket of her dress. After that, for a time, her memory lost hold of her consciousness, and what befel her remained a blank, refusing to be recalled.

When she began to come to herself she had no knowledge of where she had been, or for how long her mind had been astray; all was irretrievable confusion, crossed with cloud-like trails of blotted dreams, and vague survivals of gratitude for bread and pieces of money. Everything she became aware of surprised her, except the child in her arms. Her story had been plain to every one she met, and she had received thousands of kindnesses which her memory could not hold. At length, intentionally or not, she found herself in a neighbourhood to which she had heard James Blatherwick refer.

Here again a dead blank stopped her backward gaze - till suddenly once more she grew aware, and knew that she was aware, of being alone on a wide moor in a dim night, with her hungry child, to whom she had given the last drop of nourishment he could draw from her, wailing in her arms. Then fell upon her a hideous despair, and unable to carry him a step farther, she dropped him from her helpless hands into a bush, and there left him, to find, as she thought, some milk for him. She could sometimes even remember that she went staggering about, looking under the great stones, and into the clumps of heather, in the hope of finding something for him to drink. At last, I presume, she sank on the ground, and lay for a time insensible; anyhow, when she came to herself, she searched in vain for the child, or even the place where she had left him.

The same evening it was that Maggie came along with Andrew, and found the baby as I have already told. All that night, and a great part of the next day, Isy went searching about in vain, doubtless with intervals of repose compelled by utter exhaustion. Imagining at length that she had discovered the very spot where she left him, and not finding him, she came to the conclusion that some wild beast had come upon the helpless thing and carried him off. Then a gleam of water coming to her eye, she rushed to the peat-hag whence it was reflected, and would there have drowned herself. But she was intercepted and turned aside by a man who threw down his flauchter-spade, and ran between her and the frightful hole. He thought she was out of her mind, and tried to console her with the assurance that no child left on that moor could be in other than luck's way. He gave her a few half-pence, and directed her to the next town, with a threat of hanging if she made a second attempt of the sort. A long time of wandering followed, with ceaseless inquiry, and alternating disappointment and fresh expectation; but every day something occurred that served just to keep the life in her, and at last she reached the county-town, where she was taken to a place of shelter.

George MacDonald

CHAPTER VIII

James Blatherwick was proving himself not unaccept-
able to his native parish, where he was thought a very
rising man, inasmuch as his fluency was far ahead of
his perspicuity. He soon came to note the soutar as a
man far in advance of the rest of his parishioners; but
he saw, at the same time, that he was regarded by most
as a wild fanatic if not as a dangerous heretic; and
himself imagined that he saw in him certain indications
of a mild lunacy.

In Tiltowie he pursued the same course as elsewhere:
anxious to let nothing come between him and the
success of his eloquence, he avoided any appearance of
differing in doctrine from his congregation; and until
he should be more firmly established, would show
himself as much as possible of the same mind with
them, using the doctrinal phrases he had been accustomed to in his youth, or others so like that they would
be taken to indicate unchanged opinions, while for his
part he practised a mental reservation in regard to
them.

He had noted with some degree of pleasure in the
soutar, that he used almost none of the set phrases of
the good people of the village, who devoutly followed
the traditions of the elders; but he knew little as to
what the soutar did not believe, and still less of what

he did believe with all his heart and soul; for John MacLear could not even utter the name of God without therein making a confession of faith immeasurably beyond anything inhabiting the consciousness of the parson; and on his part soon began to note in James a total absence of enthusiasm in regard to such things of which his very calling implied at least an absolute acceptance: he would allude to any or all of them as merest matters of course! Never did his face light up when he spoke of the Son of God, of his death, or of his resurrection; never did he make mention of the kingdom of heaven as if it were anything more venerable than the kingdom of Great Britain and Ireland.

But the soul of the soutar would venture far into the twilight, searching after the things of God, opening wider its eyes, as the darkness widened around them. On one occasion the parson took upon him to remonstrate with what seemed to him the audacity of his parishioner:

"Don't you think you are just going a little too far there, Mr. MacLear?" he said.

"Ye mean ower far intil the dark, Mr. Blatherwick?"

"Yes, that is what I mean. You speculate too boldly."

"But dinna ye think, sir, that that direction it's plain the dark grows a wee thinner, though I grant ye there's nothing yet to ca' licht? Licht we may aye ken by its ain fair shinin, and by noucht else!"

"But the human soul is just as apt to deceive itself as the human eye! It is always ready to take a flash inside itself for something objective!" said Blatherwick.

"Nae doobt! nae doobt! but whan the true licht comes, ye aye ken the differ! A man *may* tak the dark for licht, but he canna take the licht for darkness!"

"And there must always be something for the light to shine upon, else the man sees nothing!" said the parson.

"There's thoucht, and possible insicht intil the man!" said the soutar to himself. - "Maybe, like the Ephesians, ye haena yet fund oot gien there be ony Holy Ghost, sir?" he said to him aloud.

"No man dares deny that!" answered the minister.

"Still a man mayna *ken't*, though he daursna deny't! Nane but them 'at follows whaur he leads, can ken that he verily is."

"We must beware of private interpretation!" suggested James.

"Gien a man hearsna a word spoken til his ain sel', he has na the word to lippen til! The Scriptur is to him but a sealed buik; he walks i' the dark. The licht is neither pairtit nor gethered. Gien a man has licht, he has nane the less that there's twa or three o' them thegither present. - Gien there be twa or three prayin thegither, ilk ane o' the three has jist what he's able to receive, and he kens 't in himsel as licht; and the fourth may hae nane. Gien it comena to ilk ane o' them, it comesna to a'. Ilk ane maun hae the revelation intil his ain sel', as gien there wasna ane mair. And gien it be sae, hoo are we to win at ony trouth no yet revealed, 'cep we gang oot intil the dark to meet it? Ye maun caw canny, I admit, i' the mirk; but ye maun caw gien ye wad win at onything!" "But suppose you know enough to keep going, and do not care to venture into the dark?"

"Gien a man hauds on practeesin what he kens, the hunger 'ill wauk in him efter something mair. I'm thinkin the angels had lang to desire afore they could luik intil certain things they sair wantit; but ye may be sure they warna left withoot as muckle licht as would lead honest fowk safe on!"

"But suppose they couldn't tell whether what they seemed to see was true light or not?"

"Syne they would hae to fa' back upo the wull o' the great Licht: we ken weel he wants us a' to see as he himsel sees! Gien we seek that Licht, we'll get it; gien we carena for't, we're jist naething and naegait, and are in sore need o' some sharp discipleen."

"I'm afraid I can't follow you quite. The fact is, I have been so long occupied with the Bible history, and the new discoveries that bear testimony to it, that I have had but little time for metaphysics."

"And what's the guid o' history, or sic metapheesics as is the vera sowl o' history, but to help ye to see Christ? and what's the guid o' seein Christ but sae to see God wi' hert and un'erstan'in baith as to ken that yer seein him? Ye min' hoo the Lord said nane could ken the Father but the man to whom the Son revealt him? Sir, it's fell time ye had a glimp o' that! Ye ken naething till ye ken God - the only ane a man can truly and railly ken!"

"Well, you're a long way ahead of me, and for the present I'm afraid there's nothing left but to say good-night to you!"

And therewith the minister departed.

"Lord," said the soutar, as he sat guiding his awl through sole and welt and upper of the shoe on his last, "there's surely something at work i' the yoong man! Surely he canna be that far frae waukin up to see and ken that he sees and kens naething! Lord, pu' doon the dyke o' learnin and self-richteousness that he canna see ower the tap o', and lat him see thee upo' the ither side o' 't. Lord, sen' him the grace o' oppen e'en to see whaur and what he is, that he may cry oot wi' the lave o' 's, puir blin' bodies, to them that winna see. 'Wauk, thoo that sleepest, and come oot o' thy grave, and see the licht o' the Father i' the face o' the Son.'"

But the minister went away intent on classifying the soutar by finding out with what sect of the middle-age mystics to place him. At the same time something strange seemed to hover about the man, refusing to be handled in that way. Something which he called his own religious sense appeared to know something of what the soutar must mean, though he could neither isolate nor define it.

Faithlessly as he had behaved to Isy, Blatherwick was not consciously, that is with purpose or intent, a deceitful man. He had, on the contrary, always cherished a strong faith in his own honour. But faith in a thing, in an idea, in a notion, is no proof, or even sign that the thing actually exists: in the present case it had no root except in the man's thought of himself, in his presentation to himself of his own reflected self. The man who thought so much of his honour was in truth a moral unreality, a cowardly fellow, a sneak who, in the hope of escaping consequences, carried himself as beyond reproof. How should such a one ever have the power of spiritual vision developed in him? How should such a one ever see God - ever exist in the same region in which the soutar had long taken up his abode? Still there was this much reality in him, and he had made this much progress that, holding fast by his resolve henceforward no more to slide, he was aware also of a dim suspicion of something he had not seen, but which he might become able to see; and was half resolved to think and read, for the future, with the intent to find out what this strange man seemed to know, or thought he knew.

Soon finding himself unable, however, try as hard as he might, to be sure of anything, he became weary of the effort, and sank back into the old, self-satisfied, blind sleep.

CHAPTER IX

Out of this quiescence, however, a pang from the past one morning suddenly waked him, and almost without consciousness of a volition, he found himself at the soutar's door. Maggie opened it with the baby in her arms, with whom she had just been having a game. Her face was in a glow, her hair tossed about, and her dark eyes flashing with excitement. To Blatherwick, without any great natural interest in life, and in the net of a haunting trouble which caused him no immediate apprehension, the young girl, of so little account in the world, and so far below him as he thought, affected him as beautiful; and, indeed, she was far more beautiful than he was able to appreciate. It must be remembered too, that it was not long since he had been refused by another; and at such a time a man is readier to fall in love afresh. Trouble then, lack of interest, and late repulse, had laid James's heart, such as it was, open to assault from a new quarter whence he foresaw no danger.

"That's a very fine baby you have!" he said. "Whose is he?"

"Mine, sir," answered Maggie, with some triumph, for she thought every one must know the story of her treasure.

"Oh, indeed; I did not know!" answered the parson, bewildered.

"At least," Maggie resumed a little hurriedly, "I have the best right to him!" and there stopped.

"She cannot possibly be his mother!" thought the minister, and resolved to question his housekeeper about the child.

"Is your father in the house?" he asked, and without waiting for an answer, went in. "Such a big boy is too heavy for you to carry!" he added, as he laid his hand on the latch of the kitchen door.

"No ae bit!" rejoined Maggie, with a little contempt at his disparagement of her strength. "And wha's to cairry him but me?"

Huddling the boy to her bosom, she went on talking to him in childish guise, as she lifted the latch for the minister: -

"Wad he hae my pet gang traivellin the warl' upo thae twa bonny wee legs o' his ain, wantin the wings he left ahint him? Na, na! they maun grow a heap stronger first. His ain mammie wad cairry him gien he war twice the size! Noo, we s' gang but the hoose and see daddy."

She bore him after the minister, and sat down with him on her own stool, beside her father, who looked up, with his hands and knees in skilful consort of labour.

"Weel, minister, hoo are ye the day? Is the yerd ony lichter upo' the tap o' ye?" he said, with a smile that was almost pauky.

"I do not understand you, Mr. MacLear!" answered James with dignity.

"Na, ye canna! Gien ye could, ye wouldna be sae comfortable as ye seem!"

"I cannot think, Mr. MacLear, why you should be rude to me!"

"Gien ye saw the hoose on fire aboot a man deid asleep, maybe ye micht be in ower great a hurry to be polite til 'im!" remarked the soutar.

"Dare you suggest, sir, that I have been drinking?" cried the parson.

"Not for a single moment, sir; and I beg yer pardon for causin ye so to mistak me: I do not believe, sir, ye war ever ance owertaen wi' drink in a' yer life! I fear I'm jist ower ready to speyk in parables, for it's no a'body that can or wull un'erstan' them! But the last time ye left me upo' this same stule, it was wi' that cry o' the Apostle o' the Gentiles i' my lug - 'Wauk up, thoo that sleepest!' For even the deid wauk whan the trumpet blatters i' their lug!"

"It seems to me that there the Apostle makes allusion to the condition of the Gentile nations, asleep in their sins! But it may apply, doubtless, to the conversion of any unbelieving man from the error of his ways."

"Weel," said the soutar, turning half round, and looking the minister full in the face, "are *ye* convertit, sir? Or are ye but turnin frae side to side i' yer coffin - seekin a sleepin assurance that ye're waukin?"

"You are plain-spoken anyway!" said the minister, rising.

"Maybe I am at last, sir! And maybe I hae been ower lang in comin to that same plainness! Maybe I was ower feart for yer coontin me ill-fashiont - what ye ca' *rude!*"

The parson was half-way to the door, for he was angry, which was not surprising. But with the latch in his hand he turned, and, lo, there in the middle of the floor, with the child in her arms, stood the beautiful Maggie, as if in act to follow him: both were staring after him.

"Dinna anger him, father," said Maggie; "he disna ken better!"

"Weel ken I, my dautie, that he disna ken better; but I canna help thinkin he's maybe no that far frae the waukin. God grant I be richt aboot that! Eh, gien he wud but wauk up, what a man he would mak! He kens a heap - only what's that whaur a man has no licht?"

"I certainly do not see things as you would have me believe you see them; and you are hardly capable of persuading me that you do, I fear!" said Blatherwick, with the angry flush again on his face, which had for a moment been dispelled by pallor.

But here the baby seeming to recognize the unsympathetic tone of the conversation, pulled down his lovely little mouth, and sent from it a dread and potent cry. Clasping him to her bosom, Maggie ran from the room with him, jostling James in the doorway as he let her pass.

"I am afraid I frightened the little man!" he said.

"'Deed, sir, it may ha' been you, or it may ha' been me 'at frichtit him," rejoined the soutar. "It's a thing I'm sair to blame in - that, whan I'm in richt earnest, I'm aye ready to speyk as gien I was angert. Sir, I humbly beg yer pardon."

"As humbly I beg yours," returned the parson; "I was in the wrong."

The heart of the old man was drawn afresh to the youth. He laid aside his shoe, and turning on his stool, took James's hand in both of his, and said solemnly and lovingly -

"This moment I wad wullin'ly die, sir, that the licht o' that uprisin o' which we spak micht brak throuw upon ye!"

"I believe you, sir," answered James; "but," he went on, with an attempt at humour, "it wouldn't be so much for you to do after all, seeing you would straightway find yourself in a much better place!"

"Maybe whaur the penitent thief sat, some auchteen hunner year ago, waitin to be called up higher!" rejoined the soutar with a watery smile.

The parson opened the door, and went home - where his knees at once found their way to the carpet.

From that night Blatherwick began to go often to the

soutar's, and soon went almost every other day, for at least a few minutes; and on such occasions had generally a short interview with Maggie and the baby, in both of whom, having heard from the soutar the story of the child, he took a growing interest.

"You seem to love him as if he were your own, Maggie!" he said one morning to the girl.

"And isna he my ain? Didna God himsel gie me the bairn intil my vera airms - or a' but?" she rejoined.

"Suppose he were to die!" suggested the minister. "Such children often do!"

"I needna think aboot that," she answered. "I would just hae to say, as mony ane has had to say afore me: 'The Lord gave,' - ye ken the rest, sir!"

But day by day Maggie grew more beautiful in the minister's eyes, until at last he was not only ready to say that he loved her, but for her sake to disregard worldly and ambitious considerations.

George MacDonald

CHAPTER X

On the morning of a certain Saturday, therefore, which day of the week he always made a holiday, he resolved to let her know without further delay that he loved her; and the rather that on the next day he was engaged to preach for a brother clergyman at Deemouth, and felt that, his fate with Maggie unknown, his mind would not be cool enough for him to do well in the pulpit. But neither disappointment nor a fresh love had yet served to set him free from his old vanity or arrogance: he regarded his approaching declaration as about to confer great honour as well as favour upon the damsel of low estate, about to be invited to share in his growing distinction. In his late disappointment he had asked a lady to descend a little from her social pedestal, in the belief that he offered her a greater than proportionate counter-elevation; and now in his suit to Maggie he was almost unable to conceive a possibility of failure. When she would have shown him into the kitchen, he took her by the arm, and leading her to the *ben-end*, at once began his concocted speech. Scarcely had she gathered his meaning, however, when he was checked by her startled look.

"And what wad ye hae me dee wi' my bairn?" she asked instantly, without sign of perplexity, smiling on the little one as at some absurdity in her arms rather than suggested to her mind.

But the minister was sufficiently in love to disregard the unexpected indication. His pride was indeed a little hurt, but he resisted any show of offence, reflecting that her anxiety was not altogether an unnatural one.

"Oh, we shall easily find some experienced mother," he answered, "who will understand better than you even how to take care of him!"

"Na, na!" she rejoined. "I hae baith a father and a wean to luik efter; and that's aboot as muckle as I'll ever be up til!"

So saying, she rose and carried the little one up to the room her father now occupied, nor cast a single glance in the direction of her would-be lover.

Now at last he was astonished. Could it mean that she had not understood him? It could not be that she did not appreciate his offer! Her devotion to the child was indeed absurdly engrossing, but that would soon come right! He could have no fear of such a rivalry, however unpleasant at the moment! That little vagrant to come between him and the girl he would make his wife!

He glanced round him: the room looked very empty! He heard her oft-interrupted step through the thin floor: she was lavishing caresses on the senseless little animal! He caught up his hat, and with a flushed face went straight to the soutar where he sat at work.

"I have come to ask you, Mr. MacLear, if you will give me your daughter to be my wife!" he said.

"Ow, sae that's it!" returned the soutar, without raising his eyes.

George MacDonald

"You have no objection, I hope?" continued the minister, finding him silent.

"What says she hersel? Ye comena to me first, I reckon!"

"She said, or implied at least, that she could not leave the child. But she cannot mean that!"

"And what for no? - There's nae need for me to objeck!"

"But I shall soon persuade her to withdraw that objection!"

"Then I should *hae* objections - mair nor ane - to put to the fore!"

"You surprise me! Is not a woman to leave father and mother and cleave to her husband?"

"Ow ay - sae be the woman is his wife! Than lat nane sun'er them! - But there's anither sayin, sir, that I doobt may hae something to dee wi' Maggie's answer!"

"And what, pray, may that be?"

"That man or woman must leave father and mother, wife and child, for the sake o' the Son o' Man."

"You surely are not papist enough to think that means a minister is not to marry?"

"Not at all, sir; but I doobt that's what it'll come til atween you and Maggie!"

"You mean that she will not marry?"

"I mean that she winna merry *you*, sir."

"But just think how much more she could do for Christ as the minister's wife!"

"I'm 'maist convinced she wad coont merryin you as tantamount to refusin to lea' a' for the Son o' Man."

"Why should she think that?"

"Because, sae far as I see, she canna think that *ye* hae left a' for *him*."

"Ah, that is what you have been teaching her! She does not say that of herself! You have not left her free to choose!"

"The queston never came up atween's. She's perfecly free to tak her ain gait - and she kens she is! - Ye dinna seem to think it possible she sud tak *his* wull raither nor yours! - that the love o' Christ should constrain her ayont the love offert her by Jeames Bletherwick! - We *hae* conversed aboot ye, sir, but niver differt!"

"But allowing us - you and me - to be of different opinions on some points, must that be a reason why she and I should not love one another?"

"No reason whatever, sir - if ye can and do: *that* point would be already settlet. But ye winna get Maggie to merry ye sae long as she disna believe ye loe her Lord as well as she loes him hersel. It's no a common love that Maggie beirs to her Lord; and gien ye loed her wi' a luve worthy o' her, ye would see that!"

"Then you will promise me not to interfere?"

"I'll promise ye naething, sir, excep to do my duty by her - sae far as I understan' what that duty is. Gien I thoucht - which the God o' my life forbid! - that Maggie didna lo'e him as weel at least as I lo'e him, I would gang upo' my auld knees til her, to entreat her to loe him wi' a' her heart and sowl and stren'th and min'; - and whan I had done that, she micht merry wha she wad - hangman or minister: no a word would I say! For trouble she maun hae, and trouble she wull get - I thank my God, who giveth to all men liberally and upbraideth not!"

"Then I am free to do my best to win her?"

"Ye are, sir; and mair - afore the morn's mornin, I winna pass a word wi' her upo the subjeck."

"Thank you, sir," returned the minister, and took his leave.

"A fine lad! a fine lad!" said the soutar aloud to himself, as he resumed the work for a moment interrupted," - but no clear - no crystal-clear - no clear like the Son o' Man!"

He looked up, and saw his daughter in the doorway.

"No a word, lassie!" he cried. "I'm no for ye this meenute. - No a word to me aboot onything or onybody the day, but what's absolute necessar!"

"As ye wull! father," rejoined Maggie. - "I'm gaein oot to seek auld Eppy; she was intil the baker's shop a meenute ago! - The bairnie's asleep."

"Vera weel! Gien I hear him, I s' atten' til 'im," answered the soutar.

"Thank ye, father," returned Maggie, and left the house.

But the minister, having to start that same afternoon for Deemouth, and feeling it impossible, things remaining as they were, to preach at his ease, had been watching the soutar's door: he saw it open and Maggie appear. For a moment he flattered himself she was coming to look for him, in order to tell him how sorry she was for her late behaviour to him. But her start when first she became aware of his presence, did not fail, notwithstanding his conceit, to satisfy him that such was not her intent. He made haste to explain his presence.

"I've been waiting all this time on the chance of seeing you, Margaret!" he said. "I am starting within an hour or so for Deemouth, but could not bear to go without telling you that your father has no objection to my saying to you what I please. He means to have a talk with you to-morrow morning, and as I cannot possibly get back from Deemouth before Monday, I must now express the hope that he will not succeed in persuading you to doubt the reality of my love. I admire your father more than I can tell you, but he seems to hold the affections God has given us of small account compared with his judgment of the strength and reality of them."

"Did he no tell ye I was free to do or say what I liked?" rejoined Maggie rather sharply.

"Yes; he did say something to that effect."

"Then, for mysel, and i' the name o' my father, I tell ye, Maister Bletherwick, I dinna care to see ye again."

"Do you mean what you say, Margaret?" rejoined the minister, in a voice that betrayed not a little genuine emotion.

"I do mean it," she answered.

"Not if I tell you that I am both ready and willing to take the child and bring him up as my own?"

"He wouldna *be* yer ain!"

"Quite as much as yours!"

"Hardly," she returned, with a curious little laugh. "But, as I daur say my father tellt ye, I canna believe ye lo'e God wi' a' yer hert."

"Dare you say that for yourself, Margaret?"

"No; but I do want to love God wi' my whole hert. Mr. Bletherwick, are ye a rael Christian? Or are ye sure ye're no a hypocreet? I wad like to ken. But I dinna believe ye ken yersel!"

"Well, perhaps I do not. But I see there is no occasion to say more!"

"Na, nane," answered Maggie.

He lifted his hat, and turned away to the coach-office.

CHAPTER XI

It would be difficult to represent the condition of mind in which Blatherwick sat on the box-seat of the Defiance coach that evening, behind four gray thorough-breds, carrying him at the rate of ten miles an hour towards Deemouth. Hurt pride, indignation, and a certain mild revenge in contemplating Maggie's disappointment when at length she should become aware of the distinction he had gained and she had lost, were its main components. He never noted a feature of the rather tame scenery that went hurrying past him, and yet the time did not seem to go slowly, for he was astonished when the coach stopped, and he found his journey at an end.

He got down rather cramped and stiff, and, as it was still early, started for a stroll about the streets to stretch his legs, and see what was going on, glad that he had not to preach in the morning, and would have all the afternoon to go over his sermon once more in that dreary memory of his. The streets were brilliant with gas, for Saturday was always a sort of market-night, and at that moment they were crowded with girls going merrily home from the paper-mill at the close of the week's labour. To Blatherwick, who had very little sympathy with gladness of any sort, the sight only called up by contrast the very different scene on which his eyes would look down the next evening from the

George MacDonald

vantage coigne of the pulpit, in a church filled with an eminently respectable congregation - to which he would be setting forth the results of certain late geographical discoveries and local identifications, not knowing that already even later discoveries had rendered all he was about to say more than doubtful.

But while, sunk in a not very profound reverie, he was in the act of turning the corner of a narrow wynd, he was all but knocked down by a girl whom another in the crowd had pushed violently against him. Recoiling from the impact, and unable to recover her equilibrium, she fell helplessly prostrate on the granite pavement, and lay motionless. Annoyed and half-angry, he was on the point of walking on, heedless of the accident, when something in the pale face among the coarse and shapeless shoes that had already gathered thick around it, arrested him with a strong suggestion of some one he had once known. But the same moment the crowd hid her from his view; and, shocked even to be reminded of Isy in such an assemblage, he turned resolutely away, and cherishing the thought of the many chances against its being she, walked steadily on. When he looked round again ere crossing the street, the crowd had vanished, the pavement was nearly empty, and a policeman who just then came up, had seen nothing of the occurrence, remarking only that the girls at the paper-mills were a rough lot.

A moment more and his mind was busy with a passage in his sermon which seemed about to escape his memory: it was still as impossible for him to talk freely about the things a minister is supposed to love best, as it had been when he began to preach. It was not, certainly, out of the fulness of the heart that *his* mouth ever spoke!

He sought the house of Mr. Robertson, the friend he had come to assist, had supper with him and his wife, and retired early. In the morning he went to his friend's church, in the afternoon rehearsed his sermon to himself, and when the evening came, climbed the pulpit-stair, and soon appeared engrossed in its rites. But as he seemed to be pouring out his soul in the long extempore prayer, he suddenly opened his eyes as if unconsciously compelled, and that moment saw, in the front of the gallery before him, a face he could not doubt to be that of Isy. Her gaze was fixed upon him; he saw her shiver, and knew that she saw and recognized him. He felt himself grow blind. His head swam, and he felt as if some material force was bending down his body sideways from her. Such, nevertheless, was his self-possession, that he reclosed his eyes, and went on with his prayer - if that could in any sense be prayer where he knew neither word he uttered, thing he thought, nor feeling that moved him. With Claudius in *Hamlet* he might have said,

My words fly up, my thoughts remain below:
Words without thoughts never to heaven go!

But while yet speaking, and holding his eyes fast that he might not see her again, his consciousness all at once returned - it seemed to him through a mighty effort of the will, and upon that he immediately began to pride himself. Instantly there-upon he was aware of his thoughts and words, and knew himself able to control his actions and speech. All the while, however, that he conducted the rest of the "service," he was constantly aware, although he did not again look at her, of the figure of Isy before him, with its gaze fixed motionless upon him, and began at last to wonder vaguely whether she might not be dead, and come back from the grave to his mind a mysterious thought-spectre. But at the close of the sermon, when the people stood up to sing, she rose with them; and the half-dazed preacher sat down, exhausted with emotion, conflict, and effort at self-command. When he rose once more for the benediction, she was gone; and yet again he took refuge in the doubt whether she had indeed been present at all.

When Mrs. Robertson had retired, and James was sitting with his host over their tumbler of toddy, a knock came to the door. Mr. Robertson went to open it, and James's heart sank within him. But in a moment his host returned, saying it was a policeman to let him know that a woman was lying drunk at the bottom of his doorsteps, and to inquire what he wished done with her.

"I told him," said Mr. Robertson, "to take the poor creature to the station, and in the morning I would see her. When she's ill the next day, you see," he added, "I may have a sort of chance with her; but it is seldom of any use."

A horrible suspicion that it was Isy herself had seized on Blatherwick; and for a moment he was half inclined to follow the men to the station; but his friend would be sure to go with him, and what might not come of it! Seeing that she had kept silent so long, however, it seemed to him more than probable that she had lost all care about him, and if let alone would say nothing. Thus he reasoned, lost in his selfishness, and shrinking from the thought of looking the disreputable creature in the eyes. Yet the awful consciousness haunted him that, if she had fallen into drunken habits and possibly worse, it was his fault, and the ruin of the once lovely creature lay at his door, and his alone.

He made haste to his room, and to bed, where for a long while he lay unable even to think. Then all at once, with gathered force, the frightful reality, the keen, bare truth broke upon him like a huge, cold wave; he had a clear vision of his guilt, and the vision was conscious of itself as *his* guilt; he saw it rounded in a gray fog of life-chilling dismay. What was he but a troth-breaker, a liar - and that in strong fact, not in feeble tongue? "What am I," said Conscience, "but a cruel, self-seeking, loveless horror - a contemptible sneak, who, in dread of missing the praises of men, crept away unseen, and left the woman to bear alone our common sin?" What was he but a whited sepulchre, full of dead men's bones and all uncleanness? - a fellow posing in the pulpit as an example to the faithful, but knowing all the time that somewhere in the land lived a woman - once a loving, trusting woman - who could with a word hold him up to the world a hypocrite and a dastard -

A fixed figure for the Time of scorn
To point his slow unmoving finger at!

He sprang to the floor; the cold hand of an injured ghost seemed clutching feebly at his throat. But, in or out of bed, what could he do? Utterly helpless, he thought, but in truth not daring to look the question as to what he could do in the face, he crept back ignominiously into his bed; and, growing a little less uncomfortable, began to reason with himself that things were not so bad as they had for that moment seemed; that many another had failed in like fashion with him, but his fault had been forgotten, and had never reappeared against him! No culprit was ever required to bear witness against himself! He must learn to discipline and repress his over-sensitiveness, otherwise it would one day seize him at a disadvantage, and betray him into self-exposure!

Thus he reasoned - and sank back once more among the all but dead; the loud alarum of his rousing conscience ceased, and he fell asleep in the resolve to get away from Deemouth the first thing in the morning, before Mr. Robertson should be awake. How much better it had been for him to hold fast his repentant mood, and awake to tell everything! but he was very far from having even approached any such resolution. Indeed no practical idea of his, however much brooded over at night, had ever lived to bear fruit in the morning; not once had he ever embodied in action an impulse toward atonement! He could welcome the thought of a final release from sin and suffering at the dissolution of nature, but he always did his best to forget that at that very moment he was suffering because of wrong he had done for which he was taking no least trouble to make amends. He had lived for himself, to the destruction of one whom he had once loved, and to the denial of his Lord and Master!

More than twice on his way home in the early morning, he all but turned to go back to the police-station, but it was, as usual, only *all but*, and he kept walking on.

CHAPTER XII

Already, ere James's flight was discovered, morning saw Mr. Robertson on his way to do what he might for the redemption of one of whom he knew little or nothing: the policemen returning from their night's duty, found him already at the door of the office. He was at once admitted, for he was well known to most of them. He found the poor woman miserably recovered from the effects of her dissipation, and looking so woebegone, that the heart of the good man was immediately filled with profoundest pity, recognizing before him a creature whose hope was wasted to the verge of despair. She neither looked up nor spoke; but what he could see of her face appeared only ashamed, neither sullen nor vengeful. When he spoke to her, she lifted her head a little, but not her eyes to his face, confessing apparently that she had nothing to say for herself; and he saw her plainly at the point of taking refuge in the Dee. Tenderly, as if to the little one he had left behind him in bed, he spoke in her scarce listening ear child-soothing words of almost inarticulate sympathy, which yet his tone carried where they were meant to go. She lifted her lost eyes at length, saw his face, and burst into tears.

"Na, na," she cried, through tearing sobs, "ye canna help me, sir! There's naething 'at you or onybody can dee for me! But I'm near the mou o' the pit, and God be

George MacDonald

thankit, I'll be ower the rim o' 't or I hae grutten my last greit oot! - For God's sake gie me a drink - a drink o' onything!"

"I daurna gie ye onything to ca' drink," answered the minister, who could scarcely speak for the swelling in his throat. "The thing to dee ye guid is a cup o' het tay! Ye canna hae had a moofu' this mornin! I hae a cab waitin me at the door, and ye'll jist get in, my puir bairn, and come awa hame wi' me! My wife'll be doon afore we win back, and she'll hae a cup o' tay ready for ye in a moment! You and me 'ill hae oor brakfast thegither."

"Ken ye what ye're sayin, sir? I daurna luik an honest wuman i' the face. I'm sic as ye ken naething aboot."

"I ken a heap aboot fowk o' a' kin's - mair a heap, I'm thinkin, nor ye ken yersel! - I ken mair aboot yersel, tee, nor ye think; I hae seen ye i' my ain kirk mair nor ance or twice. The Sunday nicht afore last I was preachin straucht intil yer bonny face, and saw ye greitin, and maist grat mysel. Come awa hame wi' me, my dear; my wife's anither jist like mysel, an'll turn naething to ye but the smilin side o' her face, I s' un'ertak! She's a fine, herty, couthy, savin kin' o' wuman, my wife! Come ye til her, and see!"

Isy rose to her feet.

"Eh, but I would like to luik ance mair intil the face o' a bonny, clean wuman!" she said. "I'll gang, sir," she went on, with sudden resolve " - only, I pray ye, sir, mak speed, and tak me oot o' the sicht o'fowk!"

" Ay, ay, come awa; we s' hae ye oot o' this in a

moment," answered Mr. Robertson. - "Put the fine doon to me," he whispered to the inspector as they passed him on their way out.

The man returned his nod, and took no further notice.

"I thoucht that was what would come o' 't!" he murmured to himself, looking after them with a smile. But indeed he knew little of what was going to come of it!

The good minister, whose heart was the teacher of his head, and who was not ashamed either of himself or his companion, showed Isy into their little breakfast-parlour, and running up the stair to his wife, told her he had brought the woman home, and wanted her to come down at once. Mrs. Robertson, who was dressing her one child, hurried her toilet, gave over the little one to the care of her one servant, and made haste to welcome the poor shivering night-bird, waiting with ruffled feathers below. When she opened the door, the two women stood for a moment silently gazing on each other - then the wife opened her arms wide, and the girl fled to their shelter; but her strength failing her on the way, she fell to the floor. Instantly the other was down by her side. The husband came to her help; and between them they got her at once on the little couch.

"Shall I get the brandy?" said Mrs. Robertson.

"Try a cup of tea," he answered.

His wife made haste, and soon had the tea poured out and cooling. But Isy still lay motionless. Her hostess raised the helpless head upon her arm, put a spoonful of the tea to her lips, and found to her joy that she tried to swallow it. The next minute she opened her eyes, and would have risen; but the rescuing hand held her down.

"I want to tell ye," moaned Isy with feeble expostulation, "'at ye dinna ken wha ye hae taen intil yer hoose! Lat me up to get my breath, or I'll no be able to tell ye."

"Drink your tea," answered the other, "and then say what you like. There's no hurry. You'll have time enough."

The poor girl opened her eyes wide, and gazed for a moment at Mrs. Robertson. Then she took the cup and drank the tea. Her new friend went on -

"You must just be content to bide where you are a day or two. Ye're no to fash yersel aboot onything: I have clothes enough to give you all the change you can want. Hold your tongue, please, and finish your tea."

"Eh, mem," cried Isy, "fowk 'ill say ill o' ye, gien they see the like o' me in yer hoose!"

"Lat them say, and say 't again! What's fowk but muckle geese!"

"But there's the minister and his character!" she persisted.

"Hoots! what cares the minister?" said his wife. "Speir at him there, what he thinks o' clash."

"'Deed," answered her husband, "I never heedit it eneuch to tell! There's but ae word I heed, and that's my Maister's!"

"Eh, but ye canna lift me oot o' the pit!" groaned the poor girl.

"God helpin, I can," returned the minister. " - But ye're no i' the pit yet by a lang road; and oot o' that road I s' hae ye, please God, afore anither nicht has darkent!"

"I dinna ken what's to come o' me!" again she groaned.

"That we'll sune see! Brakfast's to come o' ye first, and syne my wife and me we'll sit in jeedgment upo ye, and redd things up. Min' ye're to say what ye like, and naither ill fowk nor unco guid sail come nigh ye."

A pitiful smile flitted across Isy's face, and with it returned the almost babyish look that used to form part of her charm. Like an obedient child, she set herself to eat and drink what she could; and when she had evidently done her best -

"Now put up your feet again on the sofa, and tell us everything," said the minister.

"No," returned Isy; "I'm not at liberty to tell you *everything*."

"Then tell us what you please - so long as it's true, and that I am sure it will be," he rejoined.

"I will, sir," she answered.

For several moments she was silent, as if thinking how to begin; then, after a gasp or two, -

"I'm not a good woman," she began. "Perhaps I am worse than you think me. - Oh, my baby! my baby!" she cried, and burst into tears.

"There's nae that mony o' 's just what ither fowk think us," said the minister's wife. "We're in general baith better and waur nor that. - But tell me ae thing: what took ye, last nicht, straucht frae the kirk to the public? The twa haudna weel thegither!"

"It was this, ma'am," she replied, resuming the more refined speech to which, since living at Deemouth, she had been less accustomed - "I had a shock that night from suddenly seeing one in the church whom I had thought never to see again; and when I got into the street, I turned so sick that some kind body gave me whisky, and that was how, not having been used to it for some time, that I disgraced myself. But indeed, I have a much worse trouble and shame upon me than that - one you would hardly believe, ma'am!"

"I understand," said Mrs. Robertson, modifying her speech also the moment she perceived the change in that of her guest: "you saw him in church - the man that got you into trouble! I thought that must be it! - won't you tell me all about it?"

"I will not tell his name. *I* was the most in fault, for I knew better; and I would rather die than do him any more harm! - Good morning, ma'am! - I thank you kindly, sir! Believe me I am not ungrateful, whatever else I may be that is bad."

She rose as she spoke, but Mrs. Robertson got to the door first, and standing between her and it, confronted her with a smile.

"Don't think I blame you for holding your tongue, my dear. I don't want you to tell. I only thought it might be a relief to you. I believe, if I were in the same case - or, at least, I hope so - that hot pincers wouldn't draw his name out of me. What right has any vulgar inquisitive woman to know the thing gnawing at your heart like a live serpent? I will never again ask you anything about him. - There! you have my promise! - Now sit down again, and don't be afraid. Tell me what you please, and not a word more. The minister is sure to find something to comfort you."

"What can anybody say or do to comfort such as me, ma'am? I am lost - lost out of sight! Nothing can save me! The Saviour himself wouldn't open the door to a woman that left her suckling child out in the dark night! - That's what I did!" she cried, and ended with a wail as from a heart whose wound eternal years could never close.

In a while growing a little calmer -

"I would not have you think, ma'am," she resumed, "that I wanted to get rid of the darling. But my wits went all of a sudden, and a terror, I don't know of what, came upon me. Could it have been the hunger, do you think? I laid him down in the heather, and ran from him. How far I went, I do not know. All at once I came to myself, and knew what I had done, and ran to take him up. But whether I lost my way back, or what I did, or how it was, I cannot tell, only I could not find him! Then for a while I think I must have been clean out of my mind, and was always seeing him torn by the foxes, and the corbies picking out his eyes. Even now, at night, every now and then, it comes back, and I cannot get the sight out of my head! For a while it

George MacDonald

drove me to drink, but I got rid of that until just last night, when again I was overcome. - Oh, if I could only keep from seeing the beasts and birds at his little body when I'm falling asleep!"

She gave a smothered scream, and hid her face in her hands. Mrs. Robertson, weeping herself, sought to comfort her, but it seemed in vain.

"The worst of it is," Isy resumed, " - for I must confess everything, ma'am! - is that I cannot tell what I may have done in the drink. I may even have told his name, though I remember nothing about it! It must be months, I think, since I tasted a drop till last night; and now I've done it again, and I'm not fit he should ever cast a look at me! My heart's just like to break when I think I may have been false to him, as well as false to his child! If all the devils would but come and tear me, I would say, thank ye, sirs!"

"My dear," came the voice of the parson from where he sat listening to every word she uttered, "my dear, naething but the han' o' the Son o' Man'll come nigh ye oot o' the dark, saft-strokin yer hert, and closin up the terrible gash intil't. I' the name o' God, the saviour o' men, I tell ye, dautie, the day 'ill come whan ye'll smile i' the vera face o' the Lord himsel, at the thoucht o' what he has broucht ye throuw! Lord Christ, haud a guid grup o' thy puir bairn and hers, and gie her back her ain. Thy wull be deen! - and that thy wull's a' for redemption! - Gang on wi' yer tale, my lassie."

"'Deed, sir, I can say nae mair - and seem to hae nae mair to say. - I'm some - some sick like!"

She fell back on the sofa, white as death.

The parson was a big man; he took her up in his arms, and carried her to a room they had always ready on the chance of a visit from "one of the least of these."

At the top of the stair stood their little daughter, a child of five or six, wanting to go down to her mother, and wondering why she was not permitted.

"Who is it, moder?" she whispered, as Mrs. Robertson passed her, following her husband and Isy. "Is she very dead?"

"No, darling," answered her mother; "it is an angel that has lost her way, and is tired - so tired! - You must be very quiet, and not disturb her. Her head is going to ache very much."

The child turned and went down the stair, step by step, softly, saying -

"I will tell my rabbit not to make any noise - and to be as white as he can."

Once more they succeeded in bringing back to the light of consciousness her beclouded spirit. She woke in a soft white bed, with two faces of compassion bending over her, closed her eyes again with a smile of sweet content, and was soon wrapt in a wholesome slumber.

In the meantime, the caitiff minister had reached his manse, and found a ghastly loneliness awaiting him - oh, how much deeper than that of the woman he had forsaken! She had lost her repute and her baby; he had lost his God! He had never seen his shape, and had not his word abiding in him; and now the vision of him was closed in an unfathomable abyss of darkness, far,

far away from any point his consciousness could reach! The signs of God were around him in the Book, around him in the world, around him in his own existence - but the signs only! God did not speak to him, did not manifest himself to him. God was not where James Blatherwick had ever sought him; he was not in any place where was the least likelihood of his ever looking for or finding him!

CHAPTER XIII

It must be remembered that Blatherwick knew nothing of the existence of his child: such knowledge might have modified the half-conscious satisfaction with which, on his way home, he now and then saw a providence in the fact that he had been preserved from marrying a woman who had now proved herself capable of disgracing him in the very streets. But during his slow journey of forty miles, most of which he made on foot, hounded on from within to bodily motion, he had again, as in the night, to pass through many an alternation of thought and feeling and purpose. To and fro in him, up and down, this way and that, went the changing currents of self-judgment, of self-consolement, and of fresh-gathering dread. Never for one persistent minute was his mind clear, his purpose determined, his line set straight for honesty. He must live up - not to the law of righteousness, but to the show of what a minister ought to be! he must appear unto men! In a word, he must keep up the deception he had begun in childhood, and had, until of late years, practised unknowingly! Now he knew it, and went on, not knowing how to get rid of it; or rather, shrinking in utter cowardice from the confession which alone could have set him free. Now he sought only how to conceal his deception and falseness. He had no pleasure in them, but was consciously miserable in knowing himself not what he

George MacDonald

seemed - in being compelled, as he fancied himself in excuse, to look like one that had not sinned. In his heart he grumbled that God should have forsaken him so far as to allow him to disgrace himself before his conscience. He did not yet see that his foulness was ingrained; that the Ethiopian could change his skin, or the leopard his spots, as soon as he; that he had never yet looked purity in the face; that the fall which disgraced him in his own eyes was but the necessary outcome of his character - that it was no accident but an unavoidable result; that his true nature had but disclosed itself, and appeared - as everything hid must be known, everything covered must be revealed. Even *to begin* the purification without which his moral and spiritual being must perish eternally, he must dare to look on himself as he was: he *would* not recognize himself, and thought he lay and would lie hid from all. Dante describes certain of the redeemed as lying each concealed in his or her own cocoon of emitted light: James lay hidden like a certain insect in its own *gowk-spittle*. It is strange, but so it is, that many a man will never yield to see himself until he become aware of the eyes of other men fixed upon him; they seeing him, and he knowing that they see him, then first, even to himself, will he be driven to confess what he has long all but known. Blatherwick's hour was on its way, slow-coming, but no longer to be shunned. His soul was ripening to self-declaration. The ugly self must blossom, must show itself the flower, the perfection of that evil thing he counted himself! What a hold has not God upon us in this inevitable ripening of the unseen into the visible and present! The flower is there, and must appear!

In the meantime he suffered, and went on in silence, walking like a servant of the Ancient of Days, and knowing himself a whited sepulchre. Within him he felt the dead body that could not rest until it was laid bare to the sun; but all the time he comforted himself that he had not fallen a second time, and that the *once* would not be remembered against him: did not the fact that it was forgotten, most likely was never known, indicate the forgiveness of God? And so, unrepentant, he remained unforgiven, and continued a hypocrite and the slave of sin.

But the hideous thing was not altogether concealed; something showed under the covering whiteness! His mother saw that something shapeless haunted him, and often asked herself what it could be, but always shrank even from conjecturing. His father felt that he had gone from him utterly, and that his son's feeding of the flock had done nothing to bring him and his parents nearer to each other! What could be hidden, he thought, beneath the mask of that unsmiling face?

But there was a humble observer who saw deeper than the parents - John MacLear, the soutar.

One day, after about a fortnight, the minister walked into the workshop of the soutar, and found him there as usual. His hands were working away diligently, but his thoughts had for some time been brooding over the blessed fact, that God is not the God of the perfect only, but of the growing as well; not the God of the righteous only, but of such as hunger and thirst after righteousness.

"God blaw on the smoking flax, and tie up the bruised reed!" he was saying to himself aloud, when in walked the minister.

Now, as in some other mystical natures, a certain something had been developed in the soutar not unlike a spirit of prophecy - an insight which, seemingly without exercise of the will, sometimes laid bare to him in a measure the thoughts and intents of hearts in which he was more than usually interested; or perhaps it was rather a faculty, working unconsciously, of putting signs together, and drawing from them instantaneous conclusion of the fact at which they pointed. After their greeting, he suddenly looked up at his visitor with a certain fixed attention: the mere glance had shown him that he looked ill, and he now saw that something in the man's heart was eating at it like a canker. Therewith at once arose in his brain the question: could he be the father of the little one crowing in the next room? But he shut it into the darkest closet of his mind, shrinking from the secret of another soul, as from the veil of the Holy of Holies! The next moment, however, came the thought: what if the man stood in need of the offices of a friend? It was one thing to pry into a man's secret; another, to help him escape from it! As out of this thought the soutar sat looking at him for a moment, the minister felt the hot blood rush to his cheeks.

"Ye dinna luik that weel, minister," said the soutar: "is there onything the maitter wi' ye, sir?"

"Nothing worth mentioning," answered the parson. "I have sometimes a touch of headache in the early morning, especially when I have sat later than usual over my books the night before; but it always goes off during the day."

"Ow weel, sir, that's no, as ye say, a vera sairious thing! I couldna help fancyin ye had something on yer min' by ord'nar!"

"Naething, naething," answered James with a feeble laugh. " - But," he went on - and something seemed to send the words to his lips without giving him time to think - "it is curious you should say that, for I was just thinking what was the real intent of the apostle in his injunction to confess our faults one to another."

The moment he uttered the words he felt as if he had proclaimed his secret on the housetop; and he would have begun the sentence afresh, with some notion of correcting it; but again he knew the hot blood shoot to his face. - "I *must* go on with something!" he felt rather than said to himself, "or those sharp eyes will see through and through me!"

"It came into my mind," he went on, "that I should like to know what *you* thought about the passage: it cannot surely give the least ground for auricular confession! I understand perfectly how a man may want to consult a friend in any difficulty - and that friend naturally the minister; but - "

This was by no means a thing he had meant to say, but he seemed carried on to say he knew not what. It was as if, without his will, the will of God was driving the man to the brink of a pure confession - to the cleansing of his stuffed bosom "of that perilous stuff which weighs upon the heart."

"Do you think, for instance," he continued, thus driven, "that a man is bound to tell *everything* - even to the friend he loves best?"

" I think , " answered the soutar after a moment's

thought, "that we must answer the *what*, before we enter upon the *how much*. And I think, first of all we must ask - to *whom* are we bound to confess? - and there surely the answer is, to him to whom we have done the wrong. If we have been grumbling in our hearts, it is to God we must confess: who else has to do with the matter? To *Him* we maun flee the moment oor eyes are opent to what we've been aboot! But, gien we hae wranged ane o' oor fallow-craturs, wha are we to gang til wi' oor confession but that same fallow-cratur? It seems to me we maun gang to that man first - even afore we gang to God himsel. Not one moment must we indulge procrastination on the plea o' prayin! From our vera knees we maun rise in haste, and say to brother or sister, 'I've done ye this or that wrang: forgie me.' God can wait for your prayer better nor you, or him ye've wranged, can wait for your confession! Efter that, ye maun at ance fa' to your best endeevour to mak up for the wrang. 'Confess your sins,' I think it means, 'each o' ye to the ither again whom ye hae dene the offence.' - Divna ye think that's the cowmonsense o' the maitter?"

"Indeed, I think you must be right!" replied the minister, who sat revolving only how best, alas, to cover his retreat! "I will go home at once and think it all over. Indeed, I am even now all but convinced that what you say must be what the Apostle intended!"

With a great sigh, of which he was not aware, Blatherwick rose and walked from the kitchen, hoping he looked - not guilty, but sunk in thought. In truth he was unable to think. Oppressed and heavy-laden with the sense of a duty too unpleasant for performance, he went home to his cheerless manse, where his house-keeper was the only person he had to speak to, a woman incapable of comforting anybody. There he went straight to his study, but, kneeling, found he could not pray the simplest prayer; not a word would come, and he could not pray without words! He was dead, and in hell - so far perished that he felt nothing. He rose, and sought the open air; it brought him no restoration. He had not heeded his friend's advice, had not entertained the thought of the one thing possible to him - had not moved, even in spirit, toward Isy! The only comfort he could now find for his guilty soul was the thought that he could do nothing, for he did not know where Isy was to be found. When he remembered the next moment that his friend Robertson must be able to find her, he soothed his conscience with the reflection that there was no coach till the next morning, and in the meantime he could write: a letter would reach him almost as soon as he could himself!

But what then would Robertson think? He might give his wife the letter to read! She might even read it of herself, for they concealed nothing from each other! So he only walked the faster, tired himself, and earned an appetite as the result of his day's work! He ate a good dinner, although with little enjoyment, and fell fast asleep in his chair. No letter was written to Robertson that day. No letter of such sort was ever written. The spirit was not willing, and the flesh was weakness itself.

In the evening he took up a learned commentary on the Book of Job; but he never even approached the discovery of what Job wanted, received, and was satisfied withal. He never saw that what he himself needed, but did not desire, was the same thing - even a sight of God! He never discovered that, when God came to Job, Job forgot all he had intended to say to

George MacDonald

him - did not ask him a single question - knew that all was well. The student of Scripture remained blind to the fact that the very presence of the Living One, of the Father of men, proved sufficient in itself to answer every question, to still every doubt! But then James's heart was not pure like Job's, and therefore he could never have seen God; he did not even desire to see him, and so could see nothing as it was. He read with the blindness of the devil in his heart.

In Marlowe's *Faust*, the student asks Mephistopheles -

How comes it then that thou art out of hell?

And the demon answers him -

Why, this is hell, nor am I out of it;

and again -

Where we are is hell;
And where hell is there must we ever be:
... when all the world dissolves,
And every creature shall be purified,
All places shall be hell that are not heaven;

and yet again -

I tell thee I am damned, and now in hell;

and it was thus James fared; and thus he went to bed.

And while he lay there sleepless, or walked in his death to and fro in the room, his father and mother, some three miles away, were talking about him.

CHAPTER XIV

For some time they had lain silent, thinking about him by no means happily. They were thinking how little had been their satisfaction in their minister-son; and had gone back in their minds to a certain time, long before, when conferring together about him, a boy at school.

Even then the heart of the mother had resented his coldness, his seeming unconsciousness of his parents as having any share or interest in his life or prospects. Scotch parents are seldom demonstrative to each other or to their children; but not the less in them, possibly the hotter because of their outward coldness, burns the causal fire, the central, the deepest - that eternal fire, without which the world would turn to a frozen clod, the love of the parent for the child. That must burn while *the* Father lives! that must burn until the universe *is* the Father and his children, and none beside. That fire, however long held down and crushed together by the weight of unkindled fuel, must go on to gather heat, and, gathering, it must glow, and at last break forth in the scorching, yea devouring flames of a righteous indignation: the Father must and *will* be supreme, that his children perish not! But as yet *The Father* endured and was silent; and the child-parents also must endure and be still! In the meantime their son remained hidden from them as by an impervious moral hedge; he never came out from behind it, never stood clear before them, and they were unable to break through to him: within his citadel of indifference there was no angelic traitor to draw back the bolts of its iron gates, and let them in. They had gone on hoping, and hoping in vain, for some holy, lovely change in him; but at last had to confess it a relief when he left the house, and went to Edinburgh.

But the occasion to which I refer was long before that.

The two children were in bed and asleep, and the parents were lying then, as they lay now, sleepless.

"Hoo's Jeemie been gettin on the day?" said his father.

"Well enough, I suppose," answered his mother, who did not then speak Scotch quite so broad as her husband's, although a good deal broader than her mother, the wife of a country doctor, would have permitted when she was a child; "he's always busy at his books. He's a good boy, and a diligent; there's no gainsayin that! But as to hoo he's gettin on, I can beir no testimony. He never lets a word go from him as to what he's doin, one way or anither. 'What *can* he be thinkin aboot?' I say whiles to mysel - sometimes ower and ower again. When I gang intil the parlour, where he always sits till he has done his lessons, he never lifts his heid to show that he hears me, or cares wha's there or wha isna. And as soon as he's learnt them, he taks a buik and gangs up til his room, or oot aboot the hoose, or intil the cornyard or the barn, and never comes nigh me! - I sometimes won'er gien he would ever miss me deid!" she ended, with a great sigh.

" Hoot awa, wuman! dinna tak on like that," returned

her husband. "The laddie's like the lave o' laddies! They're a' jist like pup-doggies till their een comes oppen, and they ken them 'at broucht them here. He's bun' to mak a guid man in time, and he canna dee that ohn learnt to be a guid son to her 'at bore him! - Ye canna say 'at ever he contert ye! Ye hae tellt me that a hunner times!"

"I have that! But I would hae had no occasion to dwall upo' the fac', gien he had ever gi'en me, noo or than, jist a wee bit sign o' ony affection!"

"Ay, doobtless! but signs are nae preefs! The affection, as ye ca' 't, may be there, and the signs o' 't wantin! - But I ken weel hoo the hert o' ye 's workin, my ain auld dautie!" he added, anxious to comfort her who was dearer to him than son or daughter.

"I dinna think it wad be weel," he resumed after a pause, "for me to say onything til 'im aboot his behaviour til 's mither: I dinna believe he wud ken what I was aimin at! I dinna believe he has a notion o' onything amiss in himsel, and I fear he wad only think I was hard upon him, and no' fair. Ye see, gien a thing disna come o' 'tsel, no cryin upo' 't 'll gar 't lift its heid - sae lang, at least, as the man kens naething aboot it!"

"I dinna doobt ye're right, Peter," answered his wife; "I ken weel that flytin 'ill never gar love spread oot his wings - excep' it be to flee awa'! Naething but shuin can come o' flytin!"

"It micht be even waur nor shuin!" rejoined Peter." - But we better gang til oor sleeps, lass! - We hae ane anither, come what may!"

"That's true, Peter; but aye the mair I hae you, the mair I want my Jeemie!" cried the poor mother.

The father said no more. But, after a while, he rose, and stole softly to his son's room. His wife stole after him, and found him on his knees by the bedside, his face buried in the blankets, where his boy lay asleep with calm, dreamless countenance.

She took his hand, and led him back to bed.

"To think," she moaned as they went, "'at yon's the same bairnie I glowert at till my sowl ran oot at my een! I min' weel hoo I leuch and grat, baith at ance, to think I was the mother o' a man-child! and I thought I kenned weel what was i' the hert o' Mary, whan she claspit the blessed ane til her boasom!"

"May that same bairnie, born for oor remeid, bring oor bairn til his richt min' afore he's ower auld to repent!" responded the father in a broken voice.

"What for," moaned Marion, "was the hert o' a mither put intil me? What for was I made a wuman, whause life is for the beirin o' bairns to the great Father o' a' gien this same was to be my reward? - Na, na, Lord," she went on, checking herself, "I claim naething but thy wull; and weel I ken ye wouldna hae me think siclike thy wull!"

CHAPTER XV

It would be too much to say that the hearts of his parents took no pleasure in the advancement of their son, such as it was. I suspect the mother was glad to be proud where she could find no happiness - proud with the love that lay incorruptible in her being. But the love that is all on one side, though it may be stronger than death, can hardly be so strong as life! A poor, maimed, one-winged thing, such love cannot soar into any region of conscious bliss. Even when it soars into the region where God himself dwells, it is but to partake there of the divine sorrow which his heartless children cause him. My reader may well believe that father nor mother dwelt much upon what their neighbours called James's success - or cared in the least to talk about it: that they would have felt to be mere hypocrisy, while hearty and genuine relations were so far from perfect between them. Never to human being, save the one to the other, and that now but very seldom, did they allude to the bitterness which their own hearts knew; for to speak of it would have seemed almost equivalent to disowning their son. And alas the daughter was gone to whom the mother had at one time been able to bemoan herself, knowing she understood and shared in their misery! For Isobel would gladly have laid down her life to kindle in James's heart such a love to their parents as her own.

George MacDonald

We may now understand a little, into what sort of man the lad James Blatherwick had grown. When he left Stonecross for the University, it was with scarce a backward look; nothing was in his heart but eagerness for the coming conflict. Having gained there one of its highest bursaries, he never spent a thought, as he donned his red gown, on the son of the poor widow who had competed with him, and who, failing, had to leave ambition behind him and take a place in a shop - where, however, he soon became able to keep, and did keep, his mother in what was to her nothing less than happy luxury; while the successful James - well, so far my reader already knows about him.

As often as James returned home for the vacations, things, as between him and his parents, showed themselves unaltered; and by his third return, the heart of his sister had ceased to beat any faster at the thought of his arrival: she knew that he would but shake hands limply, let hers drop, and the same moment be set down to read. Before the time for taking his degree arrived, Isobel was gone to the great Father. James never missed her, and neither wished nor was asked to go home to her funeral. To his mother he was never anything more or less than quite civil; she never asked him to do anything for her. He came and went as he pleased, cared for nothing done on the farm or about the house, and seemed, in his own thoughts and studies, to have more than enough to occupy him. He had grown a powerful as well as handsome youth, and had dropped almost every sign of his country breeding. He hardly ever deigned a word in his mother-dialect, but spoke good English with a Scotch accent. Neither had he developed any of the abominable affectations by which not a few such as he have imagined to repudiate their origin.

His father had not then first to discover that his son was far too fine a gentleman to show any interest in agriculture, or put out his hand to the least share in that oldest and most dignified of callings. His mother continued to look forward, although with fading interest, to the time when he should be - the messenger of a gospel which he nowise understood; but his father did not at all share her anticipation; and she came to know ere long that to hear him preach would but renew and intensify a misery to which she had become a little accustomed in their ordinary intercourse. The father felt that his boy had either left him a long way off, or had never at any time come near him. He seemed to stand afar upon some mountain-top of conscious or imagined superiority.

James, as one having no choice, lived at *home*, so called by custom and use, but lived as one come of another breed than his parents, having with theirs but few appreciable points of contact. Most conventional of youths, he yet wrote verses in secret, and in his treasure-closet worshipped Byron. What he wrote he seldom showed, and then only to one or two of his fellow-students. Possibly he wrote only to prove to himself that he could do that also, for he never doubted his faculty in any direction. When he went to Edinburgh - to learn theology, forsooth! - he was already an accomplished mathematician, and a yet better classic, with some predilections for science, and a very small knowledge of the same: his books showed for the theology, and for the science, an occasional attempt to set his father right on some point of chemistry. His first aspiration was to show himself a gentleman in the eyes of the bubblehead calling itself Society - of which in fact he knew nothing; and the next, to have his eloquence, at present existent only in an ambitious imagination, recognized by the public. Such were the two devils, or rather the two forms of the one devil Vanity, that possessed him. He looked down on his parents, and the whole circumstance of their ordered existence, as unworthy of him, because old-fashioned and bucolic, occupied only with God's earth and God's animals, and having nothing to do with the shows of life. And yet to the simply honourable, to such of gentle breeding as despised mere show, the ways of life in their house would have seemed altogether admirable: the homely, yet not unfastidious modes and conditions of the unassuming homestead, would have appeared to them not a little attractive. But James took no interest in any of them, and, if possible, yet less in the ways of the tradesmen and craftsmen of the neighbouring village. He never felt the common humanity that made him one with them, did not in his thoughts associate himself at all with them. Had he turned his feeling into thoughts and words, he would have said, "I cannot help being the son of a farmer, but at least my mother's father was a doctor; and had I been consulted, my father should have been at least an officer in one of his majesty's services, not a treader of dung or artificial manure!" The root of his folly lay in the groundless self-esteem of the fellow; fostered, I think, by a certain literature which fed the notion, if indeed it did not plainly inculcate the *duty* of rising in the world. To such as he, the praise of men may well seem the patent of their nobility; but the man whom we call *The Saviour*, and who knew the secret of Life, warned his followers that they must not seek that sort of distinction if they would be the children of the Father who claimed them.

I have said enough, perhaps too much, of this most uninteresting of men! How he came to be born such, is not for my speculation: had he remained such, his story would not have been for my telling. How he became something better, it remains my task to try to set forth.

I now complete the talk that followed the return of the simple couple to bed. "I was jist thinkin, Peter," said Marion, after they had again lain silent for a while, "o' the last time we spak thegither aboot the laddie - it maun be nigh sax year sin syne, I'm thinkin!"

"'Deed I canna say! ye may be richt, Mirran," replied her spouse. "It's no sic a cheery subjec' 'at we sud hae muckle to say to ane anither anent it! He's a man noo, and weel luikit upo'; but it maks unco little differ to his parents! He's jist as dour as ever, and as far as man could weel be frae them he cam o'! - never a word to the ane or the ither o' 's! Gien we war twa dowgs, he couldna hae less to say til's, and micht weel hae mair! I s' warran' Frostie says mair in ae half-hoor to his tyke, nor Jeemie has said to you or me sin' first he gaed to the college!"

"Bairns is whiles a queer kin' o' a blessin!" remarked the mother. "But, eh, Peter! it's what may lie ahint the silence that frichts me!"

"Lass, ye're frichtin *me* noo! What *div* ye mean?"

"Ow naething!" returned Marion, bursting into tears. "But a' at ance it was borne in upo me, that there maun be something to accoont for the thing. At the same time I daurna speir at God himsel what that thing can be. For there's something waur noo, and has been for some time, than ever was there afore! He has sic a luik, as gien he saw nor heard onything but ae thing, the whilk ae thing keeps on inside him, and winna wheesht. It's an awfu' thing to say o' a mither's ain laddie; and to hae said it only to my ain man, and the father o' the laddie, maks my hert like to brak! - it's as gien I had been fause to my ain flesh and blude but to think it o' 'im! - Eh, Peter, what *can* it be?"

"Ow jist maybe naething ava'! Maybe he's in love, and the lass winna hear til 'im!"

"Na, Peter; love gars a man luik up, no doon at his ain feet! It gars him fling his heid back, and set his een richt afore him - no turn them in upo his ain inside! It maks a man straucht i' the back, strong i' the airm, and bauld i' the hert. - Didna it you, Peter?"

"Maybe it did; I dinna min' vera weel. - But I see love can hardly be the thing that's amiss wi' the lad. Still, even his parents maun tak tent o' jeedgin - specially ane o' the Lord's ministers - maybe ane o' the Lord's ain elec'!"

"It's awfu' to think - I daurna say 't - I daurna maist think the words o' 't, Peter, but it *wull* cry oot i' my vera hert! - Steik the door, Peter - and ticht, that no a stray stirk may hear me! - Was a minister o' the gospel ever a heepocreete, Peter? - like ane o' the auld scribes and Pharisees, Peter? - Wadna it be ower terrible, Peter, to be permittit? - Gien our ain only son was - "

But here she broke down; she could not finish the frightful sentence. The farmer again left his bed, and dropt upon a chair by the side of it. The next moment he sank on his knees, and hiding his face in his hands, groaned, as from a thicket of torture -

"God in haven, hae mercy upon the haill lot o' 's."

Then, apparently unconscious of what he did, he went wandering from the room, down to the kitchen, and out to the barn on his bare feet, closing the door of the house behind him. In the barn he threw himself, face downward, on a heap of loose straw, and there lay motionless. His wife wept alone in her bed, and hardly missed him: it required of her no reflection to understand whither he had gone, or what he was doing. He was crying, like King Lear from the bitterness of an outraged father's heart, to the Father of fathers:

"God, ye're a father yersel," he groaned; "and sae ye ken hoo it's rivin at my hert! - Na, Lord, ye dinna ken; for ye never had a doobt aboot *your* son! - Na, I'm no blamin Jeemie, Lord; I'm no cryin oot upo *him*; for ye ken weel hoo little I ken aboot him: he never opened the buik o' his hert to *me*! Oh God, grant that he hae naething to hide; but gien he has, Lord, pluck it oot o' 'im, and *him* oot o' the glaur! latna him stick there. I kenna hoo to shape my petition, for I'm a' i' the dark; but deliver him some gait, Lord, I pray thee, for his mither's sake! - ye ken what she is! - *I* dinna coont for onything, but ye ken *her*! - Lord, deliver the hert o' her frae the awfu'est o' a' her fears. - Lord, a hypocreet! a Judas-man!"

More of what he said, I cannot tell; somehow this much has reached my ears. He remained there upon the straw while hour after hour passed, pleading with the great Father for his son; his soul now lost in dull fatigue, now uttering itself in groans for lack of words, until at length the dawn looked in on the night-weary earth, and into the two sorrow-laden hearts, bringing with it a comfort they did not seek to understand.

CHAPTER XVI

But it brought no solace to the mind of the weak, hard-hearted, and guilty son. He had succeeded once more in temporarily soothing his conscience with some narcotic of false comfort, and now slept the sleep of the houseless, whose covering was narrower than he could wrap himself in. Ah, those nights! Alas for the sleepless human soul out in the eternal cold! But so heartless was James, that, if his mother had come to him in the morning with her tear-dimmed eyes, he would never have asked himself what could ail her; would never even have seen that she was unhappy; least of all would have suspected himself the cause of her red eyes and aching head, or that the best thing in him was that mental uneasiness of which he was constantly aware. Thank God, there was no way round the purifying fire! He could not escape it; he *must* pass through it!

CHAPTER XVII

Little knows the world what a power among men is the man who simply and really believes in him who is Lord of the world to save men from their sins! He may be neither wise nor prudent; he may be narrow and dim-sighted even in the things he loves best; they may promise him much, and yield him but a poor fragment of the joy that might be and ought to be his; he may present them to others clothed in no attractive hues, or in any word of power; and yet, if he has but that love to his neighbour which is rooted in, and springs from love to his God, he is always a redeeming, reconciling influence among his fellows. The Robertsons were genial of heart, loving and tender toward man or woman in need of them; their door was always on the latch for such to enter. If the parson insisted on the wrath of God against sin, he did not fail to give assurance of His tenderness toward such as had fallen. Together the godly pair at length persuaded Isobel of the eager forgiveness of the Son of Man. They assured her that he could not drive from him the very worst of sinners, but loved - nothing less than tenderly *loved* any one who, having sinned, now turned her face to the Father. She would doubtless, they said, have to see her trespass in the eyes of unforgiving women, but the Lord would lift her high, and welcome her to the home of the glad-hearted.

George MacDonald

But poor Isy, who regarded her fault as both against God and the man who had misled her, and was sick at the thought of being such as she judged herself, insisted that nothing God himself could do, could ever restore her, for nothing could ever make it that she had not fallen: such a contradiction, such an impossibility alone could make her clean! God might be ready to forgive her, but He could not love her! Jesus might have made satisfaction for her sin, but how could that make any difference in or to her? She was troubled that Jesus should have so suffered, but that could not give her back her purity, or the peace of mind she once possessed! That was gone for ever! The life before her took the appearance of an unchanging gloom, a desert region whence the gladness had withered, and whence came no purifying wind to blow from her the odours of the grave by which she seemed haunted! Never to all eternity could she be innocent again! Life had no interest for her! She was, and must remain just what she was; for, alas, she could not cease to be!

Such thoughts had at one period ravaged her life, but they had for some time been growing duller and deader: now once more revived by goodness and sympathy, they had resumed their gnawing and scorching, and she had grown yet more hateful to herself. Even the two who befriended and comforted her, could never, she thought, cease to regard her as what they knew she was! But, strange to say, with this revival of her suffering, came also a requickening of her long dormant imagination, favoured and cherished, doubtless, by the peace and love that surrounded her. First her dreams, then her broodings began to be haunted with sweet embodiments. As if the agonized question of the guilty Claudius were answered to her, to assure her that there *was* "rain enough in the sweet heavens to wash her white as snow," she sometimes would wake from a dream where she stood in blessed nakedness with a deluge of cool, comforting rain pouring upon her from the sweetness of those heavens - and fall asleep again to dream of a soft strong west wind chasing from her the offensive emanations of the tomb, that seemed to have long persecuted her nostrils as did the blood of Duncan those of the wretched Lady Macbeth. And every night to her sinful bosom came back the soft innocent hands of the child she had lost - when ever and again her dream would change, and she would be Hagar, casting her child away, and fleeing from the sight of his death. More than once she dreamed that an angel came to her, and went out to look for her boy - only to return and lay him in her arms grievously mangled by some horrid beast.

When the first few days of her sojourn with the good Samaritans were over, and she had gathered strength enough to feel that she ought no longer to be burdensome to them, but look for work, they positively refused to let her leave them before her spirit also had regained some vital tone, and she was able to "live a little"; and to that end they endeavoured to revive in her the hope of finding her lost child: setting inquiry on foot in every direction, they promised to let her know the moment when her presence should begin to cause them inconvenience.

"Let you go, child?" her hostess had exclaimed: "God forbid! Go you shall not until you go for your own sake: you cannot go for ours!"

"But I'm such a burden to you - and so useless!"

"Was the Lord a burden to Mary and Lazarus, think ye, my poor bairn?" rejoined Mrs. Robertson.

"Don't, ma'am, please!" sobbed Isy.

"Inasmuch as ye did it to one of the least of these, ye did it to me!" insisted her hostess.

"That doesna apply, ma'am," objected Isy. "I'm nane o' his!"

"Who is then? Who was it he came to save? Are you not one of his lost sheep? Are you not weary and heavy-laden? Will you never let him feel at home with you? Are *you* to say who he is to love and who he isn't? Are *you* to tell him who are fit to be counted his, and who are not good enough?"

Isy was silent for a long time. The foundations of her coming peace were being dug deeper, and laid wider.

She still found it impossible, from the disordered state of her mind at the time, to give any notion of whereabout she had been when she laid her child down, and leaving him, could not again find him. And Maggie, who loved him passionately and believed him wilfully abandoned, cherished no desire to discover one who could claim him, but was unworthy to have him. For a long time, therefore, neither she nor her father ever talked, or encouraged talk about him; whence certain questing busybodies began to snuff and give tongue. It was all very well, they said, for the cobbler and his Maggie to pose as rescuers and benefactors: but whose was the child? His growth nevertheless went on all the same, and however such hints might seem to concern him, happily they never reached him. Maggie flattered herself, indeed, that never in this world would they reach him, but would die away in the void, or like a fallen wave against the heedless shore! And yet, all the time, in the not so distant city, a loving woman was weeping and pining for lack of him, whose conduct, in the eyes of the Robertsons, was not merely blameless, but sweetly and manifestly true, constantly yielding fuel to the love that encompassed her. But, although mentally and spiritually she was growing rapidly, she seemed to have lost all hope. For, deeper in her soul, and nearer the root of her misery than even the loss of her child, lay the character and conduct of the man to whom her love seemed inextinguishable. His apostasy from her, his neglect of her, and her constantly gnawing sense of pollution, burned at the bands of her life; and her friends soon began to fear that she was on the verge of a slow downward slide, upon which there is seldom any turning.

The parson and his wife had long been on friendliest terms with the farmer of Stonecross and his wife; and, brooding on the condition of their guest, it was natural that the thought of Mrs. Blatherwick should occur to them as one who might be able to render them the help they needed for her. Difficulties were in the way, it was true, chiefly that of conveying a true conception of the nature and character of the woman in whom they desired her interest; but if Mrs. Blatherwick were once to see her, there would be no fear of the result: received at the farm, she was certain in no way to compromise them! They were confident she would never belie the character they were prepared to give her. Neither was there any one at the farm for whom it was possible to dread intercourse with her, seeing that, since the death of their only daughter, they had not had

George MacDonald

a servant in the house. It was concluded therefore between them that Mr. Robertson should visit their friends at Stonecross, and tell them all they knew about Isy.

It was a lovely morning in the decline of summer, the corn nearly full grown, but still green, without sign of the coming gold of perfection, when the minister mounted the top of the coach, to wait, silent and a little anxious, for the appearance of the coachman from the office, thrusting the waybill into the pocket of his huge greatcoat, to gather his reins, and climb heavily to his perch. A journey of four hours, through a not very interesting country, but along a splendid road, would carry him to the village where the soutar lived, and where James Blatherwick was parson! There a walk of about three miles awaited him - a long and somewhat weary way to the town-minister - accustomed indeed to tramping the hard pavements, but not to long walks unbroken by calls. Climbing at last the hill on which the farmhouse stood, be caught sight of Peter Blatherwick in a neighbouring field of barley stubble, with the reins of a pair of powerful Clydesdales in his hands, wrestling with the earth as it strove to wrench from his hold the stilts of the plough whose share and coulter he was guiding through it. Peter's delight was in the open air, and hard work in it. He was as far from the vulgar idea that a man rose in the scale of honour when he ceased to labour with his hands, as he was from the fancy that a man rose in the kingdom of heaven when he was made a bishop.

As to his higher nature, the farmer believed in God - that is, he tried to do what God required of him, and thus was on the straight road to know him. He talked little about religion, and was no partisan. When he heard people advocating or opposing the claims of this or that party in the church, he would turn away with a smile such as men yield to the talk of children. He had no time, he would say, to spend on such disputes: he had enough to do in trying to practise what was beyond dispute.

He was a reading man, who not merely drank at every open source he came across, but thought over what he read, and was, therefore, a man of true intelligence, who was regarded by his neighbours with more than ordinary respect. He had been the first in the district to lay hold of the discoveries in chemistry applicable to agriculture, and had made use of them, with notable results, upon his own farm; setting thus an example which his neighbours were so ready to follow, that the region, nowise remarkable for its soil, soon became remarkable for its crops. The note-worthiest thing in him, however, was his *humanity*, shown first and chiefly in the width and strength of his family affections. He had a strong drawing, not only to his immediate relations, but to all of his blood; who were not few, for he came of an ancient family, long settled in the neighbourhood. In his worldly affairs he was well-to-do, having added not a little to the little his father had left him; but he was no lover of money, being open-handed even to his wife, upon whom first your money-grub is sure to exercise his parsimony. There was, however, at Stonecross, little call to spend and less temptation from without, the farm itself being equal to the supply of almost every ordinary necessity.

In disposition Peter Blatherwick was a good-humoured, even merry man, with a playful answer almost always ready for a greeting neighbour.

George MacDonald

The minister did not however go on to join the farmer, but went to the house, which stood close at hand, with its low gable toward him. Late summer still lorded it in the land; only a few fleecy clouds shared the blue of the sky with the ripening sun, and on the hot ridges the air pulsed and trembled, like vaporized layers of mother-of-pearl.

At the end of the idle lever, no sleepy old horse was now making his monotonous rounds; his late radiance, born of age and sunshine, was quenched in the dark of the noonday stall. But the peacock still strutted among the ricks, as conscious of his glorious plumage, as regardless of the ugliness of his feet as ever; now and then checking the rhythmic movement of his neck, undulating green and blue, to scratch the ground with those feet, and dart his beak, with apparently spiteful greed, at some tiny crystal of quartz or pickle of grain they exposed; or, from the towering steeple of his up lifted throat, to utter his self-satisfaction in a hideous cry.

In the gable before him, Mr. Robertson passed a low window, through which he had a glimpse of the pretty, old-fashioned parlour within, as he went round to the front, to knock at the nearer of two green-painted doors.

Mrs. Blatherwick herself came to open it, and finding who it was that knocked - of all men the most welcome to her in her present mood - received him with the hearty simplicity of an evident welcome.

For was he not a minister? and was not he who caused all her trouble, a minister also? She was not, indeed, going to lay open her heart and let him see into its sorrow; for to confess her son a cause of the least anxiety to her, would be faithless and treacherous; but the unexpected appearance of Mr. Robertson brought her, nevertheless, as it were the dawn of a winter morning after a long night of pain.

She led him into the low-ceiled parlour, the green gloom of the big hydrangea that filled the front window, and the ancient scent of the withered rose-leaves in the gorgeous china basin on the gold-bordered table-cover. There the minister, after a few kind commonplaces, sat for a moment, silently pondering how to enter upon his communication. But he did not ponder long, however; for his usual way was to rush headlong at whatever seemed to harbour a lion, and come at once to the death-grapple.

Marion Blatherwick was a good-looking woman, with a quiet strong expression, and sweet gray eyes. The daughter of a country surgeon, she had been left an orphan without means; but was so generally respected, that all said Mr. Blatherwick had never done better than when he married her. Their living son seemed almost to have died in his infancy; their dead daughter, gone beyond range of eye and ear, seemed never to have left them: there was no separation, only distance between them.

"I have taken the liberty, Mrs. Blatherwick, of coming to ask your help in a great perplexity," began Mr. Robertson, with an embarrassment she had never seen in him before, and which bewildered her not a little.

"Weel, sir, it's an honour done me - a great honour, for which I hae to thank ye, I'm sure!" she answered.

"Bide ye, mem, till ye hear what it is," rejoined the minister. "We, that is, my wife and mysel, hae a puir lass at hame i' the hoose. We hae ta'en a great interest in her for some weeks past; but noo we're 'maist at oor wits' en' what to do wi' her neist. She's sair oot o' hert, and oot o' health, and out o' houp; and in fac' she stan's in sair, ay, desperate need o' a cheenge."

"Weel, that ouchtna to mak muckle o' a diffeeclety atween auld friens like oorsels, Maister Robertson! - Ye wad hae us tak her in for a whilie, till she luiks up a bit, puir thing? - Hoo auld may she be?"

"She can hardly be mair nor twenty, or aboot that - sic like as your ain bonnie lassie would hae been by this time, gien she had ripent here i'stead o' gaein awa to the gran' finishin schuil o' the just made perfec. Weel min' I her bonny face! And, 'deed, this ane's no' that unlike yer ain Isy! She something favours her."

"Eh, sir, fess her to me! My hert's waitin for her! Her mither maunna lowse her! She couldna stan' that!"

"She has nae mither, puir thing! - But ye maun dee naething in a hurry; I maun tell ye aboot her first!"

"I'm content 'at she's a frien o' yours, sir. I ken weel ye wad never hae me tak intil my hoose are that was na fit - and a' the lads aboot the place frae ae mornin til anither!"

"Indeed she *is* a frien o' mine, mem; and I hae never a dreid o' onything happenin ye wadna like. She's in ower sair trouble to cause ony anxiety. The fac' is, she's had a terrible misfortun!"

The good woman started, drew herself up a little, and said hurriedly,

"There's no a wean, is there?"

"'Deed is there, mem! - but pairt o' the meesery is, the bairn's disappeart; and she's brackin her heart aboot 'im. She's maist oot o' her min', mem! No that she's onything but perfecly reasonable, and gies never a grain o' trouble! I canna doobt she'd be a great help til ye, and that ilka minute ye saw fit to lat her bide. But she's jist huntit wi' the idea that she pat the bairnie doon, and left him, and kens na whaur. - Verily, mem, she's are o' the lambs o' the Lord's ain flock!"

"That's no the w'y the lambs o' *his* flock are i' the w'y o' behavin themsels! - I fear me, sir, ye're lattin yer heart rin awa wi' yer jeedgment!"

"I hae aye coontit Mary Magdalen are o' the Lord's ain yowies, that he left the lave i' the wilderness to luik for: this is sic anither! Gien ye help Him to come upon her, ye'll cairry her hame 'atween ye rej'icin! And ye min' hoo he stude 'atween are far waur nor her, and the ill men that would fain hae shamet her, and sent them oot like sae mony tykes - thae gran' Pharisees - wi their tails tuckit in 'atween their legs! - Sair affrontit they war, doobtless! - But I maun be gaein, mem, for we're no vera like to agree! My Maister's no o' ae min' wi' you, mem, aboot sic affairs - and sae I maun gang, and lea' ye to yer ain opingon! But I would jist remin' ye, mem, that she's at this present i' *my* hoose, wi my wife; and my wee bit lassie hings aboot her as gien she was an angel come doon to see the bonny place this warl luks frae up there. - Eh, puir lammie, the stanes oucht to be feower upo thae hill-sides!"

George MacDonald

"What for that, Maister Robertson?"

"'Cause there's so mony o' them whaur human herts oucht to be. - Come awa, doggie!" he added, rising.

"Dear me, sir! haena ye hae a grain o' patience to waur (*spend*) upon a puir menseless body?" cried Marion, wringing her hands in dismay. "To think *I* sud be nice whaur my Lord was sae free!"

"Ay," returned the minister, "and he was jist as clean as ever, wi' mony ane siclike as her inside the heart o' him! - *Gang awa, and dinna dee the like again*, was a' he said to that ane! - and ye may weel be sure she never did! And noo she and Mary are followin, wi' yer ain Isy, i' the vera futsteps o' the great shepherd, throuw the gowany leys o' the New Jerus'lem - whaur it may be they ca' her Isy yet, as they ca' this ane I hae to gang hame til."

"Ca' they her *that*, sir? - Eh, gar her come, gar her come! I wud fain cry upo *Isy* ance mair! - Sit ye doon, sir, shame upo' me! - and tak a bite efter yer lang walk! - Will ye no bide the nicht wi' 's, and gang back by the mornin's co'ch?"

"I wull that, mem - and thank ye kindly! I'm a bit fatiguit wi' the hill ro'd, and the walk a wee langer than I'm used til. - Ye maun hae peety upo my kittle temper, mem, and no drive me to ower muckle shame o' myself!" he concluded, wiping his forehead.

"And to think," cried his hostess, "that my hard hert sud hae drawn sic a word frae ane o' the Lord's servans that serve him day and nicht! I beg yer pardon, and that richt heumbly, sir! I daurna say I'll never do the like again, but I'm no sae likly to transgress a second time as the first. - Lord, keep the doors o' my lips, that ill-faured words comena thouchtless oot, and shame me and them that hear me! - I maun gang and see aboot yer denner, sir! I s' no be lang."

"Yer gracious words, mem, are mair nor meat and drink to me. I could, like Elijah, go i' the stren'th o' them - maybe something less than forty days, but it wad be by the same sort o' stren'th as that angels'-food gied the prophet!"

Marion hurried none the less for such a word; and soon the minister had eaten his supper, and was seated in the cool of a sweet summer-evening, in the garden before the house, among roses and lilies and poppy-heads and long pink-striped grasses, enjoying a pipe with the farmer, who had anticipated the hour for unyoking, and hurried home to have a talk with Mr. Robertson. The minister opened wide his heart, and told them all he knew and thought of Isy. And so prejudiced were they in her favour by what he said of her, and the arguments he brought to show that the judgment of the world was in her case tyrannous and false, that what anxiety might yet remain as to the new relation into which they were about to enter, was soon absorbed in hopeful expectation of her appearance.

"But," he concluded, "you will have to be wise as serpents, lest aiblins (*possibly*) ye kep (*intercept*) a lost sheep on her w'y back to the shepherd, and gar her lie theroot (*out of doors*), exposed to the prowlin wouf. Afore God, I wud rether share wi' her in *that* day, nor wi' them that keppit her!"

But when he reached home, the minister was startled,

indeed dismayed by the pallor that overwhelmed Isy's countenance when she heard, following his assurance of the welcome that awaited her, the name and abode of her new friends.

"They'll be wantin to ken a'thing!" she sobbed.

"Tell you them," returned the minister, "everything they have a right to know; they are good people, and will not ask more. Beyond that, they will respect your silence."

"There's but ae thing, as ye ken, sir, that I canna, and winna tell. To haud my tongue aboot that is the ae particle o' honesty left possible to me! It's enough I should have been the cause of the poor man's sin; and I'm not going to bring upon him any of the consequences of it as well. God keep the doors of my lips!"

"We will not go into the question whether you or he was the more to blame," returned the parson; "but I heartily approve of your resolve, and admire your firmness in holding to it. The time *may* come when you *ought* to tell; but until then, I shall not even allow myself to wonder who the faithless man may be."

Isy burst into tears.

"Don't call him that, sir! Don't drive me to doubt him. Don't let the thought cross my mind that he could have helped doing nothing! Besides, I deserve nothing! And for my bonny bairn, he maun by this time be back hame to Him that sent him!"

Thus assured that her secret would be respected by those to whom she was going, she ceased to show further reluctance to accept the shelter offered her. And, in truth, underneath the dread of encountering James Blatherwick's parents, lay hidden in her mind the fearful joy of a chance of some day catching, herself unseen, a glimpse of the man whom she still loved with the forgiving tenderness of a true, therefore strong heart. With a trembling, fluttering bosom she took her place on the coach beside Mr. Robertson, to go with him to the refuge he had found for her.

Once more in the open world, with which she had had so much intercourse that was other than joyous, that same world began at once to work the will of its Maker upon her poor lacerated soul; and afar in its hidden deeps the process of healing was already begun. Agony would many a time return unbidden, would yet often rise like a crested wave, with menace of overwhelming despair, but the Real, the True, long hidden from her by the lying judgments of men and women, was now at length beginning to reveal itself to her tear-blinded vision; Hope was lifting a feeble head above the tangled weeds of the subsiding deluge; and ere long the girl would see and understand how little cares the Father, whose judgment is the truth of things, what at any time his child may have been or, done, the moment that child gives herself up to be made what He would have her! Looking down into the hearts of men, He sees differences there of which the self-important world takes no heed; many that count themselves of the first, He sees the last - and what He sees, alone *is*: a gutter-child, a thief, a girl who never in this world had even a notion of purity, may lie smiling in the arms of the Eternal, while the head of a lordly house that still flourishes like a green bay-tree, may be wandering about with the dogs beyond the walls of the city.

George MacDonald

Out in the open world, I say, the power of the present God began at once to work upon Isobel, for there, although dimly, she yet looked into His open face, sketched vaguely in the mighty something we call Nature - chiefly on the great vault we call Heaven, the *Upheaved*. Shapely but undefined; perfect in form, yet limitless in depth; blue and persistent, yet ever evading capture by human heart in human eye; this sphere of fashioned boundlessness, of definite shapelessness, called up in her heart the formless children of upheavedness - grandeur, namely, and awe; hope, namely, and desire: all rushed together toward the dawn of the unspeakable One, who, dwelling in that heaven, is above all heavens; mighty and unchan-geable, yet childlike; inexorable, yet tender as never was mother; devoted as never yet was child save one. Isy, indeed, understood little of all this; yet she wept, she knew not why; and it was not for sorrow.

But when, the coach-journey over, she turned her back upon the house where her child lay, and entered the desolate hill-country, a strange feeling began to invade her consciousness. It seemed at first but an old mood, worn shadowy; then it seemed the return of an old dream; then a painful, confused, half-forgotten memory; but at length it cleared and settled into a conviction that she had been in the same region before, and had had, although a passing, yet a painful acquaintance with it; and at the last she concluded that she must be near the very spot where she had left and lost her baby. All that had, up to that moment, befallen her, seemed fused in a troubled conglomerate of hunger and cold and weariness, of help and hurt, of deliverance and returning pain: they all mingled inextricably with the scene around her, and there condensed into the memory of that one event - of which this must assuredly be the actual place! She looked upon widespread wastes of heather and peat, great stones here and there, half-buried in it, half-sticking out of it: surely she was waiting there for something to come to pass! surely behind this veil of the Seen, a child must be standing with outstretched arms, hungering after his mother! In herself that very moment must Memory be trembling into vision! At Length her heart's desire must be drawing near to her expectant soul!

But suddenly, alas! her certainty of recollection, her assurance of prophetic anticipation, faded from her, and of the recollection itself remained nothing but a ruin! And all the time it took to dawn into brilliance and fade out into darkness, had measured but a few weary steps by the side of her companion, lost in the meditation of a glad sermon for the next Sunday about the lost sheep carried home with jubilance, and forgetting how unfit was the poor sheep beside him for such a fatiguing tramp up hill and down, along what was nothing better than the stony bed of a winter-torrent.

All at once Isy darted aside from the rough track, scrambled up the steep bank, and ran like one demented into a great clump of heather, which she began at once to search through and through. The minister stopped bewildered, and stood to watch her, almost fearing for a moment that she had again lost her wits. She got on the top of a stone in the middle of the clump, turned several times round, gazed in every direction over the moor, then descended with a hopeless look, and came slowly back to him, saying -

"I beg your pardon, sir; I thought I had a glimpse of

my infant through the heather! This must be the very spot where I left him!"

The next moment she faltered feebly -

"Hae we far to gang yet, sir?" and before he could make her any answer, staggered to the bank on the roadside, fell upon it, and lay still.

The minister immediately felt that he had been cruel in expecting her to walk so far; he made haste to lay her comfortably on the short grass, and waited anxiously, doing what he could to bring her to herself. He could see no water near, but at least she had plenty of air!

In a little while she began to recover, sat up, and would have risen to resume her journey. But the minister, filled with compunction, took her up in his arms. They were near the crown of the ascent, and he could carry her as far as that! She expostulated, but was unable to resist. Light as she was, however, he found it no easy task to bear her up the last of the steep rise, and was glad to set her down at the top - where a fresh breeze was waiting to revive them both. She thanked him like a child whose father had come to her help; and they seated themselves together on the highest point of the moor, with a large, desolate land on every side of them.

"Oh, sir, but ye *are* good to me!" she murmured. "That brae just minded me o' the Hill of Difficulty in the Pilgrim's Progress!"

"Oh, you know that story?" said the minister.

"My old grannie used to make me read it to her when

she lay dying. I thought it long and tiresome then, but since you took me to your house, sir, I have remembered many things in it; I knew then that I was come to the house of the Interpreter. You've made me understand, sir!"

"I am glad of that, Isy! You see I know some things that make me very glad, and so I want them to make you glad too. And the thing that makes me gladdest of all, is just that God is what he is. To know that such a One is God over us and in us, makes of very being a most precious delight. His children, those of them that know him, are all glad just because he *is*, and they are his children. Do you think a strong man like me would read sermons and say prayers and talk to people, doing nothing but such shamefully easy work, if he did not believe what he said?"

"I'm sure, sir, you have had hard enough work with me! I am a bad one to teach! I thought I knew all that you have had such trouble to make me see! I was in a bog of ignorance and misery, but now I am getting my head up out of it, and seeing about me! - Please let me ask you one thing, sir: how is it that, when the thought of God comes to me, I draw back, afraid of him? If he be the kind of person you say he is, why can't I go close up to him?"

"I confess the same foolishness, my child, *at times*," answered the minister. "It can only be because we do not yet see God as he is - and that must be because we do not yet really understand Jesus - do not see the glory of God in his face. God is just like Jesus - exactly like him!"

And the parson fell a wondering how it could be that

George MacDonald

so many, gentle and guileless as this woman-child, recoiled from the thought of the perfect One. Why were they not always and irresistibly drawn toward the very idea of God? Why, at least, should they not run to see and make sure whether God was indeed such a one or not? whether he was really Love itself - or only loved them after a fashion? It set him thinking afresh about many things; and he soon began to discover that he had in fact been teaching a good many things without *knowing* them; for how could he *know* things that were not true, and therefore *could not* be known? He had indeed been *saying* that God was Love, but he had yet been teaching many things about him that were not lovable!

They sat thinking and talking, with silences between; and while they thought and talked, the day-star was all the time rising unnoted in their hearts. At length, finding herself much stronger, Isy rose, and they resumed their journey.

The door stood open to receive them; but ere they reached it, a bright-looking little woman, with delicate lines of ingrained red in a sorrowful face, appeared in it, looking out with questioning eyes - like a mother-bird just loosening her feet from the threshold of her nest to fly and meet them. Through the film that blinded those expectant eyes, Marion saw what manner of woman she was that drew nigh, and her motherhood went out to her. For, in the love-witchery of Isy's yearning look, humbly seeking acceptance, and in her hesitating approach half-checked by gentle apology, Marion imagined she saw her own Isy coming back from the gates of Death, and sprang to meet her. The mediating love of the minister, obliterating itself, had made him linger a step or two behind, waiting what would follow: when he saw the two folded each in the other's arms, and the fountain of love thus break forth at once from their encountering hearts, his soul leaped for joy of the new-created love - new, but not the less surely eternal; for God is Love, and Love is that which is, and was, and shall be for evermore - boundless, unconditioned, self-existent, creative! "Truly," he said in himself, "God is Love, and God is all and in all! He is no abstraction; he is the one eternal Individual God! In him Love evermore breaks forth anew into fresh personality - in every new consciousness, in every new child of the one creating Father. In every burning heart, in everything that hopes and fears and is, Love is the creative presence, the centre, the source of life, yea Life itself; yea, God himself!"

The elder woman drew herself a little back, held the poor white-faced thing at arms'-length, and looked her through the face into the heart.

"My bonny lamb!" she cried, and pressed her again to her bosom. "Come hame, and be a guid bairn, and ill man sall never touch ye, or gar ye greit ony mair! There's *my* man waitin for ye, to tak ye, and haud ye safe!"

Isy looked up, and over the shoulder of her hostess saw the strong paternal face of the farmer, full of silent welcome. For the strange emotion that filled him he did not seek to account: he had nothing to do with that; his will was lord over it!

"Come ben the hoose, lassie," he said, and led the way to the parlour, where the red sunset was shining through the low gable window, filling the place with the glamour of departing glory. "Sit ye doon upo the sofa there; ye maun be unco tired! Surely ye haena come a' the lang ro'd frae Tiltowie upo yer ain twa wee feet?"

"'Deed has she," answered the minister, who had followed them into the room; "the mair shame to me 'at loot her dee 't!"

Marion lingered outside, wiping away the tears that would keep flowing. For the one question, "What can be amiss wi' Jamie?" had returned upon her, haunting and harrying her heart; and with it had come the idea, though vague and formless, that their goodwill to the wandering outcast might perhaps do something to make up for whatever ill thing Jamie might have done. At last, instead of entering the parlour after them, she turned away to the kitchen, and made haste to get ready their supper.

Isy sank back in the wide sofa, lost in relief; and the minister, when he saw her look of conscious refuge and repose, said to himself -

"She is feeling as we shall all feel when first we know nothing near us but the Love itself that was before all worlds! - when there is no doubt more, and no questioning more!"

But the heart of the farmer was full of the old uncontent, the old longing after the heart of his boy, that had never learned to cry "*Father!*"

But soon they sat down to their meal. While they ate, hardly any one spoke, and no one missed the speech or was aware of the silence, until the bereaved Isobel thought of her child, and burst into tears. Then the mother who sorrowed with such a different, and so much bitterer sorrow, divining her thought and whence it came, rose, and from behind her said -

"Noo ye maun jist come awa wi' me, and I s' pit ye til yer bed, and lea' ye there! - Na, na; say gude nicht to naebody! - Ye'll see the minister again i' the mornin!"

With that she took Isy away, half-carrying her close-pressed, and half-leading her; for Marion, although no bigger than Isy, was much stronger, and could easily have carried her.

That night both mothers slept well, and both dreamed of their mothers and of their children. But in the morning nothing remained of their two dreams except two hopes in the one Father.

When Isy entered the little parlour, she found she had slept so long that breakfast was over, the minister smoking his pipe in the garden, and the farmer busy in his yard. But Marion heard her, and brought her breakfast, beaming with ministration; then thinking she would eat it better if left to herself, went back to her work. In about five minutes, however, Isy joined her, and began at once to lend a helping hand.

"Hoot, hoot, my dear!" cried her hostess, "ye haena taen time eneuch to make a proaper brakfast o' 't! Gang awa back, and put mair intil ye. Gien ye dinna learn to ate, we s' never get ony guid o' ye!"

"I just can't eat for gladness," returned Isy. "Ye're that good to me, that I dare hardly think aboot it; it'll gar me greit! - Lat me help ye, mem, and I'll grow hungry by dennertime!"

Mrs. Blatherwick understood, and said no more. She showed her what she might set about; and Isy, happy as a child, came and went at her commands, rejoicing. Probably, had she started in life with less devotion, she might have fared better; but the end was not yet, and the end must be known before we dare judge: result explains history. It is enough for the present to say that, with the comparative repose of mind she now enjoyed, with the good food she had, and the wholesome exercise, for Mrs. Blatherwick took care she should not work too hard, with the steady kindness shown her, and the consequent growth of her faith and hope, Isy's light-heartedness first, and then her good looks began to return; so that soon the dainty little creature was both prettier and lovelier than before. At the same time her face and figure, her ways and motions, went on mingling themselves so inextricably with Marion's impressions of her vanished Isy, that at length she felt as if she never could be able to part with her. Nor was it long before she assured herself that she was equal to anything that had to be done in the house; and that the experience of a day or two would make her capable of the work of the dairy as well. Thus Isy and her mistress, for so Isy insisted on regarding and calling her, speedily settled into their new relation.

It did sometimes cross the girl's mind, and that with a sting of doubt, whether it was fair to hide from her new friends the full facts of her sorrowful history; but to quiet her conscience she had only to reflect that for the sake of the son they loved, she must keep jealous guard over her silence. Further than James's protection, she had no design, cherished no scheme. The idea of compelling, or even influencing him to do her justice, never once crossed her horizon. On the contrary, she was possessed by the notion that she had done him a great wrong, and shrank in horror from the danger of rendering it irretrievable. She had never thought the thing out as between her and him, never even said to herself that he too had been to blame. Her exaggerated notion of the share she had in the fault, had lodged and got fixed in her mind, partly from her acquaintance with the popular judgment concerning such as she, and partly from her humble readiness to take any blame to herself. Even had she been capable of comparing the relative consequences, the injury she had done his prospects as a minister, would have seemed to her revering soul a far greater wrong than any suffering or loss he had brought upon her. For what was she beside him? What was the ruin of her life to the frustration of such prospects as his? The sole alleviation of her misery was that she seemed hitherto to have escaped involving him in the results of her lack of self-restraint, which results, she was certain, remained concealed from him, as from every one in any way concerned with him in them. In truth, never was man less worthy of it, or more devotedly shielded! And never was hidden wrong to the woman turned more eagerly and persistently into loving service to the man's parents! Many and many a time did the heart of James's mother, as she watched Isy's deft and dainty motions, regret, even with bitterness, that such a capable and love-inspiring girl should have rendered herself unworthy of her son - for, notwithstanding what she regarded as the disparity of their positions, she would gladly have welcomed Isy as a daughter, had she but been spotless, and fit to be loved by him.

In the evenings, when the work of the day was done, Isy used to ramble about the moor, in the lingering rays of the last of the sunset, and the now quickly shortening twilight. In those hours unhasting, gentle, and so spiritual in their tone that they seem to come straight from the eternal spaces where is no recalling and no forgetting, where time and space are motionless, and the spirit is at rest, Isy first began to read with conscious understanding. For now first she fell into the company of books - old-fashioned ones no doubt, but perhaps even therefore the more fit for her, who was an old-fashioned, gentle, ignorant, thoughtful child. Among the rest in the farmhouse, she came upon the two volumes of a book called The Preceptor, which contained various treatises laying down "the first principles of Polite Learning:" these drew her eager attention; and with one or other of the not very handy volumes in her hand, she would steal out of sight of the farm, and lapt in the solitude of the moor, would sit and read until at last the light could reveal not a word more. Even the Geometry she found in them attracted her not a little; the Rhetoric and Poetry drew her yet more; but most of all, the Natural History, with its engravings of beasts and birds, poor as they were, delighted her; and from these antiquated repertories she gathered much, and chiefly that most valuable knowledge, some acquaintance with her own ignorance. There also, in a garret over the kitchen, she found an English translation of Klopstock's Messiah, a poem which, in the middle of the last and in the present century, caused a great excitement in Germany, and did not a little, I believe, for the development of religious feeling in that country, where the slow-subsiding ripple of its commotion is possibly not altogether unfelt even at the present day. She read the volume through as she strolled in those twilights, not without risking many a fall over bush and stone ere practice taught her to see at once both the way for her feet over the moor, and that for her eyes over the printed page. The book both pleased and suited her, the parts that interested her most being those about the repentant angel, Abaddon; who, if I remember aright, haunted the steps of the Saviour, and hovered about the cross while he was crucified. The great question with her for a long time was, whether the Saviour must not have forgiven him; but by slow degrees it became at last clear to her, that he who came but to seek and to save the lost, could not have closed the door against one that sought return to his fealty. It was not until she knew the soutar, however, that at length she understood the tireless redeeming of the Father, who had sent men blind and stupid and ill-conditioned, into a world where they had to learn almost everything.

There were some few books of a more theological sort, which happily she neither could understand nor was able to imagine she understood, and which therefore she instinctively refused, as affording nourishment neither for thought nor feeling. There was, besides, Dr. Johnson's *Rasselas*, which mildly interested her; and a book called *Dialogues of Devils*, which she read with avidity. And thus, if indeed her ignorance did not become rapidly less, at least her knowledge of its existence became slowly greater.

And all the time the conviction grew upon her, that she had been in that region before, and that in truth she could not be far from the spot where she laid her child down, and lost him.

CHAPTER XVIII

In the meantime the said child, a splendid boy, was the delight of the humble dwelling to which Maggie had borne him in triumph. But the mind of the soutar was not a little exercised as to how far their right in the boy approached the paternal: were they justified in regarding him as their love-property, before having made exhaustive inquiry as to who could claim, and might re-appropriate him? For nothing could liberate the finder of such a thing from the duty of restoring it upon demand, seeing there could be no assurance that the child had been deliberately and finally abandoned! Maggie, indeed, regarded the baby as absolutely hers by right of rescue; but her father asked himself whether by appropriating him she might not be depriving his mother of the one remaining link between her and humanity, and so abandoning her helpless to the Enemy. Surely to take and withhold from any woman her child, must be to do what was possible toward dividing her from the unseen and eternal! And he saw that, for the sake of his own child also, and the truth in her, both she and he must make every possible endeavour to restore the child to his mother.

So the next time that Maggie brought the crowing infant to the kitchen, her father, who sat as usual under the small window, to gather upon his work all the light to be had, said, with one quick glance at the child -

"Eh, the bonny, glaid cratur! Wha can say 'at sic as he, 'at haena the twa in ane to see til them, getna frae Himsel a mair partic'lar and carefu' regaird, gien that war poassible, than ither bairns! I would fain believe that same!"

"Eh, father, but ye aye think bonny!" exclaimed Maggie. "Some hae been dingin 't in upo me 'at sic as he maist aye turn oot onything but weel, whan they step oot intil the warl. Eh, but we maun tak care o' 'im, father! Whaur *would* I be wi'oot you at my back!"

"And God at the back o' baith, bairn!" rejoined the soutar. "It's thinkable that the Almichty may hae special diffeeculty wi sic as he, but nane can jeedge o' ony thing or body till they see the hin'er en' o' 't a'. But I'm thinkin it maun aye be harder for ane that hasna his ain mither to luik til. Ony ither body, be she as guid as she may, maun be but a makshift! - For ae thing he winna get the same naitral disciplene 'at ilka mither cat gies its kitlins!"

"Maybe! maybe! - I ken I couldna ever lay a finger upo' the bonny cratur mysel!" said Maggie.

"There 'tis!" returned her father. "And I dinna think," he went on, "we could expec muckle frae the wisdom o' the mither o' 'm, gien she had him. I doobt she micht turn oot to be but a makshift hersel! There's mony aboot 'im 'at'll be sair eneuch upon 'im, but nane the wiser for that! Mony ane'll luik upon 'im as a bairn in whause existence God has had nae share - or jist as muckle share as gies him a grup o' 'im to gie 'im his licks! There's a heap o' mystery aboot a'thing, Maggie, and that frae the vera beginnin to the vera en'! It may be 'at yon bairnie's i' the waur danger jist frae haein

George MacDonald

you and me, Maggie! Eh, but I wuss his ain mither war gien back til him! And wha can tell but she's needin him waur nor he's needin her - though there maun aye be something he canna get - 'cause ye're no his ain mither, Maggie, and I'm no even his ain gutcher!"

The adoptive mother burst into a howl.

"Father, father, ye'll brak the hert o' me!" she almost yelled, and laid the child on the top of her father's hands in the very act of drawing his waxed ends.

Thus changing him perforce from cobbler to nurse, she bolted from the kitchen, and up the little stair; and throwing herself on her knees by the bedside, sought, instinctively and unconsciously, the presence of him who sees in secret. But for a time she had nothing to say even to *him*, and could only moan on in the darkness beneath her closed eyelids.

Suddenly she came to herself, remembering that she too had abandoned her child: she must go back to him!

But as she ran, she heard loud noises of infantile jubilation, and re-entering the kitchen, was amazed to see the soutar's hands moving as persistently if not quite so rapidly as before: the child hung at the back of the soutar's head, in the bight of the long jack-towel from behind the door, holding on by the gray hair of his occiput. There he tugged and crowed, while his care-taker bent over his labour, circumspect in every movement, nor once forgetting the precious thing on his back, who was evidently delighted with his new style of being nursed, and only now and then made a wry face at some movement of the human machine too abrupt for his comfort. Evidently he took it all as intended solely for his pleasure.

Maggie burst out laughing through the tears that yet filled her eyes, and the child, who could hear but not see her, began to cry a little, so rousing the mother in her to a sense that he was being treated too unceremoniously; when she bounded to liberate him, undid the towel, and seated herself with him in her lap. The grandfather, not sorry to be released, gave his shoulders a little writhing shake, laughed an amused laugh, and set off boring and stitching and drawing at redoubled speed.

"Weel, Maggie?" he said, with loving interrogation, but without looking up.

"I saw ye was richt, father, and it set me greitin sae sair that I forgot the bairn, and you, father, as weel. Gang on, please, and say what ye think fit: it's a' true!"

"There's little left for me to say, lassie, noo ye hae begun to say't to yersel. But, believe me, though ye can never be the bairn's ain mither, *she* can never be til 'im the same ye hae been a'ready, whatever mair or better may follow. The pairt ye hae chosen is guid eneuch never to be taen frae ye - i' this warl or the neist!"

"Thank ye, father, for that! I'll dee for him what I can, ohn forgotten that he's no mine but anither wuman's. I maunna tak frae her what's her ain!"

The soutar, especially while at his work, was always trying "to get," as he said, "into his Lord's company," - now endeavouring, perhaps, to understand some saying of his, or now, it might be, to discover his reason for saying it just then and there. Often, also, he would be pondering why he allowed this or that to take place in the world, for it was his house, where he was always present and always at work. Humble as diligent disciple, he never doubted, when once a thing had taken place, that it was by his will it came to pass, but he saw that evil itself, originating with man or his deceiver, was often made to subserve the final will of the All-in-All. And he knew in his own self that much must first be set right there, before the will of the Father could be done in earth as it was in heaven. Therefore in any new development of feeling in his child, he could recognize the pressure of a guiding hand in the formation of her history; and was able to understand St. John where he says, "Beloved, now are we the sons of God, and it doth not yet appear what we shall be, but we know that, when he shall appear, we shall be like him, for we shall see him as he is." For first, foremost, and deepest of all, he positively and absolutely believed in the man whose history he found in the Gospel: that is, he believed not only that such a man once was, and that every word he then spoke was true, but he believed that that man was still in the world, and that every word he then spoke, had always been, still was, and always would be true. Therefore he also believed - which was more both to the Master and to John MacLear, his disciple - that the chief end of his conscious life must be to live in His presence, and keep his affections ever, afresh and constantly, turning toward him in hope and aspiration. Hence every day he felt afresh that he too was living in the house of God, among the things of the father of Jesus.

The life-influence of the soutar had already for some time, and in some measure, been felt at Tiltowie. In a certain far-off way, men seemed to surmise what he was about, although they were, one and all, unable to estimate the nature or value of his pursuit. What their idea of him was, may in a measure be gathered from the answer of the village-fool to the passer-by who said to him: "Weel, and what's yer soutar aboot the noo?" "Ow, as usual," answered the *natural*, "turnin up ilka muckle stane to luik for his maister aneth it!" For in truth he believed that the Lord of men was very often walking to and fro in the earthly kingdom of his Father, watching what was there going on, and doing his best to bring it to its true condition; that he was ever and always in the deepest sense present in the same, where he could, if he pleased, at any moment or in any spot, appear to whom he would. Never did John MacLear lift his eyes heavenward without a vague feeling that he might that very moment, catch a sight of the glory of his coming Lord; if ever he fixed his eyes on the far horizon, it was never without receiving a shadowy suggestion that, like a sail towering over the edge of the world, the first great flag of the Lord's hitherward march might that moment be rising between earth and heaven; - for certainly He would come unawares, and then who could tell what moment be might not set his foot on the edge of the visible, and come out of the dark in which he had hitherto clothed himself as with a garment - to appear in the ancient glory of his transfiguration! Thus he was ever ready to fall a watching - and thus, also, never did he play the false prophet, with cries of "Lo here!" and "Lo there!" And even when deepest lost in watching, the lowest whisper of humanity seemed always loud enough to recall him to his "work alive" - lest he should be found asleep at His coming. His was the same live readiness that had opened the ear of Maggie to the cry of the little one on the hill-side. As his daily work was ministration to the weary feet of his Master's men, so was his soul ever awake to their sorrows and

George MacDonald

spiritual necessities.

"There's a haill warl' o' bonny wark aboot me!" he would say. "I hae but to lay my han' to what's neist me, and it's sure to be something that wants deein! I'm clean ashamt sometimes, whan I wauk up i' the mornin, to fin' mysel deein naething!"

Every evening while the summer lasted, he would go out alone for a walk, generally toward a certain wood nigh the town; for there lay, although it was of no great extent, and its trees were small, a probability of escaping for a few moments from the eyes of men, and the chance of certain of another breed showing themselves.

"No that," he once said to Maggie, "I ever cared vera muckle aboot the angels: it's the man, the perfec man, wha was there wi' the Father afore ever an angel was h'ard tell o', that sen's me upo my knees! Whan I see a man that but minds me o' *Him*, my hert rises wi' a loup, as gien it wad 'maist lea' my body ahint it. - Love's the law o' the universe, and it jist works amazin!"

One day a man, seeing him approach in the near distance, and knowing he had not perceived his presence, lay down behind a great stone to watch "the mad soutar," in the hope of hearing him say something insane. As John came nearer, the man saw his lips moving, and heard sounds issue from them; but as he passed, nothing was audible but the same words repeated several times, and with the same expression of surprise and joy as if at something for the first time discovered: - "Eh, Lord! Eh, Lord, I see! I un'erstaun'! - Lord, I'm yer ain - to the vera deith! - a' yer ain! - Thy father bless thee, Lord! - I ken ye care for noucht else! - Eh, but my hert's glaid! - that glaid, I 'maist canna speyk!"

That man ever after spoke of the soutar with a respect that resembled awe.

After that talk with her father about the child and his mother, a certain silent change appeared in Maggie. People saw in her face an expression which they took to resemble that of one whose child was ill, and was expected to die. But what Maggie felt was only resignation to the will of her Lord: the child was not hers but the Lord's, lent to her for a season! She must walk softly, doing everything for him as under the eye of the Master, who might at any moment call to her, "Bring the child: I want him now!" And she soon became as cheerful as before, but never after quite lost the still, solemn look as of one in the eternal spaces, who saw beyond this world's horizon. She talked less with her father than hitherto, but at the same time seemed to live closer to him. Occasionally she would ask him to help her to understand something he had said; but even then he would not always try to make it plain; he might answer -

"I see, lassie, ye're no just ready for 't! It's true, though; and the day maun come whan ye'll see the thing itsel, and ken what it is; and that's the only w'y to win at the trowth o' 't! In fac', to see a thing, and ken the thing, and be sure it's true, is a' ane and the same thing!" Such a word from her father was always enough to still and content the girl.

Her delight in the child, instead of growing less, went on increasing because of the *awe*, rather than *dread* of having at last to give him up.

CHAPTER XIX.

Meanwhile the minister remained moody, apparently sunk in contemplation, but in fact mostly brooding, and meditating neither form nor truth. Sometimes he felt indeed as if he were losing altogether his power of thinking - especially when, in the middle of the week, he sat down to find something to say on the Sunday. He had greatly lost interest in the questions that had occupied him while he was yet a student, and imagined himself in preparation for what he called the ministry - never thinking how one was to minister who had not yet learned to obey, and had never sought anything but his own glorification! It was little wonder he should lose interest in a profession, where all was but profession! What pleasure could that man find in holy labour who, not indeed offered his stipend to purchase the Holy Ghost, but offered all he knew of the Holy Ghost to purchase popularity? No wonder he should find himself at length in lack of talk to pay for his one thing needful! He had always been more or less dependent on commentaries for the joint he provided - and even for the cooking of it: was it any wonder that his guests should show less and less appetite for his dinners?

The hungry sheep looked up and were not fed!

To have food to give them, he must think! To think, he

must have peace! To have peace, he must forget himself! to forget himself, he must repent, and walk in the truth! to walk in the truth, he must love God and his neighbour! - Even to have interest in the dry bone of criticism, which was all he could find in his larder, he must broil it - and so burn away in the slow fire of his intellect, now dull and damp enough from lack of noble purpose, every scrap of meat left upon it! His last relation to his work, his fondly cherished intellect, was departing from him, to leave him lord of a dustheap! In the unsavoury mound he grubbed and nosed and scraped dog-like, but could not uncover a single fragment that smelt of provender. The morning of Saturday came, and he recognized with a burst of agonizing sweat, that he dared not even imagine his appearance before his congregation: he had not one written word to read to them; and extempore utterance was, from conscious vacancy, impossible to him; he could not even call up one meaningless phrase to articulate! He flung his concordance sprawling upon the floor, snatched up his hat and clerical cane, and, scarce knowing what he did, presently found himself standing at the soutar's door, where he had already knocked, without a notion of what he was come to seek. The old parson, generally in a mood to quarrel with the soutar, had always walked straight into his workshop, and greeted him crouched over his work; but the new parson always waited on the doorstep for Maggie to admit him.

She had opened the door wide ere he knew why he had come, or could think of anything to say. And now he was in greater uneasiness than usual at the thought of the cobbler's deep-set black eyes about to be fixed upon him, as if to probe his very thoughts.

"Do you think your father would have time," he asked humbly, "to measure me for a pair of light boots?"

Mr. Blatherwick was very particular about his foot-gear, and had hitherto always fitted himself at Deemouth; but he had at length learned that nothing he could there buy approached in quality, either of material or workmanship, what the soutar supplied to his poorest customer: he would mend anything worth mending, but would never *make* anything inferior.

"Ye'll get what ye want at such and such place," he would answer, "and I doobtna it'll be as guid as can be made at the siller; but for my ain pairt, ye maun excuse me!"

"'Deed, sir, he'll be baith glad and prood to mak ye as guid a pair o' beets as he can compass," answered Maggie. "Jist step in here, sir, and lat him ken what ye want. My bairn's greitin, and I maun gang til 'im; it's seldom he cries oot!"

The minister walked in at the open door of the kitchen, and met the eyes of the soutar expectant.

"Ye're welcome, sir!" said MacLear, and returned his eyes to what he had for a moment interrupted.

"I want you to make me a nice pair of boots, if you please," said the parson, as cheerily as he could. "I am rather particular about the fit, I fear!"

"And what for no, sir?" answered the soutar. "I'll do what I can onygait, I promise ye - but wi' mair readiness nor confidence as to the fit; for I canna profess assurance o' fittin' the first time, no haein the necessar instinc' frae the mak' o' the man to the shape o' the fut, sir."

"Of course I should like to have them both neat and comfortable," said the parson.

"In coorse ye wad, sir, and sae would I! For I confess I wad fain hae my customers tak note o' my success in followin the paittern set afore me i' the first oreeginal fut!"

"But you will allow, I suppose, that a foot is seldom as perfect now as when the divine idea of the member was first embodied by its maker?" rejoined the minister.

"Ow, ay; there's been mony an interferin circumstance; but whan His kingdom's come, things 'll tak a turn for the redemption o' the feet as weel as the lave o' the body - as the apostle Paul says i' the twenty-third verse o' the aucht chapter o' his epistle to the Romans; - only I'm weel aveesed, sir, 'at there's no sic a thing as *adoption* mintit at i' the original Greek. That can hae no pairt i' what fowk ca's the plan o' salvation - as gien the consumin fire o' the Love eternal was to be ca'd a *plan*! Hech, minister, it scunners me! But for the fut, it's aye perfec' eneuch to be *my* pattern, for it's the only ane I hae to follow! It's Himsel sets the shape o' the shune this or that man maun weir!"

"That's very true - and the same applies to everything a man cannot help. A man has both the make of his mind and of his circumstances to do the best he can with, and sometimes they don't seem to fit each other - so well as, I hope, your boots will fit my feet."

"Ye're richt there, sir - only that no man's bun' to follow his inclinations or his circumstances, ony mair than he's bun' to alter his fut to the shape o' a ready-made beet! - But hoo wull ye hae them made, sir? - I mean what sort o' butes wad ye hae me mak?"

"Oh, I leave that to you, Mr. MacLear! - a sort of half Wellington, I suppose - a neat pair of short boots."

"I understand, sir."

"And now tell me," said the minister, moved by a sudden impulse, coming he knew not whence, "what you think of this new fad, if it be nothing worse, of the English clergy - I mean about the duty of confessing to the priest. - I see they have actually prevailed upon that wretched creature we've all been reading about in the papers lately, to confess the murder of her little brother! Do you think they had any right to do that? Remember the jury had acquitted her."

"And has she railly confessed? I *am* glaid o' that! I only wuss they could get a haud o' Madeline Smith as weel, and persuaud *her* to confess! Eh, the state o' that puir crater's conscience! It 'maist gars me greit to think o' 't! Gien she wad but confess, houp wad spring to life in her sin-oppressed soul! Eh, but it maun be a gran' lichtenin to that puir thing! I'm richt glaid to hear o' 't."

"I didn't know, Mr. MacLear, that you favoured the power and influence of the priesthood to such an extent! We Presbyterian clergy are not in the way of doing the business of detectives, taking upon us to act as the agents of human justice! There is no one, guilty or not, but is safe with us!"

"As with any confessor, Papist or Protestant," rejoined the soutar. "If I understand your news, sir, it means that they persuaded the poor soul to confess her guilt, and so put herself safe in the hands of God!"

"And is not that to come between God and the sinner?"

"Doubtless, sir - in order to bring them together; to persuade the sinner to the first step toward reconciliation with God, and peace in his own mind."

"That he could take without the intervention of the priest!"

"Yes, but not without his own consenting will! And in this case, she would not, and did not confess without being persuaded to it!"

"They had no right to threaten her!"

"Did they threaten her? If they did, they were wrong. - And yet I don't know! In any case they did for her the very best thing that could be done! For they did get her, you tell me, to confess - and so cast from her the horror of carrying about in her secret heart the knowledge of an unforgiven crime! Christians of all denominations hold, I presume, that, to be forgiven, a sin must be confessed!"

"Yes, to God - that is enough! No mere man has a right to know the sins of his neighbour!"

"Not even the man against whom the sin was committed?"

"Suppose the sin has never come abroad, but remains

hidden in the heart, is a man bound to confess it? Is he, for instance, bound to tell his neighbour that he used to hate him, and in his heart wish him evil?"

"The time micht come whan to confess even that would ease a man's hert! But in sic a case, the man's first duty, it seems to me, would be to watch for an opportunity o' doin that neebour a kin'ness. That would be the deid blow to his hatred! But where a man has done an act o' injustice, a wrang to his neebour, he has no ch'ice, it seems to me, but confess it: that neebour is the one from whom first he has to ask and receive forgiveness; and that neebour alone can lift the burden o' 't aff o' him! Besides, the confession may be but fair, to baud the blame frae bein laid at the door o' some innocent man! - And the author o' nae offence can affoord to forget," ended the soutar, "hoo the Lord said, 'There's naething happit-up, but maun come to the licht'!"

It seems to me that nothing could have led the minister so near the presentation of his own false position, except the will of God working in him to set him free. He continued, driven by an impulse he neither understood nor suspected -

"Suppose the thing not known, however, or likely to be known, and that the man's confession, instead of serving any good end, would only destroy his reputation and usefulness, bring bitter grief upon those who loved him, and nothing but shame to the one he had wronged - what would you say then? - You will please to remember, Mr. MacLear, that I am putting an entirely imaginary case, for the sake of argument only!"

"Eh, but I doobt - I doobt yer imaiginary case!" murmured the soutar to himself, hardly daring even to think his thought clearly, lest somehow it might reveal itself.

"In that case," he replied, "it seems to me the offender wad hae to cast aboot him for ane fit to be trustit, and to him reveal the haill affair, that he may get his help to see and do what's richt: it maks an unco differ to luik at a thing throuw anither man's een, i' the supposed licht o' anither man's conscience! The wrang dune may hae caused mair evil, that is, mair injustice, nor the man himsel kens! And what's the reputation ye speak o', or what's the eesefu'ness o' sic a man? Can it be worth onything? Isna his hoose a lee? isna it biggit upo the san'? What kin' o' a usefulness can that be that has hypocrisy for its fundation? Awa wi' 't! Lat him cry oot to a' the warl', 'I'm a heepocrit! I'm a worm, and no man!' Lat him cry oot to his makker, 'I'm a beast afore thee! Mak a man o' me'!'"

As the soutar spoke, overcome by sympathy with the sinner, whom he could not help feeling in bodily presence before him, the minister, who had risen when he began to talk about the English clergy and confession, stood hearing with a face pale as death.

"For God's sake, minister," continued the soutar, "gien ye hae ony sic thing upo yer min', hurry and oot wi' 't! I dinna say *to me*, but to somebody - to onybody! Mak a clean breist o' 't, afore the Adversary has ye again by the thrapple!"

But here started awake in the minister the pride of superiority in station and learning: a shoemaker, from whom he had just ordered a pair of boots, to take such a liberty, who ought naturally to have regarded him as necessarily spotless! He drew himself up to his lanky height, and made reply -

"I am not aware, Mr. MacLear, that I have given you any pretext for addressing me in such terms! I told you, indeed, that I was putting a case, a very possible one, it is true, but not the less a merely imaginary one! You have shown me how unsafe it is to enter into an argument on any supposed case with one of limited education! It is my own fault, however; and I beg your pardon for having thoughtlessly led you into such a pitfall! - Good morning!"

As the door closed behind the parson, he began to felicitate himself on having so happily turned aside the course of a conversation whose dangerous drift he seemed now first to recognize; but he little thought how much he had already conveyed to the wide-eyed observation of one well schooled in the symptoms of human unrest.

"I must set a better watch over my thoughts lest they betray me!" he reflected; thus resolving to conceal himself yet more carefully from the one man in the place who would have cut for him the snare of the fowler.

"I was ower hasty wi' 'im!" concluded the soutar on his part. "But I think the truth has some grup o' 'im. His conscience is waukin up, I fancy, and growlin a bit; and whaur that tyke has ance taen haud, he's no ready to lowsen or lat gang! We maun jist lie quaiet a bit, and see! His hoor 'ill come!"

The minister being one who turned pale when angry,

walked home with a face of such corpse-like whiteness, that a woman who met him said to herself, "What
can ail the minister, bonny laad! He's luikin as scared
as a corp! I doobt that fule body the soutar's been
angerin him wi' his havers!"

The first thing he did when he reached the manse, was
to turn, nevertheless, to the chapter and verse in the
epistle to the Romans, which the soutar had indicated,
and which, through all his irritation, had, strangely
enough, remained unsmudged in his memory; but the
passage suggested nothing, alas! out of which he could
fabricate a sermon. Could it have proved otherwise
with a heart that was quite content to have God no
nearer him than a merely adoptive father? He found at
the same time that his late interview with the soutar
had rendered the machinery of his thought-factory no
fitter than before for weaving a tangled wisp of loose
ends, which was all he could command, into the
homogeneous web of a sermon; and at last was driven
to his old stock of carefully preserved preordination
sermons; where he was unfortunate enough to make
choice of the one least of all fitted to awake
comprehension or interest in his audience.

His selection made, and the rest of the day thus cleared
for inaction, he sat down and wrote a letter. Ever since
his fall he had been successfully practising the art of
throwing a morsel straight into one or other of the
throats of the triple-headed Cerberus, his conscience -
which was more clever in catching such sops, than
they were in choking the said howler; and one of them,
the letter mentioned, was the sole wretched result of
his talk with the soutar. Addressed to a late divinity-
classmate, he asked in it incidentally whether his old
friend had ever heard anything of the little girl - he

could just remember her name and the pretty face of her - Isy, general slavey to her aunt's lodgers in the Canongate, of whom he was one: he had often wondered, he said, what had become of her, for he had been almost in love with her for a whole half-year! I cannot but take the inquiry as the merest pretence, with the sole object of deceiving himself into the notion of having at least made one attempt to discover Isy. His friend forgot to answer the question, and James Blatherwick never alluded to his having put it to him.

CHAPTER XX

Never dawned Sunday upon soul more wretched. He had not indeed to climb into his watchman's tower without the pretence of a proclamation, but on that very morning his father had put the mare between the shafts of the gig to drive his wife to Tiltowie and their son's church, instead of the nearer and more accessible one in the next parish, whither they oftener went. Arrived there, it was not wonderful they should find themselves so dissatisfied with the spiritual food set before them, as to wish heartily they had remained at home, or driven to the nearer church. The moment the service was over, Mr. Blatherwick felt much inclined to return at once, without waiting an interview with his son; for he had no remark to make on the sermon that would be pleasant either for his son or his wife to hear; but Marion combated the impulse with entreaties that grew almost angry, and Peter was compelled to yield, although sullenly. They waited in the churchyard for the minister's appearance.

"Weel, Jeemie," said his father, shaking hands with him limply, "yon was some steeve parritch ye gied us this mornin! - and the meal itsel was baith auld and soor!"

The mother gave her son a pitiful smile, as if in deprecation of her husband's severity, but said not a word; and James, haunted by the taste of failure the sermon had left in his own mouth, and possibly troubled by sub-conscious motions of self-recognition, could hardly look his father in the face, and felt as if he had been rebuked by him before all the congregation.

"Father," he replied in a tone of some injury, "you do not know how difficult it is to preach a fresh sermon every Sunday!"

"Ca' ye yon fresh, Jeemie? To me it was like the fuistit husks o' the half-faimisht swine! Man, I wuss sic provender would drive yersel whaur there's better and to spare! Yon was lumps o' brose in a pig-wash o' stourum! The tane was eneuch to choke, and the tither to droon ye!"

James made a wry face, and the sight of his annoyance broke the ice gathering over the well-spring in his mother's heart; tears rose in her eyes, and for one brief moment she saw the minister again her bairn. But he gave her no filial response; ambition, and greed of the praise of men, had blocked in him the movements of the divine, and corrupted his wholesomest feelings, so that now he welcomed freely as a conviction the suggestion that his parents had never cherished any sympathy with him or his preaching; which reacted in a sudden flow of resentment, and a thickening of the ice on his heart. Some fundamental shock must dislodge that rooted, overmastering ice, if ever his wintered heart was to feel the power of a reviving Spring!

The threesum family stood in helpless silence for a few moments; then the father said to the mother -

"I doobt we maun be settin oot for hame, Mirran!"

"Will you not come into the manse, and have something before you go?" said James, not without anxiety lest his housekeeper should be taken at unawares, and their acceptance should annoy her: he lived in constant dread of offending his housekeeper!

"Na, I thank ye," returned his father: "it wad taste o' stew!" (*blown dust*).

It was a rude remark; but Peter was not in a kind mood; and when love itself is unkind, it is apt to be burning and bitter and merciless.

Marion burst into tears. James turned away, and walked home with a gait of wounded dignity. Peter went in haste toward the churchyard gate, to interrupt with the bit his mare's feed of oats. Marion saw his hands tremble pitifully as he put the headstall over the creature's ears, and reproached herself that she had given him such a cold-hearted son. She climbed in a helpless way into the gig, and sat waiting for her husband.

"I'm that dry 'at I could drink cauld watter!" he said, as he took his place beside her.

They drove from the place of tombs, but they carried death with them, and left the sunlight behind them.

Neither spoke a word all the way. Not until she was dismounting at their own door, did the mother venture her sole remark, "Eh, sirs!" It meant a world of unexpressed and inexpressible misery. She went straight up to the little garret where she kept her Sunday bonnet, and where she said her prayers when in especial misery. Thence she descended after a while to her bedroom, there washed her face, and sadly prepared for a hungerless encounter with the dinner Isy had been getting ready for them - hoping to hear something about the sermon, perhaps even some little word about the minister himself. But Isy too must share in the disappointment of that vainly shining Sunday morning! Not a word passed between her master and mistress. Their son was called the pastor of the flock, but he was rather the porter of the sheepfold than the shepherd of the sheep. He was very careful that the church should be properly swept and sometimes even garnished; but about the temple of the Holy Ghost, the hearts of his sheep, he knew nothing, and cared as little. The gloom of his parents, their sense of failure and loss, grew and deepened all the dull hot afternoon, until it seemed almost to pass their endurance. At last, however, it abated, as does every pain, for life is at its root: thereto ordained, it slew itself by exhaustion. "But," thought the mother, "there's Monday coming, and what am I to do then?" With the new day would return the old trouble, the gnawing, sickening pain that she was childless: her daughter was gone, and no son was left her! Yet the new day when it came, brought with it its new possibility of living one day more!

But the minister was far more to be pitied than those whose misery he was. All night long he slept with a sense of ill-usage sublying his consciousness, and dominating his dreams; but with the sun came a doubt whether he had not acted in unseemly fashion, when he turned and left his father and mother in the churchyard. Of course they had not treated him well; but what would his congregation, some of whom might have been lingering in the churchyard, have thought, to see him leave them as he did? His only thought, however, was to take precautions against their natural judgment of his behaviour.

After his breakfast, he set out, his custom of a Monday morning, for what he called a quiet stroll; but his thoughts kept returning, ever with fresh resentment, to the soutar's insinuation - for such he counted it - on the Saturday. Suddenly, uninvited, and displacing the phantasm of her father, arose before him the face of Maggie; and with it the sudden question, What then was the real history of the baby on whom she spent such an irrational amount of devotion. The soutar's tale of her finding him was too apocryphal! Might not Maggie have made a slip? Or why should the pretensions of the soutar be absolutely trusted? Surely he had, some time or other, heard a rumour! A certain satisfaction arose with the suggestion that this man, so ready to believe evil of his neighbour, had not kept his own reputation, or that of his house, perhaps, undefiled. He tried to rebuke himself the next moment, it is true, for having harboured a moment's satisfaction in the wrong-doing of another: it was unbefitting the pastor of a Christian flock! But the thought came and came again, and he took no continuous trouble to cast it out. When he went home, he put a question or two to his housekeeper about the little one, but she only smiled paukily, and gave him no answer.

After his two-o'clock dinner, he thought it would be Christian-like to forgive his parents: he would therefore call at Stonecross - which would tend to wipe out any undesirable offence on the minds of his parents, and also to prevent any gossip that might injure him in his sacred profession! He had not been to see them for a long time; his visits to them gave him

George MacDonald

no satisfaction; but he never dreamed of attributing that to his own want of cordiality. He judged it well, however, to avoid any appearance of evil, and therefore thought it might be his duty to pay them in future a hurried call about once a month. For the past, he excused himself because of the distance, and his not being a good walker! Even now that he had made up his mind he was in no haste to set out, but had a long snooze in his armchair first: it was evening when he climbed the hill and came in sight of the low gable behind which he was born.

Isy was in the garden gathering up the linen she had spread to dry on the bushes, when his head came in sight at the top of the brae. She knew him at once, and stooping behind the gooseberries, fled to the back of the house, and so away to the moor. James saw the white flutter of a sheet, but nothing of the hands that took it. He had heard that his mother had a nice young woman to help her in the house, but cherished so little interest in home-affairs that the news waked in him no curiosity.

Ever since she came to Stonecross, Isy had been on the outlook lest James should unexpectedly surprise her, and so be himself surprised into an involuntary disclosure of his relation to her; and not even by the long deferring of her hope to see him yet again, had she come to pretermit her vigilance. She did not intend to avoid him altogether, only to take heed not to startle him into any recognition of her in the presence of his mother. But when she saw him approaching the house, her courage failed her, and she fled to avoid the danger of betraying both, herself and him. She was in truth ashamed of meeting him, in her imagination feeling guiltily exposed to his just reproaches. All the time he remained that evening with his mother, she kept watching the house, not once showing herself until he was gone, when she reappeared as if just returned from the moor, where Mrs. Blatherwick imagined her still indulging the hope of finding her baby, concerning whom her mistress more than doubted the very existence, taking the supposed fancy for nothing but a half-crazy survival from the time of her insanity before the Robertsons found her.

The minister made a comforting peace with his mother, telling her a part of the truth, namely, that he had been much out of sorts during the week, and quite unable to write a new sermon; and that so he had been driven at the very last to take an old one, and that so hurriedly that he had failed to recall correctly the subject and nature of it; that he had actually begun to read it before finding that it was altogether unsuitable - at which very moment, fatally for his equanimity, he discovered his parents in the congregation, and was so dismayed that he could not recover his self-possession, whence had ensued his apparent lack of cordiality! It was a lame, yet somewhat plausible excuse, and served to silence for the moment, although it was necessarily so far from satisfying his mother's heart. His father was out of doors, and him James did not see.

CHAPTER XXI

As time went on, the terror of discovery grew rather than abated in the mind of the minister. He could not tell whence or why it should be so, for no news of Isy reached him, and he felt, in his quieter moments, almost certain that she could not have passed so completely out of his horizon, if she were still in the world. When most persuaded of this, he felt ablest to live and forget the past, of which he was unable to recall any portion with satisfaction. The darkness and silence left over it by his unrepented offence, gave it, in his retrospect, a threatening aspect - out of which at any moment might burst the hidden enemy, the thing that might be known, and must not be known! He derived, however, a feeble and right cowardly comfort from the reflection that he had done nothing to hide the miserable fact, and could not now. He even persuaded himself that if he could he *would* not do anything now to keep it secret; he would leave all to that Providence which seemed hitherto to have wrought on his behalf: he would but keep a silence which no gentleman must break! - And why should that come abroad which Providence itself concealed? Who had any claim to know a mere passing fault, which the partner in it must least of all desire exposed, seeing it would fall heavier upon her than upon him? Where was any call for that confession, about which the soutar had maundered so foolishly? If, on the other hand, his secret should threaten to creep out, he would not, he flattered himself, move a finger to keep it hidden! He would that moment disappear in some trackless solitude, rejoicing that he had nothing left to wish undisclosed! As to the charge of hypocrisy that was sure to follow, he was innocent: he had never said anything he did not believe! he had made no professions beyond such as were involved in his position! he had never once posed as a man of Christian experience - like the soutar for instance! Simply and only he had been overtaken in a fault, which he had never repeated, never would repeat, and which he was willing to atone for in any way he could!

On the following Saturday, the soutar was hard at work all day long on the new boots the minister had ordered of him, which indeed he had almost forgotten in anxiety about the man for whom he had to make them. For MacLear was now thoroughly convinced that the young man had "some sick offence within his mind," and was the more anxious to finish his boots and carry them home the same night, that he knew his words had increased the sickness of that offence, which sickness might be the first symptom of returning health. For nothing attracted the soutar more than an opportunity of doing anything to lift from a human soul, were it but a single fold of the darkness that compassed it, and so let the light nearer to the troubled heart. As to what it might be that was harassing the minister's soul, he sternly repressed in himself all curiosity. The thought of Maggie's precious little foundling did indeed once more occur to him, but he tried all he could to shut it out. He did also desire that the minister should confess, but he had no wish that he should unbosom himself to him: from such a possibility, indeed, he shrank; while he did hope to persuade him to seek counsel of some one capable of giving him true advice. He also hoped that, his displeasure gradually passing, he would resume his friendly intercourse with himself; for somehow there was that in the gloomy parson which powerfully attracted the cheery and hopeful soutar, who hoped his troubled abstraction might yet prove to be heart-hunger after a spiritual good which he had not begun to find: he might not yet have understood, he thought, the good news about God - that he was just what Jesus seemed to those that saw the glory of God in his face. The minister could not, the soutar thought, have learned much of the truth concerning God; for it seemed to wake in him no gladness, no power of life, no strength to *be*. For *him* Christ had not risen, but lay wrapt in his winding sheet! So far as James's feeling was concerned, the larks and the angels must all be mistaken in singing as they did!

At an hour that caused the soutar anxiety as to whether the housekeeper might not have retired for the night, he rang the bell of the manse-door; which in truth did bring the minister himself from his study, to confront MacLear on the other side of the threshold, with the new boots in his hand.

But the minister had come to see that his behaviour in his last visit to the soutar must have laid him open to suspicion from him; and he was now bent on removing what he counted the unfortunate impression his words might have made. Wishing therefore to appear to cherish no offence over his parishioner's last words to him ere they parted, and so obliterate any suggestion of needed confession lurking behind his own words with which he had left him, he now addressed him with an *abandon* which, gloomy in spirit as he habitually was, he could yet assume in a moment when the masking instinct was aroused in him -

"Oh, Mr. MacLear," he said jocularly, "I am glad you have just managed to escape breaking the Sabbath! You have had a close shave! It wants ten minutes, hardly more, to the awful midnight hour!"

"I doobt, sir, it would hae broken the Sawbath waur, to fail o' my word for the sake o' a steik or twa that maittered naething to God or man!" returned the soutar.

"Ah, well, we won't argue about it! but if we were inclined to be strict, the Sabbath began some " - here he looked at his watch - "some five hours and three-quarters ago; that is, at six of the clock, on the evening of Saturday!"

"Hoot, minister, ye ken ye're wrang there! for, Jewwise, it began at sax o' the Friday nicht! But ye hae made it plain frae the poopit that ye hae nae supperstition aboot the first day o' the week, the whilk alane has aucht to dee wi' hiz Christians! - We're no a' Jews, though there's a heap o' them upo' this side the Tweed! I, for my pairt, confess nae obligation but to drap workin, and sit doon wi' clean han's, or as clean as I can weel mak them, to the speeritooal table o' my Lord, whaur I aye try as weel to weir a clean and a cheerfu' face - that is, sae far as the sermon will permit - and there's aye a pyke o' mate somewhaur intil 't! For isna it the bonny day whan the Lord wad hae us sit doon and ait wi himsel, wha made the h'avens and the yirth, and the waters under the yirth that haud it up! And wilna he, upo this day, at the last gran' merridge-feast, poor oot the bonny reid wine, and say, 'Sit ye doon, bairns, and tak o' my best'!"

"Ay, ay, Mr. MacLear; that's a fine way to think of the Sabbath!" rejoined the minister, "and the very way I am in the habit of thinking of it myself! - I'm greatly obliged to you for bringing home my boots; but indeed I could have managed very well without them!"

"Ay, sir, maybe; I dinna doobt ye hae pairs and pairs o' beets; but ye see *I* couldna dee *wi'oot* them, for I had *promised*."

The word struck the minister to the heart. "He means something!" he said to himself. " - But I never promised the girl anything! I *could* not have done it! I never thought of such a thing! I never said anything to bind me!"

He never saw that, whether he had promised or not, his deed had bound him more absolutely than any words.

All this time he was letting the soutar stand on the doorstep, with the new boots in his hand.

"Come in," he said at last, "and put them there in the window. It's about time we were all going to bed, I think - especially myself, to-morrow being sermon-day!"

The soutar betook himself to his home and to bed, sorry that he had said nothing, yet having said more than he knew.

The next evening he listened to the best sermon he had yet heard from that pulpit - a summary of the facts bearing on the resurrection of our Lord; - with which sermon, however, a large part of the congregation was anything but pleased; for the minister had admitted the impossibility of reconciling, in every particular, the differing accounts of the doings and seeings of those who bore witness to it.

" - As gien," said the soutar, "the Lord wasna to shaw himsel till a' that had seen he was up war agreed as to their recollection o' what fouk had reportit!"

He went home edified and uplifted by his fresh contemplation of the story of his Master's victory: thank God! he thought; his pains were over at last! and through death he was lord for ever over death and evil, over pain and loss and fear, who was already through his father lord of creation and life, and of all things visible and invisible! He was Lord also of all thinking and feeling and judgment, able to give repentance and restoration, and to set right all that selfwill had set wrong! So greatly did the heart of his humble disciple rejoice in him, that he scandalized the reposing sabbath-street, by breaking out, as he went home, into a somewhat unmelodious song, "They are all gone down to hell with the weapons of their war!" to a tune nobody knew but himself, and which he could never have sung again. "O Faithful and True," he broke out once more as he reached his own house; but checked himself abruptly, saying, "Tut, tut, the fowk'll think I hae been drinkin'! - Eh," he continued to himself as he went in, "gien I micht but ance hear the name that no man kens but Himsel!"

The next day he was very tired, and could get through but little work; so, on the Tuesday he felt it would be right to take a holiday. Therefore he put a large piece of oatcake in his pocket, and telling Maggie he was going to the hills, "to do nae thing and a'thing, baith at ance, a' day," disappeared with a backward look and lingering smile.

He went brimful of expectation, and was not disappointed in those he met by the way.

After walking some distance in quiescent peace, and having since noontide met no one - to use his own fashion of speech - by which he meant that no special thought had arisen uncalled-for in his mind, always regarding such a thought as a word direct from the First Thought, he turned his steps toward Stonecross. He had known Peter Blatherwick for many years, and honoured him as one in whom there was no guile; and now the desire to see him came upon him: he wanted to share with him the pleasure and benefit he had gathered from Sunday's sermon, and show the better quality of the food their pastor had that day laid before his sheep. He knocked at the door, thinking to see the mistress, and hear from her where her husband was likely to be found; but to his surprise, the farmer came himself to the door, where he stood in silence, with a look that seemed to say, "I know you; but what can you be wanting with me?" His face was troubled, and looked not only sorrowful, but scared as well. Usually ruddy with health, and calm with content, it was now blotted with pallid shades, and seemed, as he held the door-handle without a word of welcome, that of one aware of something unseen behind him.

"What ails ye, Mr. Bletherwick?" asked the soutar, in a voice that faltered with sympathetic anxiety. "Surely - I houp there's naething come ower the mistress!"

"Na, I thank ye; she's vera weel. But a dreid thing has befa'en her and me. It's little mair nor an hoor sin syne 'at oor Isy - ye maun hae h'ard tell o' Isy, 'at we baith had sic a fawvour for - a' at ance she jist drappit doon deid as gien shotten wi' a gun! In fac I thoucht for a meenut, though I h'ard nae shot, that sic had been the case. The ae moment she steed newsin wi' her mistress i' the kitchie, and the neist she was in a heap upo' the fleer o' 't! - But come in, come in."

"Eh, the bonnie lassie!" cried the shoemaker, without moving to enter; "I min' upo' her weel, though I believe I never saw her but ance! - a fine, delicat pictur o' a lassie, that luikit up at ye as gien she made ye kin'ly welcome to onything she could gie or get for ye!"

"Aweel, as I'm tellin ye," said the farmer, "she's awa'; and we'll see her no more till the earth gies up her deid! The wife's in there wi' what's left o' her, greitin as gien she wad greit her een oot. Eh, but she lo'ed her weel: - Doon she drappit, and no even a moment to say her prayers!"

"That maitters na muckle - no a hair, in fac!" returned the soutar. "It was the Father o' her, nane ither, that took her. He wantit her hame; and he's no are to dee onything ill, or at the wrang moment! Gien a meenut mair had been ony guid til her, thinkna ye she wud hae had that meenut!"

"Willna ye come in and see her? Some fowk canna bide to luik upo the deid, but ye're no are o' sic!"

"Na; it's trowth I daurna be nane o' sic. I s' richt wullinly gang wi' ye to luik upo the face o' ane 'at's won throuw!"

"Come awa' than; and maybe the Lord 'ill gie ye a

word o' comfort for the mistress, for she taks on terrible aboot her. It braks my hert to see her!"

"The hert o' baith king and cobbler's i' the ae han' o' the Lord," answered the soutar solemnly; "and gien my hert indite onything, my tongue 'ill be ready to speyk the same."

He followed the farmer - who trode softly, as if he feared disturbing the sleeper - upon whom even the sudden silences of the world would break no more.

Mr. Blatherwick led the way to the parlour, and through it to a closet behind, used as the guest-chamber. There, on a little white bed with dimity curtains, lay the form of Isobel. The eyes of the soutar, in whom had lingered yet a hope, at once revealed that he saw she was indeed gone to return no more. Her lovely little face, although its beautiful eyes were closed, was even lovelier than before; but her arms and hands lay straight by her sides; their work was gone from them; no voice would call her any more! she might sleep on, and take her rest!

"I had but to lay them straucht," sobbed her mistress; "her een she had closed hersel as she drappit! Eh, but she *was* a bonny lassie - and a guid! - hardly less nor ain bairn to me!"

"And to me as weel!" supplemented Peter, with a choked sob.

"And no ance had I paid her a penny wage!" cried Marion, with sudden remorseful reminiscence.

"She'll never think o' wages noo!" said her husband.

"We'll sen' them to the hospital, and that'll ease yer min', Mirran!"

"Eh, she was a dacent, mensefu, richt lo'able cratur!" cried Marion. "She never *said* naething to jeedge by, but I hae a glimmer o' houp 'at she *may* ha' been ane o' the Lord's ain."

"Is that a' ye can say, mem?" interposed the soutar. "Surely ye wadna daur imaigine her drappit oot o' *his* han's!"

"Na," returned Marion; "but I wad richt fain ken her fair intil them! Wha is there to assure 's o' her faith i' the atonement?"

"Deed, I kenna, and I carena, mem! I houp she had faith i' naething, thing nor thoucht, but the Lord himsel! Alive or deid, we're in his han's wha dee'd for us, revealin his Father til 's," said the soutar; "- and gien she didna ken Him afore, she wull noo! The holy All-in-all be wi' her i' the dark, or whatever comes! - O God, hand up her heid, and latna the watters gang ower her!"

So-called Theology rose, dull, rampant, and indignant; but the solemn face of the dead interdicted dispute, and Love was ready to hope, if not quite to believe. Nevertheless to those guileless souls, the words of the soutar sounded like blasphemy: was not her fate settled, and for ever? Had not death in a moment turned her into an immortal angel, or an equally immortal devil? Only how, at such a moment, with the peaceful face before them, were they to argue the possibility that she, the loving, the gentle, whose fault they knew but by her own voluntary confession, was

George MacDonald

now as utterly indifferent to the heart of the living God, as if He had never created her - nay even had become hateful to him! No one spoke; and the soutar, after gazing on the dead for a while, prayer over-flowing his heart, but never reaching his lips, turned slowly, and departed without a word.

As he reached his own door, he met the minister, and told him of the sorrow that had befallen his parents, adding that it was plain they were in sore need of his sympathy. James, although marvelling at their being so much troubled by the death of merely a servant, was roused by the tale to the duty of his profession; and although his heart had never yet drawn him either to the house of mourning or the house of mirth, he judged it becoming to pay another visit to Stonecross, thinking it, however, rather hard that he should have to go again so soon. It pleased the soutar to see him face about at once, however, and start for the farm with a quicker stride than, since his return to Tiltowie as its minister, he had seen him put forth.

James had not the slightest foreboding of whom he was about to see in the arms of Death. But even had he had some feeling of what was awaiting him, I dare not even conjecture the mood in which he would have approached the house - whether one of compunction, or of relief. But utterly unconscious of the discovery toward which he was rushing, he hurried on, with a faint pleasure at the thought of having to expostulate with his mother upon the waste of such an unnecessary expenditure of feeling. Toward his father, he was aware of a more active feeling of disapproval, if not indeed one of repugnance. James Blatherwick was of such whose sluggish natures require, for the melting of their stubbornness, and their remoulding into forms of strength and beauty, such a concentration of the love of God that it becomes a consuming fire.

George MacDonald

CHAPTER XXII

The night had fallen when he reached the farm. The place was silent; its doors were all shut; and when he opened the nearest, seldom used but for the reception of strangers, not a soul was to be seen; no one came to meet him, for no one had even thought of him, and certainly no one, except it were the dead, desired his coming. He went into the parlour, and there, from the dim chamber beyond, whose door stood open, appeared his mother. Her heart big with grief, she clasped him in her arms, and laid her cheek against his bosom: higher she could not reach, and nearer than his breast-bone she could not get to him. No endearment was customary between them: James had never encouraged or missed any; neither did he know how to receive such when offered.

"I am distressed, mother," he began, "to see you so upset; and I cannot help thinking such a display of feeling unnecessary. If I may say so, it seems to me unreasonable. You cannot, in such a brief period as this new maid of yours has spent with you, have developed such an affection for her, as this - " he hesitated for a word, " - as this *bouleversement* would seem to indicate! The young woman can hardly be a relative, or I should surely have heard of her existence! The suddenness of the occurrence, of which I heard only from my shoemaker, MacLear, must have wrought disastrously upon your nerves! Come, come, dear mother! you must indeed compose yourself! It is quite unworthy of you, to yield to such a paroxysm of unnatural and uncalled-for grief! Surely it is the part of a Christian like you, to meet with calmness, especially in the case of one you have known so little, that inevitable change which neither man nor woman can avoid longer than a few years at most! Of course, the appalling instantaneousness of it in the present case, goes far to explain and excuse your emotion, but now at least, after so many hours have elapsed, it is surely time for reason to resume her sway! Was it not Schiller who said, 'Death cannot be an evil, for it is universal'? - At all events, it is not an unmitigated evil!" he added - with a sigh, as if for his part he was prepared to welcome it.

During this prolonged and foolish speech, the gentle woman, whose mother-heart had loved the poor girl that bore her daughter's name, had been restraining her sobs behind her handkerchief; but now, as she heard her son's cold commonplaces, it was, perhaps, a little wholesome anger that roused her, and made her able to speak.

"Ye didna ken her, laddie," she cried, "or ye wad never mint at layin yer tongue upon her that gait! - 'Deed na, ye wadna! - But I doobt gien ever ye could hae come to ken her as she was - sic a bonny, herty sowl as ance dwalt in yon white-faced, patient thing, lyin i' the chaumer there - wi' the stang oot o' her hert at last, and left the sharper i' mine! But me and yer father - eh, weel we lo'ed her! for to hiz she was like oor ain Isy, - ay, mair a dochter nor a servan - wi'a braw lovin kin'ness in her, no to be luikit for frae ony son, and sic as we never had frae ony afore but oor ain Isy. - Jist

George MacDonald

gang ye intil the closet there, gien ye wull, and ye'll see what'll maybe saften yer hert a bit, and lat ye unerstan' what mak o' a thing's come to the twa auld fowk ye never cared muckle aboot!"

James felt bitterly aggrieved by this personal remark of his mother. How unfair she was! What had *he* ever done to offend her? Had he not always behaved himself properly - except indeed in that matter of which neither she, nor living soul else, knew anything, or would ever know! What right had she then to say such things to him! Had he not fulfilled the expectations with which his father sent him to college? had he not gained a position whose reflected splendour crowned them the parents of James Blatherwick? She showed him none of the consideration or respect he had so justly earned but never demanded! He rose suddenly, and with never a thought save to leave his mother so as to manifest his displeasure with her, stalked heedlessly into the presence of the more heedless dead.

The night had indeed fallen, but, the little window of the room looking westward, and a bar of golden light yet lying like a resurrection stone over the spot where the sun was buried, a pale sad gleam, softly vanishing, hovered, hardly rested, upon the lovely, still, unlooking face, that lay white on the scarcely whiter pillow. Coming out of the darker room, the sharp, low light blinded him a little, so that he saw without any certainty of perception; yet he seemed to have something before him not altogether unfamiliar, giving him a suggestion as of something he had known once, perhaps ought now to recognize, but had forgotten: the reality of it seemed to be obscured by the strange autumnal light entering almost horizontally.

Concluding himself oddly affected by the sight of a room he had regarded with some awe in his childhood, and had not set foot in it for a long time, he drew a little nearer to the bed, to look closer at the face of this paragon of servants, whose loss was causing his mother a sorrow so unreasonably poignant.

The sense of her resemblance to some one grew upon him; but not yet had he begun to recognize the death-changed countenance; he became assured only that he *had* seen that still face before, and that, would she but open those eyes, he should know at once who she was.

Then the true suspicion flashed upon him: good God! *could it be* the dead Isy? Of course not! It was the merest illusion! a nonsensical fancy, caused by the irregular mingling of the light and darkness! In the daytime he could not have been so befooled by his imagination! He had always known the clearness, both physical and mental, with which he saw everything! Nevertheless, the folly had power to fix him staring where he stood, with his face leant close to the face of the dead. It was only like, it could not be the same! and yet he could not turn and go from it! Why did he not, by the mere will in whose strength he took pride, force his way out of the room? He stirred not a foot; he stared and stood. And as he stared, the dead face seemed to come nearer him through the darkness, growing more and more like the only girl he had ever, though even then only in fancy, loved. If it was not she, how could the dead look so like the living he had once known? At length what doubt was left, changed suddenly to assurance that it must be she. And - dare I say it? - it brought him a sense of relief! He breathed a sigh of such false, rascally peace as he had not known since his sin, and with that sigh he left the room.

George MacDonald

Passing his mother, who still wept in the now deeper dusk of the parlour, with the observation that there was no moon, and it would be quite dark before he reached the manse, he bade her good-night, and went out.

When Peter, who unable to sit longer inactive had gone to the stable, re-entered, foiled in the attempt to occupy himself, and sat down by his wife, she began to talk about the funeral preparations, and the persons to be invited. But such sorrow overtook him afresh, that even his wife, herself inconsolable over her loss, was surprised at the depth of his grief for one who was no relative. It seemed to him indelicate, almost heartless of her to talk so soon of burying the dear one but just gone from their sight: it was unnecessary dispatch, and suggested a lack of reverence!

"What for sic a hurry?" he expostulated. "Isna there time eneuch to put oot o' yer sicht what ye ance lo'ed sae weel? Lat me be the nicht; the morn 'ill be here sene eneuch! Lat my sowl rest a moment wi' deith, and haud awa wi' yer funeral. 'Sufficient til the day,' ye ken!"

"Eh dear, but I'm no like you, Peter! Whan the sowl's gane, I tak no content i' the presence o' the puir worthless body, luikin what it never mair can be! Na, I wad be rid o' 't, I confess! - But be it as ye wull, my ain man! It's a sair hert ye hae as weel as me i' yer body this nicht; and we maun beir ane anither's burdens! The dauty may lie as we hae laid her, the nicht throuw, and naething said: there's little to be dene for her; she's a bonny clean corp as ever was, and may weel lie a week afore we put her awa'! - There's no need for ony to watch her; tyke nor baudrins 'ill never come near her. - I hae aye won'ert what for fowk wad sit up wi the deid:

yet I min' me weel they aye did i' the auld time."

In this she showed, however, and in this alone, that the girl she lamented was not her own daughter; for when the other Isy died, her body was never for a moment left with the eternal spaces, as if she might wake, and be terrified to find herself alone. Then, as if God had forgotten them, they went to bed without saying their usual prayers together: I fancy the visit of her son had been to Marion like the chill of a wandering iceberg.

In the morning the farmer, up first as usual, went into the death-chamber and sat down by the side of the bed, reproaching himself that he had forgotten "worship" the night before.

And as he sat looking at the white face, he became aware of what might be a little tinge of colour - the faintest possible - upon the lips. He knew it must be a fancy, or at best an accident without significance - for he had heard of such a thing! Still, even if his eyes were deceiving him, he must shrink from hiding away such death out of sight! The merest counterfeit of life was too sacred for burial! Just such might the little daughter of Jairus have looked when the Lord took her by the hand ere she arose!

Thus feeling, and thus seeming to see on the lips of the girl a doubtful tinge of the light of life, it was no wonder that Peter could not entertain the thought of her immediate burial. They must at least wait some sign, some unmistakable proof even, of change begun!

Instead, therefore, of going into the yard to set in motion the needful preparations for the harvest at hand, he sat on with the dead: he could not leave her until his wife should come to take his place and keep her company! He brought a bible from the next room, sat down again, and waited beside her. In doubtful, timid, tremulous hope, not worthy of the name of hope - a mere sense of a scarcely possible possibility, he waited what he would not consent to believe he waited for. He would not deceive himself; he would give his wife no hint, but wait to see how she saw! He would put to her no leading question even, but watch for any start or touch of surprise she might betray!

By and by Marion appeared, gazed a moment on the dead, looked pitifully in her husband's face, and went out again.

"She sees naething!" said Peter to himself. "I s' awa' to my wark! - Still I winna hae her laid aside afore I'm a wheen surer o' what she is - leevin sowl or deid clod!"

With a sad sense of vanished self-delusion, he rose and went out. As he passed through the kitchen, his wife followed him to the door. "Ye'll see and sen' a message to the vricht *(carpenter)* the day?" she whispered.

"I'm no likly to forget!" he answered; "but there's nae hurry, seem there's no life concernt!"

"Na, nane; the mair's the pity!" she answered; and Peter knew, with a glad relief, that his wife was coming to herself from the terrible blow.

She sent the cowboy to the Cormacks' cottage, to tell Eppie to come to her.

The old woman came, heard what details there were to the sad story, shook her head mournfully, and found nothing to say; but together they set about preparing the body for burial. That done, the mind of Mrs. Blatherwick was at ease, and she sat expecting the visit of the carpenter. But the carpenter did not come.

On the Thursday morning the soutar came to inquire after his friends at Stanecross, and the gudewife gave him a message to Willie Wabster, the *vricht*, to see about the coffin.

But the soutar, catching sight of the farmer in the yard, went and had a talk with him; and the result was that he took no message to the carpenter; and when Peter went in to his dinner, he still said there was no hurry: why should she be so anxious to heap earth over the dead? For still he saw, or fancied he saw, the same possible colour on Isy's cheek - like the faintest sunset-red, or that in the heart of the palest blush-rose, which is either glow or pallor as you choose to think it. So the first week of Isy's death passed, and still she lay in state, ready for the grave, but unburied.

Not a few of the neighbours came to see her, and were admitted where she lay; and some of them warned Marion that, when the change came, it would come suddenly; but still Peter would not hear of her being buried "with that colour on her cheek!" And Marion had come to see, or to imagine with her husband that she saw the colour. So, each in turn, they kept watching her: who could tell but the Lord might be going to work a miracle for them, and was not in the meantime only trying them, to see how long their patience and hope would endure!

The report spread through the neighbourhood, and reached Tiltowie, where it speedily pervaded street and lane: - "The lass at Stanecross, she's lyin deid, and luikin as alive as ever she was!" From street and lane the people went crowding to see the strange sight, and would have overrun the house, but had a reception by no means cordial: the farmer set men at every door, and would admit no one. Angry and ashamed, they all turned and went - except a few of the more inquisitive, who continued lurking about in the hope of hearing something to carry home and enlarge upon.

As to the minister, he insisted upon disbelieving the whole thing, and yet was made not a little uncomfortable by the rumour. Such a foe to superstition that in his mind he silently questioned the truth of all records of miracles, to whomsoever attributed, he was yet haunted by a fear which he dared not formulate. Of course, whatever might take place, it could be no miracle, but the mere natural effect of natural causes! None the less, however, did he dread what might happen: he feared Isy herself, and what she might disclose! For a time he did not dare again go near the place. The girl might be in a trance! she might revive suddenly, and call out his name! She might even reveal all! She had always been a strange girl! What if, indeed, she were even being now kept alive to tell the truth, and disgrace him before all the world! Horrible as was the thought, might it not be well, in view of the possibility of her revival, that he should be present to hear anything she might say, and take precaution against it? He resolved, therefore, to go to Stonecross, and make inquiry after her, heartily hoping to find her undoubtedly and irrecoverably dead.

In the meantime, Peter had been growing more and more expectant, and had nearly forgotten all about the coffin, when a fresh rumour came to the ears of

William Webster, the coffin-maker, that the young woman at Stonecross was indeed and unmistakably gone; whereupon he, having lost patience over the uncertainty that had been crippling his operations, questioned no more what he had so long expected, set himself at once to his supposed task, and finished what he had already begun and indeed half ended. The same night that the minister was on his way to the farm, he passed Webster and his man carrying the coffin home through the darkness: he descried what it was, and his heart gave a throb of satisfaction. The men reaching Stonecross in the pitch-blackness of a gathering storm, they stupidly set up their burden on end by the first door, and went on to the other, where they made a vain effort to convey to the deaf Eppie a knowledge of what they had done. She making them no intelligible reply, there they left the coffin leaning up against the wall; and, eager to get home ere the storm broke upon them, set off at what speed was possible to them on the rough and dark road to Tiltowie, now in their turn meeting and passing the minister on his way.

By the time James arrived at Stonecross, it was too dark for him to see the ghastly sentinel standing at the nearer door. He walked into the parlour; and there met his father coming from the little chamber where his wife was seated.

"Isna this a most amazin thing, and houpfu' as it's amazing?" cried his father. "What *can* there be to come oot o' 't? Eh, but the w'ys o' the Almichty are truly no to be mizzered by mortal line! The lass maun surely be intendit for marvellous things, to be dealt wi' efter sic an extra-ordnar fashion! Nicht efter nicht has the tane or the tither o' hiz twa been sittin here aside her, lattin the hairst tak its chance, and i' the daytime lea'in 'maist

George MacDonald

a' to the men, me sleepin and they at their wark; and here the bonny cratur lyin, as quaiet as gien she had never seen tribble, for thirteen days, and no change past upon her, no more than on the three holy bairns i' the fiery furnace! I'm jist in a trimle to think what's to come oot o' 't a'! God only kens! we can but sit still and wait his appearance! What think ye, Jeemie? - Whan the Lord was deid upo' the cross, they waitit but twa nichts, and there he was up afore them! here we hae waitit, close on a haill fortnicht - and naething even to pruv that she's deid! still less ony sign that ever she'll speyk word til's again! - What think ye o' 't, man?"

"Gien ever she returns to life, I greatly doobt she'll ever bring back her senses wi' her!" said the mother, joining them from the inner chamber.

"Hoot, ye min' the tale o' the lady - Lady Fanshawe, I believe they ca'd her? She cam til hersel a' richt i' the en'!" said Peter.

"I don't remember the story," said James. "Such old world tales are little to be heeded."

"I min' naething aboot it but jist that muckle," said his father. "And I can think o' naething but that bonny lassie lyin there afore me naither deid nor alive! I jist won'er, Jeames, that ye're no as concernt, and as fillt wi' doobt and even dreid anent it as I am mysel!"

"We're all in the hands of the God who created life and death," returned James, in a pious tone.

The father held his peace.

" And He'll bring licht oot o' the vera dark o' the

grave!" said the mother.

Her faith, or at least her hope, once set agoing, went farther than her husband's, and she had a greater power of waiting than he. James had sorely tried both her patience and her hope, and not even now had she given him up.

"Ye'll bide and share oor watch this ae nicht, Jeames?" said Peter. "It's an elrische kin o' a thing to wauk up i' the mirk mids, wi' a deid corp aside ye! - No 'at even yet I gie her up for deid! but I canna help feelin some eerie like - no to say fleyt! Bide, man, and see the nicht oot wi' 's, and gie yer mither and me some hert o' grace."

James had little inclination to add another to the party, and began to murmur something about his house-keeper. But his mother cut him short with the indignant remark -

"Hoot, what's *she*? - Naething to you or ony o' 's! Lat her sit up for ye, gien she likes! Lat her sit, I say, and never waste thoucht upo' the queyn!"

James had not a word to answer. Greatly as he shrank from the ordeal, he must encounter it without show of reluctance! He dared not even propose to sit in the kitchen and smoke. With better courage than will, he consented to share their vigil. "And then," he reflected, "if she should come to herself, there would be the advantage he had foreseen and even half desired!"

His mother went to prepare supper for them. His father rose, and saying he would have a look at the night, went toward the door; for even his strange situation could not entirely smother the anxiety of the husband-man. But James glided past him to the door, determined not to be left alone with that thing in the chamber.

But in the meantime the wind had been rising, and the coffin had been tilting and resettling on its narrower end. At last, James opening the door, the gruesome thing fell forward just as he crossed the threshold, knocked him down, and settled on the top of him. His father, close behind him, tumbled over the obstruction, divined, in the light of a lamp in the passage, what the prostrate thing was, and scrambling to his feet with the only oath he had, I fully believe, ever uttered, cried: "Damn that fule, Willie Wabster! Had he naething better to dee nor sen' to the hoose coffins naebody wantit - and syne set them doon like rotten-traps *(rat-traps)* to whomel puir Jeemie!" He lifted the thing from off the minister, who rose not much hurt, but both amazed and offended at the mishap, and went to his mother in the kitchen.

"Dinna say muckle to yer mither, Jeames laad," said his father as he went; "that is, dinna explain preceesely hoo the ill-faured thing happent. *I'll* hae amen's *(amends, vengeance)* upon him!" So saying, he took the offensive vehicle, awkward burden as it was, in his two arms, and carrying it to the back of the cornyard, shoved it over the low wall into the dry ditch at its foot, where he heaped dirty straw from the stable over it.

"It'll be lang," he vowed to himsel, "or Willie Wabster hear the last o' this! - and langer yet or he see the glint o' the siller he thoucht he was yirnin by 't! - It's come and cairry 't hame himsel he sall, the muckle idiot! He may turn 't intil a breid-kist, or what he likes, the gomf!"

"Fain wud I screw the reid heid o' 'im intil that same kist, and hand him there, short o' smorin!" he muttered as he went back to the house. - "Faith, I could 'maist beery him ootricht!" he concluded, with a grim smile.

Ere he re-entered the house, however, he walked a little way up the hill, to cast over the vault above him a farmer's look of inquiry as to the coming night, and then went in, shaking his head at what the clouds boded.

Marion had brought their simple supper into the parlour, and was sitting there with James, waiting for him. When they had ended their meal, and Eppie had removed the remnants, the husband and wife went into the adjoining chamber and sat down by the bedside, where James presently joined them with a book in his hand. Eppie, having *rested* the fire in the kitchen, came into the parlour, and sat on the edge of a chair just inside the door.

Peter had said nothing about the night, and indeed, in his wrath with the carpenter, had hardly noted how imminent was the storm; but the air had grown very sultry, and the night was black as pitch, for a solid mass of cloud had blotted out the stars: it was plain that, long before morning, a terrible storm must break. But midnight came and went, and all was very still.

Suddenly the storm was upon them, with a forked, vibrating flash of angry light that seemed to sting their eyeballs, and was replaced by a darkness that seemed to crush them like a ponderous weight. Then all at once the weight itself seemed torn and shattered into sound - into heaps of bursting, roaring, tumultuous billows. Another flash, yet another and another followed, each with its crashing uproar of celestial avalanches. At the first flash Peter had risen and gone to the larger window of the parlour, to discover, if possible, in what direction the storm was travelling. Marion, feeling as if suddenly unroofed, followed him, and James was left alone with the dead. He sat, not daring to move; but when the third flash came, it flickered and played so long about the dead face, that it seemed for minutes vividly visible, and his gaze was fixed on it, fascinated. The same moment, without a single preparatory movement, Isy was on her feet, erect on the bed.

A great cry reached the ears of the father and mother. They hurried into the chamber: James lay motionless and senseless on the floor: a man's nerve is not necessarily proportioned to the hardness of his heart! The verity of the thing had overwhelmed him.

Isobel had fallen, and lay gasping and sighing on the bed. She knew nothing of what had happened to her; she did not yet know herself - did not know that her faithless lover lay on the floor by her bedside.

When the mother entered, she saw nothing - only heard Isy's breathing. But when her husband came with a candle, and she saw her son on the floor, she forgot Isy; all her care was for James. She dropped on her knees beside him, raised his head, held it to her bosom, and lamented over him as if he were dead. She even felt annoyed with the poor girl's moaning, as she struggled to get back to life. Why should she whose history was such, be the cause of mishap to her reverend and honoured son? Was she worth one of his little fingers! Let her moan and groan and sigh away there - what did it matter! she could well enough wait a bit! She would see to her presently, when her precious son was better!

Very different was the effect upon Peter when he saw Isy coming to herself. It was a miracle indeed! It could be nothing less! White as was her face, there was in it an unmistakable look of reviving life! When she opened her eyes and saw her master bending over her, she greeted him with a faint smile, closed her eyes again, and lay still. James also soon began to show signs of recovery, and his father turned to him.

With the old sullen look of his boyhood, he glanced up at his mother, still overwhelming him with caresses and tears.

"Let me up," he said querulously, and began to wipe his face. "I feel so strange! What can have made me turn so sick all at once?"

"Isy's come to life again!" said his mother, with modified show of pleasure.

"Oh!" he returned.

"Ye're surely no sorry for that!" rejoined his mother, with a reaction of disappointment at his lack of sympathy, and rose as she said it.

"I'm pleased to hear it - why not?" he answered. "But she gave me a terrible start! You see, I never expected it, as you did!"

"Weel, ye *are* hertless, Jeernie!" exclaimed his father.

"Hae ye nae spark o' fellow-feelin wi' yer ain mither, whan the lass comes to life 'at she's been fourteen days murnin for deid? But losh! she's aff again! - deid or in a dwaum, I kenna! - Is't possible she's gaein to slip frae oor hand yet?"

James turned his head aside, and murmured something inaudibly.

But Isy had only fainted. After some eager ministrations on the part of Peter, she came to herself once more, and lay panting, her forehead wet as with the dew of death.

The farmer ran out to a loft in the yard, and calling the herd-boy, a clever lad, told him to rise and ride for the doctor as fast as the mare could lay feet to the road.

"Tell him," he said, "that Isy has come to life, and he maun munt and ride like the vera mischeef, or she'll be deid again afore he wins til her. Gien ye canna get the tae doctor, awa wi' ye to the tither, and dinna ley him till ye see him i' the saiddle and startit. Syne ye can ease the mere, and come hame at yer leisur; he'll be here lang afore ye! - Tell him I'll pey him ony fee he likes, be't what it may, and never compleen! - Awa' wi' ye like the vera deevil!"

"I didna think ye kenned hoo *he* rade," answered the boy pawkily, as he shot to the stable. "Weel," he added, "ye maunna gley asklent at the mere whan she comes hame some saipy-like!"

When he returned on the mare's back, the farmer was waiting for him with the whisky-bottle in his hand.

"Na, na!" he said, seeing the lad eye the bottle, "it's no for you! ye want a' the sma' wit ye ever hed: it's no *you* 'at has to gallop; ye hae but to stick on! - Hae, Susy!"

He poured half a tumblerful into a soup-plate, and held it out to the mare, who, never snuffing at it, licked it up greedily, and immediately started of herself at a good pace.

Peter carried the bottle to the chamber, and got Isy to swallow a little, after which she began to recover again. Nor did Marion forget to administer a share to James, who was not a little in want of it.

When, within an hour, the doctor arrived full of amazed incredulity, he found Isy in a troubled sleep, and James gone to bed.

CHAPTER XXIII

The next day, Isy, although very weak, was greatly better. She was, however, too ill to get up; and Marion seemed now in her element, with two invalids, both dear to her, to look after. She hardly knew for which to be more grateful - her son, given helpless into her hands, unable to repel the love she lavished upon him; or the girl whom God had taken from the very throat of the swallowing grave. But her heart, at first bubbling over with gladness, soon grew calmer, when she came to perceive how very ill James was. And before long she began to fear she must part with her child, whose lack of love hitherto made the threatened separation the more frightful to her. She turned even from the thought of Isy's restoration, as if that were itself an added wrong. From the occasional involuntary association of the two in her thought, she would turn away with a sort of meek loathing. To hold her James for one moment in the same thought with any girl less spotless than he, was to disgrace herself!

James was indeed not only very ill, but growing slowly worse; for he lay struggling at last in the Backbite of Conscience, who had him in her unrelaxing jaws, and was worrying him well. Whence the holy dog came we know, but how he got a hold of him to begin his saving torment, who shall understand but the maker of men and of their secret, inexorable friend! Every beginning is infinitesimal, and wrapt in the mystery of creation.

Its results only, not its modes of operation or their stages, I may venture attempting to convey. It was the wind blowing where it listed, doing everything and explaining nothing. That wind from the timeless and spaceless and formless region of God's feeling and God's thought, blew open the eyes of this man's mind so that he saw, and became aware that he saw. It blew away the long-gathered vapours of his self-satisfaction and conceit; it blew wide the windows of his soul, that the sweet odour of his father's and mother's thoughts concerning him might enter; and when it entered, he knew it for what it was; it blew back to him his own judgments of them and their doings, and he saw those judgments side by side with his new insights into their real thoughts and feelings; it blew away the desert sands of his own moral dulness, indifference, and selfishness, that had so long hidden beneath them the watersprings of his own heart, existent by and for love and its gladness; it cleared all his conscious being, made him understand that he had never hitherto loved his mother or his father, or any neighbour; that he had never loved God one genuine atom, never loved the Lord Christ, his Master, or cared in the least that he had died for him; had never at any moment loved Isy - least of all when to himself he pleaded in his own excuse that he had loved her. That blowing wind, which he could not see, neither knew whence it came, and yet less whither it was going, began to blow together his soul and those of his parents; the love in his father and in his mother drew him; the memories of his childhood drew him; for the heart of God himself was drawing him, as it had been from the first, only now first he began to feel its drawing; and as he yielded to that drawing and went nearer, God drew ever more and more strongly; until at last - I know not, I say, how God did it, or whereby he made the soul of James Blatherwick different from what it had been - but at last it grew capable of loving, and did love: first, he yielded to love because he could not help it; then he willed to love because he could love; then, become conscious of the power, he loved the more, and so went on to love more and more. And thus did James become what he had to become - or perish.

But for this liberty, he had to pass through wild regions of torment and horror; he had to become all but mad, and know it; his body, and his soul as well, had to be parched with fever, thirst, and fear; he had to sleep and dream lovely dreams of coolness and peace and courage; then wake and know that all his life he had been dead, and now first was alive; that love, new-born, was driving out the gibbering phantoms; that now indeed it was good to be, and know others alive about him; that now life was possible, because life was to love, and love was to live. What love was, or how it was, he could not tell; he knew only that it was the will and the joy of the Father and the Son.

Long ere he arrived at this, however, the falsehood and utter meanness of his behaviour to Isy had become plain to him, bringing with it such an overpowering self-contempt and self-loathing, that he was tempted even to self-destruction to escape the knowledge that he was himself the very man who had been such, and had done such things. "To know my deed, 'twere best not know myself!" he might have said with Macbeth. But he must live on, for how otherwise could he make any atonement? And with the thought of reparation, and possible forgiveness and reconcilement, his old love for Isy rushed in like a flood, grown infinitely nobler, and was uplifted at last into a genuine self-abandoning devotion. But until this final change arrived, his occasional paroxysms of remorse touched almost on madness, and for some time it seemed doubtful whether his mind must not retain a permanent tinge of insanity. He conceived a huge disgust of his office and all its requirements; and sometimes bitterly blamed his parents for not interfering with his choice of a profession that was certain to be his ruin.

One day, having had no delirium for some hours, he suddenly called out as they stood by his bed -

"Oh, mother! oh, father! *why* did you tempt me to such hypocrisy? *Why* did you not bring me up to walk at the plough-tail? *Then* I should never have had to encounter the damnable snares of the pulpit! It was that which ruined me - the notion that I must take the minister for my pattern, and live up to my idea of *him*, before even I had begun to cherish anything real in me! It was the road royal to hypocrisy! Without that rootless, worthless, devilish fancy, I might have been no worse than other people! Now I am lost! Now I shall never get back to bare honesty, not to say innocence! They are both gone for ever!"

The poor mother could only imagine it his humility that made him accuse himself of hypocrisy, and that because he had not fulfilled to the uttermost the smallest duty of his great office.

"Jamie, dear," she cried, laying her cheek to his, "ye maun cast yer care upo' Him that careth for ye! He kens ye hae dene yer best - or if no yer vera best - for wha daur say that? - ye hae at least dene what ye could!"

"Na, na!" he answered, resuming the speech of his boyhood - a far better sign of him than his mother understood, "I ken ower muckle, and that muckle ower weel, to lay sic a flattering unction to my sowl! It's jist as black as the fell mirk! 'Ah, limed soul, that, struggling to be free, art more engaged!'"

"Hoots, ye're dreamin, laddie! Ye never was engaged to onybody - at least that ever I h'ard tell o'! But, ony gait, fash na ye aboot that! Gien it be onything o' sic a natur that's troublin ye, yer father and me we s' get ye clear o' 't!"

"Ay, there ye're at it again! It was *you* 'at laid the bird-lime! Ye aye tuik pairt, mither, wi' the muckle deil that wad na rist till he had my sowl in his deepest pit!"

"The Lord kens his ain: he'll see that they come throuw unscaumit!"

"The Lord disna mak ony hypocreet o' purpose doobtless; but gien a man sin efter he has ance come to the knowledge o' the trowth, there remaineth for him - ye ken the lave o' 't as weel as I dee mysel, mother! My only houp lies in a doobt - a doobt, that is, whether I *had* ever come til a knowledge o' the trowth - or hae yet! - Maybe no!"

"Laddie, ye're no i' yer richt min'. It's fearsome to hearken til ye!"

"It'll be waur to hear me roarin wi' the rich man i' the lowes o' hell!"

"Peter! Peter!" cried Marion, driven almost to distraction, "here's yer ain son, puir fallow, blasphemin like ane o' the condemned! He jist gars me creep!"

Receiving no answer, for her husband was nowhere near at the moment, she called aloud in her desperation -

"Isy! Isy! come and see gien ye can dee onything to quaiet this ill bairn."

Isy heard, and sprang from her bed.

"Comin, mistress!" she answered; "comin this moment."

They had not met since her resurrection, as Peter always called it.

"Isy! Isy!" cried James, the moment he heard her approaching, "come and hand the deil aff o' me!"

He had risen to his elbow, and was looking eagerly toward the door.

She entered. James threw wide his arms, and with glowing eyes clasped her to his bosom. She made no resistance: his mother would lay it all to the fever! He broke into wild words of love, repentance, and devotion.

"Never heed him a hair, mem; he's clean aff o' his heid!" she said in a low voice, making no attempt to free herself from his embrace, but treating him like a delirious child. "There maun be something aboot me, mem, that quaiets him a bit! It's the brain, ye ken, mem! it's the het brain! We maunna contre him! he maun hae his ain w'y for a wee!"

But such was James's behaviour to Isy that it was impossible for the mother not to perceive that, incredible as it might seem, this must be far from the first time they had met; and presently she fell to examining her memory whether she herself might not have seen Isy before ever she came to Stonecross; but she could find no answer to her inquiry, press the question as she might. By and by, her husband came in to have his dinner, and finding herself compelled, much against her will, to leave the two together, she sent up Eppie to take Isy's place, with the message that she was to go down at once. Isy obeyed, and went to the kitchen; but, perturbed and trembling, dropped on the first chair she came to. The farmer, already seated at the table, looked up, and anxiously regarding her, said -

"Bairn, ye're no fit to be aboot! Ye maun caw canny, or ye'll be ower the burn yet or ever ye're safe upo' this side o' 't! Preserve's a'! ir we to lowse ye twise in ae month?"

"Jist answer me ae queston, Isy, and I'll speir nae mair," said Marion.

"Na, na, never a queston!" interposed Peter; - "no ane afore even the shaidow o' deith has left the hoose! - Draw ye up to the table, my bonny bairn: this isna a time for ceremony, and there's sma' room for that ony day!"

Finding, however, that she sat motionless, and looked far more death-like than while in her trance, he got up, and insisted on her swallowing a little whisky; when she revived, and glad to put herself under his nearer protection, took the chair he had placed for her beside him, and made a futile attempt at eating. "It's sma' won'er the puir thing hasna muckle eppiteet," remarked Mrs. Blatherwick, "considerin the w'y yon ravin laddie up the stair has been cairryin on til her!"

"What! Hoo's that?" questioned her husband with a start.

"But ye're no to mak onything o' that, Isy!" added her mistress.

"Never a particle, mem!" returned Isy. "I ken weel it stan's for naething but the heat o' the burnin brain! I'm richt glaid though, that the sicht o' me did seem to comfort him a wee!"

"Weel, I'm no sae sure!" answered Marion. "But we'll say nae mair anent that the noo! The guidman says no; and his word's law i' this hoose."

Isy resumed her pretence of breakfast. Presently Eppie came down, and going to her master, said -

"Here's An'ra, sir, come to speir efter the yoong minister and Isy: am I to gar him come in?"

"Ay, and gie him his brakfast," shouted the farmer.

The old woman set a chair for her son by the door, and proceeded to attend to him. James was left alone.

Silence again fell, and the appearance of eating was resumed, Peter being the only one that made a reality of it. Marion was occupied with many thinkings, specially a growing doubt and soreness about Isy. The hussy had a secret! She had known something all the

George MacDonald

time, and had been taking advantage of her unsuspiciousness! It would be a fine thing for her, indeed, to get hold of the minister! but she would see him dead first! It was too bad of the Robertsons, whom she had known so long and trusted so much! They knew what they were doing when they passed their trash upon her! She began to distrust ministers! What right had they to pluck brands from the burning at the expense o' dacent fowk! It was to do evil that good might come! She would say that to their faces! Thus she sat thinking and glooming.

A cry of misery came from the room above. Isy started to her feet. But Marion was up before her.

"Sit doon this minute," she commanded.

Isy hesitated.

"Sit doon this moment, I tell ye!" repeated Marion imperiously. "Ye hae no business there! I'm gaein til 'im mysel!" And with the word she left the room.

Peter laid down his spoon, then half rose, staring bewildered, and followed his wife from the room.

"Oh my baby! my baby!" cried Isy, finding herself alone. "If only I had you to take my part! It was God gave you to me, or how could I love you so? And the mistress winna believe that even I had a bairnie! Noo she'll be sayin I killt my bonny wee man! And yet, even for *his* sake, I never ance wisht ye hadna been born! And noo, whan the father o' 'im's ill, and cryin oot for me, they winna lat me near 'im!"

The last words left her lips in a wailing shriek.

Then first she saw that her master had reentered. Wiping her eyes hurriedly, she turned to him with a pitiful, apologetic smile.

"Dinna be sair vext wi' me, sir: I canna help bein glaid that I had him, and to tyne him has gien me an unco sair hert!"

She stopped, terrified: how much had he heard? she could not tell what she might not have said! But the farmer had resumed his breakfast, and went on eating as if she had not spoken. He had heard nearly all she said, and now sat brooding on her words.

Isy was silent, saying in her heart - "If only he loved me, I should be content, and desire no more! I would never even want him to say it! I would be so good to him, and so silent, that he could not help loving me a little!"

I wonder whether she would have been as hopeful had she known how his mother had loved him, and how vainly she had looked for any love in return! And when Isy vowed in her heart never to let James know that she had borne him a son, she did not perceive that thus she would withhold the most potent of influences for his repentance and restoration to God and his parents. She did not see James again that night; and before she fell asleep at last in the small hours of the morning, she had made up her mind that, ere the same morning grew clear upon the moor, she would, as the only thing left her to do for him, be far away from Stonecross. She would go back to Deemouth, and again seek work at the paper-mills!

CHAPTER XXIV

She woke in the first of the gray dawn, while the house was in utter stillness, and rising at once, rose and dressed herself with soundless haste. It was hard indeed to go and leave James thus in danger, but she had no choice! She held her breath and listened, but all was still. She opened her door softly; not a sound reached her ear as she crept down the stair. She had neither to unlock nor unbolt the door to leave the house, for it was never made fast. A dread sense of the old wandering desolation came back upon her as she stepped across the threshold, and now she had no baby to comfort her! She was leaving a mouldy peace and a withered love behind her, and had once more to encounter the rough coarse world! She feared the moor she had to cross, and the old dreams she must there encounter; and as she held on her way through them, she felt, in her new loneliness, and the slow-breaking dawn, as if she were lying again in her trance, partly conscious, but quite unable to move, thinking she was dead, and waiting to be buried. Then suddenly she knew where she was, and that God was not gone, but her own Maker was with her, and would not forsake her.

Of the roads that led from the farm she knew only that by which Mr. Robertson had brought her, and that would guide her to the village where they had left the coach: there she was sure to find some way of returning to Deemouth! Feeble after her prolonged inaction, and the crowd of emotions succeeding her recovery, she found the road very weary, and long ere she reached Tiltowie, she felt all but worn out. At the only house she had come to on the way, she stopped and asked for some water. The woman, the only person she had seen, for it was still early morning, and the road was a lonely one, perceived that she looked ill, and gave her milk instead. In the strength of that milk she reached the end of her first day's journey; and for many days she had not to take a second.

Now Isy had once seen the soutar at the farm, and going about her work had heard scraps of his conversation with the mistress, when she had been greatly struck by certain things he said, and had often since wished for the opportunity of a talk with him. That same morning then, going along a narrow lane, and hearing a cobbler's hammer, she glanced through a window close to the path, and at once recognized the soutar. He looked up as she obscured his light, and could scarce believe his eyes when, so early in the day, he saw before him Mistress Blatherwick's maid, concerning whom there had been such a talk and such a marvelling for weeks. She looked ill, and he was amazed to see her about so soon, and so far from home. She smiled to him feebly, and passed from his range with a respectful nod. He sprang to his feet, bolted out, and overtook her at once.

"I'm jist gaein to drop my wark, mem, and hae my brakfast: wull ye no come in and share wi' an auld man and a yoong lass? Ye hae come a gey bit, and luik some fatiguit!"

"Thank ye kindly, sir," returned Isy. "I *am* a bit tired! - But I won'er ye kenned me!"

"Weel, I canna jist say I ken ye by the name fowk ca' ye; and still less div I ken ye by the name the Lord ca's ye; but nowther maitters muckle to her that kens He has a name growin for her - or raither, a name she's growin til! Eh, what a day will that be whan ilk habitant o' the holy city 'ill tramp the streets o' 't weel kenned and weel kennin!"

"Ay, sir! I 'maist un'erstan' ye ootricht, for I h'ard ye ance sayin something like that to the mistress, the nicht ye broucht hame the maister's shune to Stanecross. And, eh, I'm richt glaid to see ye again!"

They were already in the house, for she had followed him in almost mechanically; and the soutar was setting for her the only chair there was, when the cry of a child reached their ears. The girl started to her feet. A rosy flush of delight overspread her countenance; she fell a-trembling from head to foot, and it seemed uncertain whether she would succeed in running to the cry, or must fall to the floor.

"Ay," exclaimed the soutar, with one of his sudden flashes of unquestioning insight, "by the luik o' ye, ye ken that for the cry o' yer ain bairn, my bonny lass! Ye'll hae been missin him, sair, I doobt! - There! sit ye doon, and I'll hae him i' yer airms afore ae meenut!"

She obeyed him and sat down, but kept her eyes fixed on the door, wildly expectant. The soutar made haste, and ran to fetch the child. When he returned with him in his arms, he found her sitting bolt upright, with her hands already apart , held out to receive him , and her eyes alive as he had never seen eyes before.

"My Jamie! my ain bairn!" she cried, seizing him to her bosom with a grasp that, trembling, yet seemed to cling to him desperately, and a look almost of defiance, as if she dared the world to take him from her again. "O my God!" she cried, in an agony of thankfulness, "I ken ye noo! I ken ye noo! Never mair wull I doobt ye, my God! - Lost and found! - Lost for a wee, and found again for ever!"

Then she caught sight of Maggie, who had entered behind her father, and stood staring at her motionless, - with a look of gladness indeed, but not all of gladness.

"I ken fine," Isy broke out, with a trembling, yet eager, apologetic voice, "ye're grudgin me ilka luik at him! I ken't by mysel! Ye're thinkin him mair yours nor mine! And weel ye may, for it's you that's been motherin him ever since I lost my wits! It's true I ran awa' and left him; but ever sin' syne, I hae soucht him carefully wi' tears! And ye maunna beir me ony ill will - for there!" she added, holding him out to Maggie! "I haena kissed him yet! - no ance! - But ye wull lat me kiss him afore ye tak him awa'? - my ain bairnie, whause vera comin I had prepared shame for! - Oh my God! - But he kens naething aboot it, and winna ken for years to come! And nane but his ain mammie maun brak the dreid trowth til him! - and by that time he'll lo'e her weel eneuch to be able to bide it! I thank God that I haena had to shue the birds and the beasts aff o' his bonny wee body! It micht hae been, but for you, my bonnie lass! - and for you, sir!" she went on, turning to the soutar.

Maggie caught the child from her offering arms, and

held up his little face for his mother to kiss; and so held him until, for the moment, Isy's mother-greed was satisfied. Then she sat down with him in her lap, and Isy stood absorbed in regarding him. At last she said, with a deep sigh -

"Noo I maun awa', and I dinna ken hoo I'm to gang! I hae found him and maun leave him! - but I houp no for vera lang! - Maybe ye'll keep him yet a whilie - say for a week mair? He's been sae lang disused til a wan'erin life, that I doobt it mayna weel agree wi' him; and I maun awa' back to Deemooth, gien I can get onybody to gie me a lift."

"Na, na; that'll never dee," returned Maggie, with a sob. "My father'll be glaid eneuch to keep him; only we hae nae richt ower him, and ye maun hae him again whan ye wull."

"Ye see I hae nae place to tak him til!" pleaded Isy.

"Gien ye dinna want him, gie him to me: I want him!" said Maggie eagerly.

"Want him!" returned Isy, bursting into tears; "I hae lived but upo the bare houp o' gettin him again! I hae grutten my een sair for the sicht o' 'im! Aften hae I waukent greetin ohn kenned for what! - and noo ye tell me I dinna want him, 'cause I hae nae spot but my breist to lay his heid upo! Eh, guid fowk, keep him till I get a place to tak him til, and syne haudna him a meenute frae me!"

All this time the soutar had been watching the two girls with a divine look in his black eyes and rugged face; now at last he opened his mouth and said:

"Them 'at haps the bairn, are aye sib *(related)* to the mither! - Gang ben the hoose wi' Maggie, my dear; and lay ye doon on her bed, and she'll lay the bairnie aside ye, and fess yer brakfast there til ye. Ye winna be easy to sair *(satisfy)*, haein had sae little o' 'im for sae lang! - Lea' them there thegither, Maggie, my doo," he went on with infinite tenderness, "and come and gie me a han' as sune as ye hae maskit the tay, and gotten a lof o' white breid. I s' hae my parritch a bit later."

Maggie obeyed at once, and took Isy to the other end of the house, where the soutar had long ago given up his bed to her and the baby.

When they had all breakfasted, the soutar and Maggie in the kitchen, and Isy and the bairnie in the ben en', Maggie took her old place beside her father, and for a long time they worked without word spoken.

"I doobt, father," said Maggie at length, "I haena been atten'in til ye properly! I fear the bairnie 's been garrin me forget ye!"

"No a hair, dautie!" returned the soutar. "The needs o' the little are stude aye far afore mine, and *had* to be seen til first! And noo that we hae the mither o' 'im, we'll get on faumous! - Isna she a fine cratur, and richt mitherlike wi' the bairn? That was a' I was concernt aboot! We'll get her story frae her or lang, and syne we'll ken a hantle better hoo to help her on! And there can be nae fear but, atween you and me, and the Michty at the back o' 's, we s' get breid eneuch for the quaternion o' 's!"

He laughed at the odd word as it fell from his mouth and the Acts of Apostles. Maggie laughed too, and wiped her eyes.

Before long, Maggie recognized that she had never been so happy in her life. Isy told them as much as she could without breaking her resolve to keep secret a certain name; and wrote to Mr. Robertson, telling him where she was, and that she had found her baby. He came with his wife to see her, and so a friendship began between the soutar and him, which Mr. Robertson always declared one of the most fortunate things that had ever befallen him.

"That soutar-body," he would say, "kens mair aboot God and his kingdom, the hert o' 't and the w'ys o' 't, than ony man I ever h'ard tell o' - and *that* heumble! - jist like the son o' God himsel!"

Before many days passed, however, a great anxiety laid hold of the little household: wee Jamie was taken so ill that the doctor had to be summoned. For eight days he had much fever, and his appealing looks were pitiful to see. When first he ceased to run about, and wanted to be nursed, no one could please him but the soutar himself, and he, at once discarding his work, gave himself up to the child's service. Before long, however, he required defter handling, and then no one would do but Maggie, to whom he had been more accustomed; nor could Isy get any share in the labour of love except when he was asleep: as soon as he woke, she had to encounter the pain of hearing him cry out for Maggie, and seeing him stretch forth his hands, even from his mother's lap, to one whom he knew better than her. But Maggie was very careful over the poor mother, and would always, the minute he was securely asleep, lay him softly upon her lap. And Maggie soon got so high above her jealousy, that one of the happiest moments in her life was when first the child consented to leave her arms for those of his mother. And when he was once more able to run about, Isy took her part with Maggie in putting hand and needle to the lining of the more delicate of the soutar's shoes.

CHAPTER XXV

There was great concern, and not a little alarm at Stonecross because of the disappearance of Isy. But James continued so ill, that his parents were unable to take much thought about anybody else. At last, however, the fever left him, and he began to recover, but lay still and silent, seeming to take no interest in anything, and remembered nothing he had said, or even that he had seen Isy. At the same time his wakened conscience was still at work in him, and had more to do with his enfeebled condition than the prolonged fever. At length his parents were convinced that he had something on his mind that interfered with his recovery, and his mother was confident that it had to do with "that deceitful creature, Isy." To learn that she was safe, might have given Marion some satisfaction, had she not known her refuge so near the manse; and having once heard where she was, she had never asked another question about her. Her husband, however, having overheard certain of the words that fell from Isy when she thought herself alone, was intently though quietly waiting for what must follow.

"I'm misdoobtin sair, Peter," began Marion one morning, after a long talk with the cottar's wife, who had been telling her of Isy's having taken up her abode with the soutar, "I'm sair misdoobtin whether that hizzie hadna mair to dee nor we hae been jaloosin, wi

Jamie's attack, than the mere scare he got. It seems to me he's lang been broodin ower something we ken noucht aboot."

"That would be nae ferlie, woman! Whan was it ever we kent onything gaein on i' that mysterious laddie! Na, but his had need be a guid conscience, for did ever onybody ken eneuch aboot it or him to say richt or wrang til 'im! But gien ye hae a thoucht he's ever wranged that lassie, I s' hae the trowth o' 't, gien it cost him a greitin! He'll never come to health o' body or min' till he's confest, and God has forgien him. He maun confess! He maun confess!"

"Hoot, Peter, dinna be sae suspicious o' yer ain. It's no like ye to be sae maisterfu' and owerbeirin. I wad na lat ae ill thoucht o' puir Jeemie inside this auld heid o' mine! It's the lassie, I'll tak my aith, it's that Isy's at the bothom o' 't!"

"Ye're some ready wi' yer aith, Mirran, to what ye ken naething aboot! I say again, gien he's dene ony wrang to that bonnie cratur - and it wudna tak ower muckle proof to convince me o' the same, he s' tak his stan', minister or no minister, upo the stele o' repentance!"

"Daur ye to speyk that gait aboot yer ain son - ay, and mine the mair gien *ye* disown him, Peter Bletherwick! - and the Lord's ain ordeent minister forbye!" cried Marion, driven almost to her wits' end, but more by the persistent haunting of her own suspicion, which she could not repress, than the terror of her husband's threat. "Besides, dinna ye see," she added cunningly, "that that would be to affront the lass as weel? - *He* wadna be the first to fa' intil the snare o' a designin wuman, and wad it be for his ain father to expose him to public contemp? *Your* pairt sud be to cover up his sin - gien it were a multitude, and no ae solitary bit faut!"

"Daur *ye* speyk o' a thing like that as a bit faut? - Ca' ye leein and hypocrisy a bit faut? I alloo the sin itsel mayna be jist damnable, but to what bouk mayna it come wi ither and waur sins upo the back o' 't? - Wi leein, and haudin aff o' himsel, a man may grow a cratur no fit to be taen up wi the taings! Eh me, but my pride i' the laddie! It 'ill be sma' pride for me gien this fearsome thing turn oot to be true!"

"And wha daur say it's true?" rejoined Marion almost fiercely.

"Nane but himsel; and gien it be sae, and he disna confess, the rod laid upon him 'ill be the rod o' iron, 'at smashes a man like a muckle crock. - I maun tak Jamie throuw han' *(to task)*!"

"Noo jist tak ye care, Peter, 'at ye dinna quench the smokin flax."

"I'm mair likly to get the bruised reed intil my nakit loof *(palm)*!" returned Peter. " But I s' say naething till he's a wee better, for we maunna drive him to despair! - Eh gien he would only repent! What is there I wadna dee to clear him - that is, to ken him innocent o' ony wrang til her! I wad dee wi thanksgivin!"

"Weel, I kenna that we're jist called upon sae far as that!" said Marion. "A lass is aye able to tak care o' hersel!"

"I wud! I wud! - God hae mercy upo' the twa o' them!"

In the afternoon James was a good deal better. When his father went in to see him, his first words were -

"I doobt, father, I'm no likly to preach ony mair: I've come to see 'at I never was fit for the wark, neither had I ever ony ca' til't."

"It may be sae, Jeemie," answered his father; "but we'll haud awa frae conclusions till ye're better, and able to jeedge wi'oot the bias o' ony thrawin distemper."

"Oh father," James went on, and to his delight Peter saw, for the first time since he was the merest child, tears running down his cheeks, now thin and wan; "Oh father, I hae been a terrible hypocreet! But my een's come open at last! I see mysel as I am!"

"Weel, there's God hard by, to tak ye by the han' like Enoch! Tell me," Peter went on, "hae ye onything upo yer min', laddie, 'at ye wud like to confess and be eased o'? There's nae papistry in confessin to yer ain auld father!"

James lay still for a few moments; then he said, almost inaudibly -

"I think I could tell my mother better nor you, father."

"It'll be a' ane whilk o' 's ye tell. The forgiein and the forgettin 'ill be ae deed - by the twa o' 's at ance! I s' gang and cry doon the stair til yer mother to come up and hear ye." For Peter knew by experience that good motions must be taken advantage of in their first ripeness. "We maunna try the speerit wi ony delays!" he added, as he went to the head of the stair, where he called aloud to his wife. Then returning to the bedside,

George MacDonald

he resumed his seat, saying, "I'll jist bide a minute till she comes."

He was loath to let in any risk between his going and her coming, for he knew how quickly minds may change; but the moment she appeared, he left the room, gently closing the door behind him.

Then the trembling, convicted soul plucked up what courage his so long stubborn and yet cringing heart was capable of, and began.

"Mother, there was a lass I cam to ken in Edinburgh, whan I was a divinity student there, and - "

"Ay, ay, I ken a' aboot it!" interrupted his mother, eager to spare him; " - an ill-faured, designin limmer, 'at micht ha kent better nor come ower the son o' a respectable wuman that gait! - Sic like, I doobtna, wad deceive the vera elec'!"

"Na, na, mother, she was nane o' that sort! She was baith bonny and guid, and pleasant to the hert as to the sicht: she wad hae saved me gien I had been true til her! She was ane o' the Lord's makin, as he has made but feow!"

"Whatfor didna she haud frae ye till ye had merried her than? Dinna tell me she didna lay hersel oot to mak a prey o' ye!"

"Mother, i' that sayin ye hae sclandert yersel! - I'll no say a word mair!"

"I'm sure neither yer father nor mysel wud hae stede i' yer gait ! " said Marion , retreating from the false position she had taken.

She did not know herself, or how bitter would have been her opposition; for she had set her mind on a distinguished match for her Jamie!

"God knows how I wish I had keepit a haud o' mysel! Syne I micht hae steppit oot o' the dirt o' my hypocrisy, i'stead o' gaein ower the heid intil't! I was aye a hypocrite, but she would maybe hae fun' me oot, and garred me luik at mysel!"

He did not know the probability that, if he had not fallen, he would have but sunk the deeper in the worst bog of all, self-satisfaction, and none the less have played her false, and left her to break her heart.

If any reader of this tale should argue it better then to do wrong and repent, than to resist the devil, I warn him, that in such case he will not repent until the sorrows of death and the pains of hell itself lay hold upon him. An overtaking fault may be beaten with few stripes, but a wilful wrong shall be beaten with many stripes. The door of the latter must share, not with Judas, for he did repent, although too late, but with such as have taken from themselves the power of repentance.

"Was there no mark left o' her disgrace?" asked his mother. "Wasna there a bairn to mak it manifest?"

"Nane I ever heard tell o'."

"In that case she's no muckle the waur, and ye needna gang lamentin: *she* 'll no be the ane to tell! and *ye* maunna, for her sake! Sae tak ye comfort ower what's gane and dune wi', and canna come back, and maunna happen again. - Eh, but it's a' God's-mercy there was nae bairn!"

Thus had the mother herself become an evil councillor, crying Peace! peace! when there was no peace, and tempting her son to go on and become a devil! But one thing yet rose up for the truth in his miserable heart - his reviving and growing love for Isy. It had seemed smothered in selfishness, but was alive and operative: God knows how - perhaps through feverish, incoherent, forgotten dreams.

He had expected his mother to aid his repentance, and uphold his walk in the way of righteousness, even should the way be that of social disgrace. He knew well that reparation must go hand in hand with repentance where the All-wise was judge, and selfish Society dared not urge one despicable pretence for painting hidden shame in the hues of honour. James had been the cowering slave of a false reputation; but his illness and the assaults of his conscience had roused him, set repentance before him, brought confession within sight, and purity within reach of prayer.

"I maun gang til her," he cried, "the meenute I'm able to be up! - Whaur is she, mother?"

"Upo nae accoont see her, Jamie! It wad be but to fa' again intil her snare!" answered his mother, with decision in her look and tone. "We're to abstain frae a' appearance o' evil - as ye ken better nor I can tell ye."

"But Isy's no an appearance o' evil, mother!"

"Ye say weel there, I confess! Na, she's no an appearance; she's the vera thing! Haud frae her, as ye wad frae the ill ane himsel."

"Did she never lat on what there had been atween 's?"

"Na, never. She kenned weel what would come o' that!"

"What, mother?"

"The ootside o' the door."

"Think ye she ever tauld onybody?"

"Mony ane, I doobtna."

"Weel, I dinna believe 't, I hae nae fear but she's been dumb as deith!"

"Hoo ken ye that? - What for said she never ae word aboot ye til yer ain mither?"

"'Cause she was set on haudin her tongue. Was she to bring an owre true tale o' me to the vera hoose I was born in? As lang as I haud til my tongue, she'll never wag hers! - Eh, but she's a true ane! *She's* ane to lippen til!"

"Weel, I alloo, she's deen as a wuman sud - the faut bein a' her ain!"

"The faut bein' a' mine, mother, she wouldna tell what would disgrace me!"

" She micht hae kenned her secret would be safe

wi' me!"

"*I* micht hae said the same, but for the w'y ye spak o' her this vera meenut! - Whaur is she, mother? Whaur's Isy?"

"'Deed, she's made a munelicht flittin o' 't!"

"I telled ye she would never tell upo me! - Hed she ony siller?"

"Hoo can *I* tell?"

"Did ye pey her ony wages?"

"She gae me no time! - But she's no likly to tell noo; for, hearin her tale, wha wad tak her in?"

"Eh, mother, but ye *are* hard-hertit!"

"I ken a harder, Jamie!"

"That's me! - and ye're richt, mother! But, eh, gien ye wad hae me loe ye frae this meenut to the end o' my days, be but a wee fair to Isy: *I* hae been a damnt scoon'rel til her!"

"Jamie; Jamie! ye're provokin the Lord to anger - sweirin like that in his vera face - and you a minister!"

"I provokit him a heap waur whan I left Isy to dree her shame! Divna ye min' hoo the apostle Peter cursed, whan he said to Simon, 'Gang to hell wi' yer siller!'"

"She's telt the soutar, onygait!"

"What! has *he* gotten a hand o' her?"

"Ay, has he! - And dinna ye think it'll be a' ower the toon lang or this!"

"And hoo will ye meet it, mother?"

"We maun tell yer father, and get him to quaiet the soutar! - For *her*, we maun jist stap her mou wi' a bunch o' bank-notts!"

"That wad jist mak it 'maist impossible for even her to forgie you or me aither ony langer!"

"And wha's she to speyk o' forgivin!"

The door opened, and Peter entered. He strode up to his wife, and stood over her like an angel of vengeance. His very lips were white with wrath.

"Efter thirty years o' merried life, noo first to ken the wife o' my boasom for a messenger o' Sawtan!" he panted. "Gang oot o' my sicht, wuman!"

She fell on her knees, and held up her two hands to him.

"Think o' Jamie, Peter!" she pleaded. "I wad tyne my sowl for Jamie!"

"Ay, and tyne his as weel!" he returned. "Tyne what's yer ain to tyne, wuman - and that's no your sowl, nor yet Jamie's! He's no yours to save, but ye're deein a' ye can to destroy him - and aiblins ye'll succeed! for ye wad sen' him straucht awa to hell for the sake o' a guid name - a lee! A hypocrisy! - Oot upo ye for a Christian

George MacDonald

mither, Mirran! - Jamie, I'm awa to the toon, upo my twa feet, for the mere's cripple: the vera deil's i' the hoose and the stable and a', it would seem! - I'm awa to fess Isy hame! And, Jamie, ye'll jist tell her afore me and yer mother, that as sene 's ye're able to crawl to the kirk wi' her, ye'll merry her afore the warl', and tak her hame to the manse wi' ye!"

"Hoot, Peter! Wad ye disgrace him afore a' the beggars o' Tiltowie?"

"Ay, and afore God, that kens a'thing ohn onybody tellt him! Han's and hert I s' be clear o' this abomination!"

"Merry a wuman 'at was ta'en wi' a wat finger! - a maiden that never said *na*! - Merry a lass that's nae maiden, nor ever will be! - Hoots!"

"And wha's to blame for that?"

"Hersel."

"Jeemie! Jist Jeemie! - I'm fair scunnert at ye , Mirran! - Oot o' my sicht, I tell ye! - Lord, I kenna hoo I'm to win ower 't! - No to a' eternity, I doobt!"

He turned from her with a tearing groan, and went feeling for the open door, like one struck blind.

"Oh, father, father!" cried James, "forgie my mither afore ye gang, or my hert 'ill brak. It's the awfu'est thing o' ony to see you twa striven!"

"She's no sorry, no ae bit sorry!" said Peter.

" I am, I am, Peter!" cried Marion, breaking down at

once, and utterly. "Dee what ye wull, and I'll dee the same - only lat it be dene quaietly, 'ithoot din or proclamation! What for sud a'body ken a'thing! Wha has the richt to see intil ither fowk's herts and lives? The wail' could ill gang on gien that war the gait o' 't!"

"Father," said James, "I thank God that noo ye ken a'! Eh, sic a weicht as it taks aff o' me! I'll be hale and weel noo in ae day! - I think I'll gang wi' ye to Isy, mysel! - But I'm a wee bit sorry ye cam in jist that minute! I wuss ye had harkit a wee langer! For I wasna giein-in to my mother; I was but thinkin hoo to say oot what was in me, ohn vext her waur nor couldna be helpit. Believe me, father, gien ye can; though I doobt sair ye winna be able!"

"I believe ye, my bairn; and I thank God I hae that muckle pooer o' belief left in me! I confess I was in ower great a hurry, and I'm sure ye war takin the richt gait wi' yer puir mither. - Ye see she loed ye sae weel that she could think o' nae thing or body but yersel! That's the w'y o' mithers, Jamie, gien ye only kenned it! She was nigh sinnin an awfu sin for your sake, man!"

Here he turned again to his wife. "That's what comes o' lovin the praise o' men, Mirran! Easy it passes intil the fear o' men, and disregaird o' the Holy! - I s' awa doon to the soutar, and tell him the cheenge that's come ower us a': he'll no be a hair surprised!"

"I'm ready, father - or will be in ae minute!" said James, making as if to spring out of bed.

"Na, na; ye're no fit!" interposed his father. "I would hae to be takin ye upo my back afore we wis at the fut o' the brae! - Bide ye at hame, and keep yer mither company."

"Ay, bide, Jamie; and I winna come near ye," sobbed his mother.

"Onything to please ye, mother! - but I'm fitter nor my father thinks," said James as he settled down again in bed.

So Peter went, leaving mother and son silent together.

At last the mother spoke.

"It's the shame o' 't, Jamie!" she said.

"The shame was i' the thing itsel, mother, and in hidin frae that shame!" he answered. "Noo, I hae but the dregs to drink, and them I maun glog ower wi' patience, for I hae weel deserved to drink them! - But, eh, my bonnie Isy, she maun hae suffert sair! - I daur hardly think what she maun hae come throuw!"

"Her mither couldna hae broucht her up richt! The first o' the faut lay i' the upbringin!"

"There's anither whause upbringin wasna to blame: *my* upbringin was a' it oucht to hae been - and see hoo ill *I* turnt oot!"

"It wasna what it oucht! I see 't a' plain the noo! I was aye ower feart o' garrin ye hate me! - Oh, Isy, Isy, I hae dene ye wrang! I ken ye cud never hae laid yersel oot to snare him - it wasna in ye to dee 't!"

"Thank ye, mother! It was, railly and truly, a' my wyte!

And noo my life sail gang to mak up til her!"

" And I maun see to the manse!" rejoined his mother. " - And first in order o' a', that Jinse o' yours 'ill hae to gang!"

"As ye like, mother. But for the manse, I maun clear oot o' that! I'll speak nae mair frae that poopit! I hae hypocreesit in 't ower lang! The vera thoucht o' 't scunners me!"

"Speyk na like that o' the poopit, Jamie, whaur sae mony holy men hae stede up and spoken the word o' God! It frichts me to hear ye! Ye'll be a burnin and a shinin licht i' that poopit for mony a lang day efter we're deid and hame!"

"The mair holy men that hae there witnessed, the less daur ony livin lee stan' there braggin and blazin i' the face o' God and man! It's shame o' mysel that gars me hate the place, mother! Ance and no more wull I stan' there, making o' 't my stele o' repentance; and syne doon the steps and awa, like Adam frae the gairden!"

"And what's to come o' Eve? Are ye gaein, like him, to say, 'The wuman thoo giedest til me - it was a' her wyte'?"

"Ye ken weel I'm takin a' the wyte upo mysel!"

"But hoo can ye tak it a', or even ony fair share o' 't, gien up there ye stan' and confess? Ye maun hae some care o' the lass - that is, gien efter and a' ye're gaein to mak o' her yer wife, as ye profess. - And what are ye gaein to turn yer han' til neist, seem ye hae a'ready laid it til the pleuch and turnt back?"

"To the pleuch again, mother - the rael pleuch this time! Frae the kirk door I'll come hame like the prodigal to my father's hoose, and say til him, 'Set me to the pleuch, father. See gien I canna be something *like* a son to ye, efter a"!"

So wrought in him that mighty power, mysterious in its origin as marvellous in its result, which had been at work in him all the time he lay whelmed under feverish phantasms.

His repentance was true; he had been dead, and was alive again! God and the man had met at last! As to *how* God turned the man's heart, Thou God, knowest. To understand that, we should have to go down below the foundations themselves, underneath creation, and there see God send out from himself man, the spirit, distinguished yet never divided from God, the spirit, for ever dependent upon and growing in Him, never completed and never ended, his origin, his very life being infinite; never outside of God, because *in* him only he lives and moves and grows, and *has* his being. Brothers, let us not linger to ask! let us obey, and, obeying, ask what we will! thus only shall we become all we are capable of being; thus only shall we learn all we are capable of knowing! The pure in heart shall see God; and to see him is to know all things.

Something like this was the meditation of the soutar, as he saw the farmer stride away into the dusk of the gathering twilight, going home with glad heart to his wife and son.

Peter had told the soutar that his son was sorely troubled because of a sin of his youth and its long concealment: now he was bent on all the reparation he could make. "Mr. Robertson," said Peter, "broucht the lass to oor hoose, never mentionin Jamie, for he didna ken they war onything til ane anither; and for her, she never said ae word aboot him to Mirran or me."

The soutar went to the door, and called Isy. She came, and stood humbly before her old master.

"Weel, Isy," said the farmer kindly, "ye gied 's a clever slip yon morning and a gey fricht forbye! What possessed ye, lass, to dee sic a thing?"

She stood distressed, and made no answer.

"Hoot, lassie, tell me!" insisted Peter; "I haena been an ill maister til ye, have I?"

"Sir, ye hae been like the maister o' a' til me! But I canna - that is, I maunna - or raither, I'm determined no to explain the thing til onybody."

"Thoucht ye my wife was feart the minister micht fa' in love wi ye?"

"Weel, sir, there micht hae been something like that intil 't! But I wantit sair to win at my bairn again; for i' that trance I lay in sae lang, I saw or h'ard something I took for an intimation that he was alive, and no that far awa. - And - wad ye believe't, sir? - i' this vera hoose I fand him, and here I hae him, and I'm jist as happy the noo as I was meeserable afore! Is 't ill o' me at I *canna* be sorry ony mair?"

"Na, na," interposed the soutar: "whan the Lord wad lift the burden, it wad be baith senseless and thankless to grup at it! In His name lat it gang, lass!"

"And noo," said Mr. Blatherwick, again taking up his probe, "ye hae but ae thing left to confess - and that's wha's the father o' 'im!"

"Na, I canna dee that, sir; it's enough that I have disgracet *myself*! You wouldn't have me disgrace another as well! What good would that be?"

"It wad help ye beir the disgrace."

"Na, no a hair, sir; *he* cudna stan' the disgrace half sae weel 's me! I reckon the man the waiker vessel, sir; the woman has her bairn to fend for, and that taks her aff o' the shame!"

"Ye dinna tell me he gies ye noucht to mainteen the cratur upo?"

"I tell ye naething, sir. He never even kenned there *was* a bairn!"

"Hoot, toot! ye canna be sae semple! It's no poassible ye never loot him ken!"

"'Deed no; I was ower sair ashamit! Ye see it was a' my wyte! - and it was naebody's business! My auntie said gien I wouldna tell, I micht put the door atween 's; and I took her at her word; for I kenned weel *she* couldna keep a secret, and I wasna gaein to hae *his* name mixed up wi' a lass like mysel! And, sir, ye maunna try to gar me tell, for I hae no richt, and surely ye canna hae the hert to gar me! - But that ye *sanna*, ony gait!"

"I dinna blame ye , Isy ! But there's jist ae thing I'm determined upo - and that is that the rascal sail merry ye!"

Isy's face flushed; she was taken too much at unawares to hide her pleasure at such a word from *his* mouth. But the flush faded, and presently Mr. Blatherwick saw that she was fighting with herself, and getting the better of that self. The shadow of a pawky smile flitted across her face as she answered -

"Surely ye wouldna merry me upon a rascal, sir! Ill as I hae behaved til ye, I can hardly hae deservit that at yer han'!"

"That's what he'll hae to dee though - jist merry ye aff han'! I s' *gar* him."

"I winna hae him garred! It's me that has the richt ower him, and no anither, man nor wuman! He sanna be garred! What wad ye hae o' me - thinkin I would tak a man 'at was garred! Na, na; there s' be nae garrin! - And ye canna gar *him* merry me gien *I* winna hae him! The day's by for that! - A garred man! My certy! - Na, I thank ye!"

"Weel, my bonny leddy," said Peter, "gien I had a prence to my son, - providit he was worth yer takin - I wad say to ye, 'Hae, my leddy!'"

"And I would say to you, sir, 'No - gien he bena willin,'" answered Isy, and ran from the room.

"Weel, what think ye o' the lass by this time, Mr. Bletherwick?" said the soutar, with a flash in his eye.

"I think jist what I thoucht afore," answered Peter: "she's ane amo' a million!"

"I'm no that sure aboot the proportion!" returned MacLear. "I doobt ye micht come upo twa afore ye wan throw the million! - A million's a heap o' women!"

"All I care to say is, that gien Jeemie binna ready to lea' father and mother and kirk and steeple, and cleave to that wuman and her only, he's no a mere gomeril, but jist a meeserable, wickit fule! and I s' never speyk word til 'im again, wi my wull, gien I live to the age o' auld Methuselah!"

"Tak tent what ye say, or mint at sayin, to persuaud him: - Isy 'ill be upo ye!" said the soutar laughing. " - But hearken to me, Mr. Bletherwick, and sayna a word to the minister aboot the bairnie."

"Na, na; it'll be best to lat him fin' that oot for himsel. - And noo I maun be gaein, for I hae my wallet fu'!"

He strode to the door, holding his head high, and with never a word more, went out. The soutar closed the door and returned to his work, saying aloud as he went, "Lord, lat me ever and aye see thy face, and noucht mair will I desire - excep that the haill warl, O Lord, may behold it likewise. The prayers o' the soutar are endit!"

Peter Blatherwick went home joyous at heart. His son was his son, and no villain! - only a poor creature, as is every man until he turns to the Lord, and leaves behind him every ambition, and all care about the judgment of men. He rejoiced that the girl he and Marion had befriended would be a strength to his son: she whom his wife would have rejected had proved herself indeed right noble! And he praised the father of men, that the very backslidings of those he loved had brought about their repentance and uplifting.

"Here I am!" he cried as he entered the house. "I hae seen the lassie ance mair, and she's better and bonnier nor ever!"

"Ow ay; ye're jist like a' the men I ever cam across!" rejoined Marion smiling; " - easy taen wi' the skin-side!"

"Doobtless: the Makker has taen a heap o' pains wi the skin! - Ony gait, yon lassie's ane amang ten thoosan! Jeemie sud be on his k-nees til her this vera moment - no sitting there glowerin as gien his twa een war twa bullets - fired aff, but never won oot o' their barrels!"

"Hoot! wad ye hae him gang on his k-nees til ony but the Ane!"

"Aye wad I - til ony ane that's nearer His likness nor himsel - and that ane's oor Isy! - I wadna won'er, Jeemie, gien ye war fit for a drive the morn! In that case, I s' caw ye doon to the toon, and lat ye say yer ain say til her."

James did not sleep much that night, and nevertheless was greatly better the next day - indeed almost well.

Before noon they were at the soutar's door. The soutar opened it himself, and took the minister straight to the ben-end of the house, where Isy sat alone. She rose, and with downcast eyes went to meet him.

"Isy," he faltered, "can ye forgie me? And wull ye merry me as sene's ever we can be cried? - I'm as ashamed o' mysel as even ye would hae me!"

"Ye haena sae muckle to be ashamet o' as *I* hae, sir: it was a' my wyte!"

"And syne no to haud my face til't! - Isy, I hae been a scoonrel til ye! I'm that disgustit at mysel 'at I canna luik ye i' the face!"

"Ye didna ken whaur I was! I ran awa that naebody micht ken."

"What rizzon was there for onybody to ken? I'm sure ye never tellt!"

Isy went to the door and called Maggie. James stared after her, bewildered.

"There was this rizzon," she said, re-entering with the child, and laying him in James's arms.

He gasped with astonishment, almost consternation.

"Is this mine?" he stammered.

"Yours and mine, sir," she replied. "Wasna God a heap better til me nor I deserved? - Sic a bonnie bairn! No a mark, no a spot upon him frae heid to fut to tell that he had no business to be here! - Gie the bonnie wee man a kiss, Mr. Blatherwick. Haud him close to ye, sir, and he'll tak the pain oot o' yer heart: aften has he taen 't oot o' mine - only it aye cam again! - He's yer ain son, sir! He cam to me bringin the Lord's forgiveness, lang or ever I had the hert to speir for 't. Eh, but we maun dee oor best to mak up til God's bairn for the wrang we did him afore he was born! But he'll be like his great Father, and forgie us baith!"

As soon as Maggie had given the child to his mother, she went to her father, and sat down beside him, crying softly. He turned on his leather stool, and looked at her.

"Canna ye rejice wi' them that rejice, noo that ye hae nane to greit wi', Maggie, my doo?" he said. "Ye haena lost ane, and ye hae gaint twa! Haudna the glaidness back that's sae fain to come to the licht i' yer grudgin hert, Maggie! God himsel 's glaid, and the Shepherd's glaid, and the angels are a' makin sic a flut-flutter wi' their muckle wings 'at I can 'maist see nor hear for them!"

Maggie rose, and stood a moment wiping her eyes. The same instant the door opened, and James entered with the little one in his arms. He laid him with a smile in Maggie's.

"Thank you, sir!" said the girl humbly, and clasped the child to her bosom; nor, after that, was ever a cloud of jealousy to be seen on her face. I will not say she never longed or even wept after the little one, whom she still regarded as her very own, even when he was long gone away with his father and mother; indeed she mourned for him then like a mother from whom death has taken away her first-born and only son; neither did she see much difference between the two forms of loss; for Maggie felt in her heart that life nor death could destroy the relation that already existed between them: she could not be her father's daughter and not understand that! Therefore, like a bereaved mother, she only gave herself the more to her father.

I will not dwell on the delight of James and Isobel, thus restored to each other, the one from a sea of

George MacDonald

sadness, the other from a gulf of perdition. The one had deserved many stripes, the other but a few: needful measure had been measured to each; and repentance had brought them together.

Before James left the house, the soutar took him aside, and said -

"Daur I offer ye a word o' advice, sir?"

"'Deed that ye may!" answered the young man with humility: "and I dinna see hoo it can be possible for me to hand frae deein as ye tell me; for you and my father and Isy atween ye, hae jist saved my vera sowl!"

"Weel, what I wad beg o' ye is, that ye tak no further step o' ony consequence, afore ye see Maister Robertson, and mak him acquant wi the haill affair."

"I'm vera willin," answered James; "and I doobtna Isy 'ill be content."

"Ye may be vera certain, sir, that she'll be naething but pleased: she has a gran' opingon, and weel she may, o' Maister Robertson. Ye see, sir, I want ye to put yersels i' the han's o' a man that kens ye baith, and the half o' yer story a'ready - ane, that is, wha'll jeedge ye truly and mercifully, and no condemn ye affhan'. Syne tak his advice what ye oucht to dee neist."

"I will - and thank you, Mr. MacLear! Ae thing only I houp - that naither you, sir, nor he will ever seek to pursuaud me to gang on preachin. Ae thing I'm set upon, and that is, to deliver my sowl frae hypocrisy, and walk softly a' the rest o' my days! Happy man wad I hae been, had they set me frae the first to caw the pleuch, and cut the corn, and gether the stooks intil the barn - i'stead o' creepin intil a leaky boat to fish for men wi' a foul and tangled net! I'm affrontit and jist scunnert at mysel! - Eh, the presumption o' the thing! But I hae been weel and richteously punished! The Father drew his han' oot o' mine, and loot me try to gang my lane; sae doon I cam, for I was fit for naething but to fa': naething less could hae broucht me to mysel - and it took a lang time! I houp Mr. Robertson will see the thing as I dee mysel! - Wull I write and speir him oot to Stanecross to advise wi my father aboot Isy? That would bring him! There never was man readier to help! - But it's surely my pairt to gang to *him*, and mak my confession, and boo til his judgment! - Only I maun tell Isy first!"

Isy was not only willing, but eager that Mr. and Mrs. Robertson should know everything.

"But be sure," she added, "that you let them know you come of yourself, and I never asked you."

Peter said he could not let him go alone, but must himself go with him, for he was but weakly yet - and they must not put it off a single day, lest anything should transpire and be misrepresented.

The news which father and son carried them, filled the Robertsons with more than pleasure; and if their reception of him made James feel the repentant prodigal he was, it was by its heartiness, and their jubilation over Isy.

The next Sunday, Mr. Robertson preached in James's pulpit, and published the banns of marriage between James Blatherwick and Isobel Rose. The two following

Sundays he repeated his visit to Tiltowie for the same purpose; and on the Monday married them at Stonecross. Then was also the little one baptized, by the name of Peter, in his father's arms - amid much gladness, not unmingled with shame. The soutar and his Maggie were the only friends present besides the Robertsons.

Before the gathering broke up, the farmer put the big Bible in the hands of the soutar, with the request that he would lead their prayers; and this was very nearly what he said: - "O God, to whom we belang, hert and soul, body and blude and banes, hoo great art thou, and hoo close to us, to hand the richt ower us o' sic a gran' and fair, sic a just and true ownership! We bless thee hertily, rejicin in what thoo hast made us, and still mair in what thoo art thysel! Tak to thy hert, and hand them there, these thy twa repentant sinners, and thy ain little ane and theirs, wha's innocent as thoo hast made him. Gie them sic grace to bring him up, that he be nane the waur for the wrang they did him afore he was born; and lat the knowledge o' his parents' faut haud him safe frae onything siclike! and may they baith be the better for their fa', and live a heap the mair to the glory o' their Father by cause o' that slip! And gien ever the minister should again preach thy word, may it be wi' the better comprehension, and the mair fervour; and to that en' gie him to un'erstan' the hicht and deepth and breid and len'th o' thy forgivin love. Thy name be gloryfeed! Amen!"

"Na, na, I'll never preach again!" whispered James to the soutar, as they rose from their knees.

"I winna be a'thegither sure o' that!" returned the soutar. "Doobtless ye'll dee as the Spirit shaws ye!"

James made no answer, and neither spoke again that night.

The next morning, James sent to the clerk of the synod his resignation of his parish and office.

No sooner had Marion, repentant under her husband's terrible rebuke, set herself to resist her rampant pride, than the indwelling goodness swelled up in her like a reviving spring, and she began to be herself again, her old and lovely self. Little Peter, with his beauty and his winsome ways, melted and scattered the last lingering rack of her fog-like ambition for her son. Twenty times in a morning would she drop her work to catch up and caress her grandchild, overwhelming him with endearments; while over the return of his mother, her second Isy, now her daughter indeed, she soon became jubilant.

From the first publication of the banns, she had begun cleaning and setting to rights the parlour, meaning to make it over entirely to Isy and James; but the moment Isy discovered her intent, she protested obstinately: it should not, could not, must not be! The very morning after the wedding she was down in the kitchen, and had put the water on the fire for the porridge before her husband was awake. Before her new mother was down, or her father-in-law come in from his last preparations for the harvest, it was already boiling, and the table laid for breakfast.

"I ken weel," she said to her mother, "that I hae no richt to contre ye; but ye was glaid o' my help whan first I cam to be yer servan-lass; and what for shouldna things be jist the same noo? I ken a' the w'ys o' the place, and that they'll lea' me plenty o' time for the

George MacDonald

bairnie: ye maun jist lat me step again intil my ain auld place! and gien onybody comes, it winna tak me a minute to mak mysel tidy as becomes the minister's wife! - Only he says that's to be a' ower noo, and there'll be no need!"

With that she broke into a little song, and went on with her work, singing.

At breakfast, James made request to his father that he might turn a certain unused loft into a room for Isy and himself and little Peter. His father making no objection, he set about the scheme at once, but was interrupted by the speedy advent of an exceptionally plentiful harvest.

The very day the cutting of the oats began, James appeared on the field with the other scythe-men, prepared to do his best. When his father came, however, he interfered, and compelled him to take the thing easier, because, unfit by habit and recent illness, it would be even dangerous for him to emulate the others. But what delighted his father even more than his good-will, was the way he talked with the men and women in the field: every show of superiority had vanished from his bearing and speech, and he was simply himself, behaving like the others, only with greater courtesy.

When the hour for the noonday meal arrived, Isy appeared with her mother-in-law and old Eppie, carrying their food for the labourers, and leading little Peter in her hand. For a while the whole company was enlivened by the child's merriment; after which he was laid with his bottle in the shadow of an overarching stook, and went to sleep, his mother watching him, while she took her first lesson in gathering and binding the sheaves. When he woke, his grandfather sent the whole family home for the rest of the day.

"Hoots, Isy, my dauty," he said, when she would fain have continued her work, "wad ye mak a slave-driver o' me, and bring disgrace upo the name o' father?"

Then at once she obeyed, and went with her husband, both of them tired indeed, but happier than ever in their lives before.

CHAPTER XXVI

The next morning James was in the field with the rest long before the sun was up. Day by day he grew stronger in mind and in body, until at length he was not only quite equal to the harvest-work, but capable of anything required of a farm servant.

His deliverance from the slavery of Sunday prayers and sermons, and his consequent sense of freedom and its delight, greatly favoured his growth in health and strength. Before the winter came, however, he had begun to find his heart turning toward the pulpit with a waking desire after utterance. For, almost as soon as his day's work ceased to exhaust him, he had begun to take up the study of the sayings and doings of the Lord of men, full of eagerness to verify the relation in which he stood toward him, and, through him, toward that eternal atmosphere in which he lived and moved and had his being, God himself.

One day, with a sudden questioning hunger, he rose in haste from his knees, and turned almost trembling to his Greek Testament, to find whether the words of the Master, "If any man will do the will of the Father," meant "If any man *is willing* to do the will of the Father;" and finding that just what they did mean, he was thenceforward so far at rest as to go on asking and hoping; nor was it then long before he began to feel he had something worth telling, and must tell it to any that would hear. And heartily he betook himself to pray for that spirit of truth which the Lord had promised to them that asked it of their Father in heaven.

He talked with his wife about what he had found; he talked with his father about it; he went to the soutar, and talked with him about it.

Now the soutar had for many years made a certain use of his Sundays, by which he now saw he might be of service to James: he went four miles into the country to a farm on the other side of Stonecross, to hold there a Sunday-school. It was the last farm for a long way in that direction: beyond it lay an unproductive region, consisting mostly of peat-mosses, and lone barren hills - where the waters above the firmament were but imperfectly divided from the waters below the firmament. For there roots of the hills coming rather close together, the waters gathered and made marshy places, with here and there a patch of ground on which crops could be raised. There were, however, many more houses, such as they were, than could have been expected from the appearance of the district. In one spot, indeed, not far from the farm I have mentioned, there was a small, thin hamlet. A long way from church or parish-school, and without any, nearer than several miles, to minister to the spiritual wants of the people, it was a rather rough and ignorant place, with a good many superstitions - none of them in their nature specially mischievous, except indeed as they blurred the idea of divine care and government - just the country for bogill-baes and brownie-baes, boodies and water-kelpies to linger and disport themselves, long after they had elsewhere disappeared!

When, therefore, the late minister came seeking his counsel, the soutar proposed, without giving any special reason for it, that he should accompany him the next Sunday afternoon, to his school at Bogiescratt; and James consenting, the soutar undertook to call for him at Stonecross on his way.

"Mr. MacLear," said James, as they walked along the rough parish road together, "I have but just arrived at a point I ought to have reached before even entertaining a thought of opening my mouth upon anything belonging to religion. Perhaps I knew some little things *about* religion; certainly I knew nothing *of* religion; least of all had I made any discovery for myself *in* religion; and before that, how can a man understand or know anything whatever concerning it? Even now I may be presuming, but now at last, if I may dare to say so, I do seem to have begun to recognize something of the relation between a man and the God who made him; and with the sense of that, as I ventured to hint when I saw you last Friday, there has risen in my mind a desire to communicate to my fellow-men something of what I have seen and learned. One thing I dare to hope - that, at the first temptation to show-off, I shall be made aware of my danger, and have the grace given me to pull up. And one thing I have resolved upon - that, if ever I preach again, I will never again write a sermon. I know I shall make many blunders, and do the thing very badly; but failure itself will help to save me from conceit - will keep me, I hope, from thinking of myself at all, enabling me to leave myself in God's hands, willing to fail if he please. Don't you think, Mr. MacLear, we may even now look to God for what we ought to say, as confidently as if, like the early Christians, we stood accused before the magistrates?" "I div that, Maister Jeames!" answered the soutar.

"Hide yersel in God, sir, and oot o' that secret place, secret and safe, speyk - and fear naething. And never ye mint at speykin *doon* to your congregation. Luik them straucht i' the een, and say what at the moment ye think and feel; and dinna hesitate to gie them the best ye hae."

"Thank you, thank you, sir! I think I understand," replied James. - "If ever I speak again, I should like to begin in your school!"

"Ye sall - this vera nicht, gien ye like," rejoined the soutar. "I think ye hae something e'en noo upo yer min' 'at ye would like to say to them - but we'll see hoo ye feel aboot it efter I hae said a word to them first!"

"When you have said what you want to say, Mr. MacLear, give me a look; and if I *have* anything to say, I will respond to your sign. Then you can introduce me, saying what you will. Only dinna spare me; use me after your judgment."

The soutar held out his hand to his disciple, and they finished their journey in silence.

When they reached the farm-house, the small gathering was nearly complete. It was mostly of farm-labourers; but a few of the congregation worked in a quarry, where serpentine lay under the peat. In this serpentine occurred veins of soapstone, occasionally of such a thickness as to be itself the object of the quarrier: it was used in the making of porcelain; and small quantities were in request for other purposes.

When the soutar began, James was a little shocked at first to hear him use his mother-tongue as in his ordinary conversation; but any sense of its unsuitableness vanished presently, and James soon began to feel that the vernacular gave his friend additional power of expression, and therewith of persuasion.

"My frien's, I was jist thinkin, as I cam ower the hill," he began, "hoo we war a' made wi' differin pooers - some o' 's able to dee ae thing best, and some anither; and that led me to remark, that it was the same wi' the warl we live in - some pairts o' 't fit for growin aits, and some bere, and some wheat, or pitatas; and hoo ilk varyin rig had to be turnt til its ain best eese. We a' ken what a lot o' eeses the bonny green-and-reid-mottlet marble can be put til; but it wadna do weel for biggin hooses, specially gien there war mony streaks o' saipstane intil 't. Still it's no 'at the saipstane itsel's o' nae eese, for ye ken there's a heap o' eeses it can be put til. For ae thing, the tailor taks a bit o' 't to mark whaur he's to sen' the shears alang the claith, when he's cuttin oot a pair o' breeks; and again they mix't up wi the clay they tak for the finer kin's o' crockery. But upo' the ither han' there's ae thing it's eesed for by some, 'at canna be considert a richt eese to mak o' 't: there's ae wull tribe in America they tell me o', 'at ait a hantle o' 't - and that's a thing I can*not* un'erstan'; for it diz them, they say, no guid at a', 'cep, maybe, it be jist to fill-in the toom places i' their stammacks, puir reid craturs, and haud their ribs ohn stucken thegither - and maybe that's jist what they ait it for! Eh, but they maun be sair hungert afore they tak til the vera dirt! But they're only savage fowk, I'm thinkin, 'at hae hardly begun to be men ava!

"Noo ye see what I'm drivin' at? It's this - that things hae aye to be put to their richt eeses! But there are guid eeses and better eeses, and things canna *aye* be putten to their *best* eeses; only, whaur they can, it's a shame to put them to ony ither but their best! Noo, what's the best eese o' a man? - what's a man made for? The carritchis (*catechism*) says, *To glorifee God*. And hoo is he to dee that? Jist by deein the wull o' God. For the ae perfec' man said he was born intil the warl for that ae special purpose, to dee the wull o' him that sent him. A man's for a heap o' eeses, but that ae eese covers them a'. Whan he's deein' the wull o' God, he's deein jist a'thing.

"Still there are vahrious wy's in which a man can be deein the wull o' his Father in h'aven, and the great thing for ilk ane is to fin' oot the best w'y *he* can set aboot deein that wull.

"Noo here's a man sittin aside me that I maun help set to the best eese he's fit for - and that is, tellin ither fowk what he kens aboot the God that made him and them, and stirrin o' them up to dee what He would hae them dee. The fac is, that the man was ance a minister o' the Kirk o' Scotlan'; but whan he was a yoong man, he fell intil a great faut: - a yoong man's faut - I'm no gaein to excuse 't - dinna think it! - Only I chairge ye, be ceevil til him i' yer vera thouchts, rememberin hoo mony things ye hae dene yersels 'at ye hae to be ashamit o', though some o' them may never hae come to the licht; for, be sure o' this, he has repentit richt sair. Like the prodigal, he grew that ashamit o' what he had dene, that he gied up his kirk, and gaed hame to the day's darg upon his father's ferm. And that's what he's at the noo, thof he be a scholar, and that a ripe ane! And by his repentance he's learnt a heap that he didna ken afore, and that he couldna hae learnt ony ither w'y than by turnin wi' shame frae the path o' the transgressor. I hae broucht him wi' me this day, sirs, to tell ye something - he hasna said to me what - that the Lord in his mercy has tellt him. I'll say nae mair: Mr. Bletherwick, wull ye please tell's what the Lord has putten it intil yer min' to say?"

The soutar sat down; and James got up, white and trembling. For a moment or two he was unable to speak, but overcoming his emotion, and falling at once into the old Scots tongue, he said -

"My frien's, I hae little richt to stan' up afore ye and say onything; for, as some o' ye ken, if no afore, at least noo, frae what my frien' the soutar has jist been tellin ye, I was ance a minister o' the kirk, but upon a time I behavet mysel that ill, that, whan I cam to my senses, I saw it my duty to withdraw, and mak room for anither to tak up my disgracet bishopric, as was said o' Judas the traitor. But noo I seem to hae gotten some mair licht, and to ken some things I didna ken afore; sae, turnin my back upo' my past sin, and believin God has forgien me, and is willin I sud set my han' to his pleuch ance mair, I hae thoucht to mak a new beginnin here in a quaiet heumble fashion, tellin ye something o' what I hae begoud, i' the mercy o' God, to un'erstan' a wee for mysel. Sae noo, gien yell turn, them o' ye that has broucht yer buiks wi' ye, to the saeventh chapter o' John's gospel, and the saeventeenth verse, ye'll read wi me what the Lord says there to the fowk o Jerus'lem: *Gien ony man be wullin to dee His wull, he'll ken whether what I tell him comes frae God, or whether I say 't only oot o' my ain heid.* Luik at it for yersels, for that's what it says i' the Greek, the whilk is plainer than the English to them that un'erstan' the auld Greek tongue: Gien onybody *be wullin* to dee the wull o' God, he'll ken whether my teachin comes frae God, or I say 't o' mysel."

From that he went on to tell them that, if they kept trusting in God, and doing what Jesus told them, any mistake they made would but help them the better to understand what God and his son would have them do. The Lord gave them no promise, he said, of knowing what this or that man ought to do; but only of knowing what the man himself ought to do. And he illustrated this by the rebuke the Lord gave Peter when, leaving inquiry into the will of God that he might do it, he made inquiry into the decree of God concerning his friend that he might know it; seeking wherewithal, not to prophesy, but to foretell. Then he showed them the difference between the meaning of the Greek word, and that of the modern English word *prophesy*.

The little congregation seemed to hang upon his words, and as they were going away, thanked him heartily for thus talking to them.

That same night as James and the soutar were going home together, they were overtaken by an early snowstorm, and losing their way, were in the danger, not a small one, of having to pass the night on the moor. But happily, the farmer's wife, in whose house was their customary assembly, had, as they were taking their leave, made the soutar a present of some onion bulbs, of a sort for which her garden was famous: exhausted in conflict with the freezing blast, they had lain down, apparently to die before the morning, when the soutar bethought himself of the onions; and obeying their nearer necessity, they ate instead of keeping them to plant; with the result that they were so refreshed, and so heartened for battle with the wind and snow, that at last, in the small hours of the morning, they reached home, weary and nigh frozen.

All through the winter, James accompanied the soutar to his Sunday-school, sometimes on his father's old gig-horse, but oftener on foot. His father would occasionally go also; and then the men of Stonecross began to go, with the cottar and his wife; so that the little company of them gradually increased to about thirty men and women, and about half as many children. In general, the soutar gave a short opening address; but he always made "the minister" speak; and thus James Blatherwick, while encountering many hidden experiences, went through his apprenticeship to extempore preaching; and, hardly knowing how, grew capable at length of following out a train of thought in his own mind even while he spoke, and that all the surer from the fact that, as it rose, it found immediate utterance; and at the same time it was rendered the more living and potent by the sight of the eager faces of his humble friends fixed upon him, as they drank in, sometimes even anticipated, the things he was saying. He seemed to himself at times almost to see their thoughts taking reality and form to accompany him whither he led them; while the stream of his thought, as it disappeared from his consciousness and memory, seemed to settle in the minds of those who heard him, like seed cast on open soil - some of it, at least, to grow up in resolves, and bring forth fruit. And all the road as the friends returned, now in moonlight, now in darkness and rain, sometimes in wind and snow, they had such things to think of and talk about, that the way never seemed long. Thus dwindled by degrees Blatherwick's self-reflection and self-seeking, and, growing divinely conscious, he grew at the same time divinely self-oblivious. Once, upon such a home-coming, as his wife was helping him off with his wet boots, he looked up in her face and said -

"To think, Isy, that here am I, a dull, selfish creature, so long desiring only for myself knowledge and influence, now at last grown able to feel in my heart all the way home, that I took every step, one after the other, only by the strength of God in me, caring for me as my own making father! - Ken ye what I'm trying to say, Isy, my dear?"

"I canna be a'thegither certain I un'erstan'," answered his wife; "but I'll keep thinkin aboot it, and maybe I'll come til't!"

"I can desire no more," answered James, "for until the Lord lat ye see a thing, hoo can you or I or onybody see the thing that *he* maun see first! And what is there for us to desire, but to see things as God sees them, and would hae us see them? I used to think the soutar a puir fule body whan he was sayin the vera things I'm tryin to say noo! I saw nae mair what he was efter than that puir collie there at my feet - maybe no half sae muckle, for wha can tell what he mayna be thinkin, wi' that far awa luik o' his!"

"Div ye think, Jeames, that ever we'll be able to see inside thae doggies, and ken what they're thinkin?"

"I wouldna won'er what we mayna come til; for ye ken Paul says, 'A' things are yours, and ye are Christ's, and Christ is God's!' Wha can tell but the vera herts o' the doggies may ae day lie bare and open to *oor* herts, as to the hert o' Him wi' whom they and we hae to do! Eh, but the thouchts o' a doggie maun be a won'erfu' sicht! And syne to think o' the thouchts o' Christ aboot that doggie! We'll ken them, I daurna weel doobt, some day! I'm surer aboot that nor aboot kennin the thouchts o' the doggie himsel!"

Another Sunday night, having come home through a terrible storm of thunder and lightning, he said to Isy -

"I hae been feelin, a' the w'y hame, as gien, afore lang, I micht hae to gie a wider testimony. The apostles and the first Christians, ye see, had to beir testimony to the fac' that the man that was hangt and dee'd upo the cross, the same was up again oot o' the grave, and gangin aboot the warl; noo I canna beir testimony to that, for I wasna at that time awaur o' onything; but I might weel be called upon to beir testimony to the fac' that, whaur ance he lay deid and beeried, there he's come alive at last - that is, i' the sepulchre o' my hert! For I hae seen him noo, and ken him noo - the houp o' glory in my hert and my life! Whatever he said ance, that I believe for ever."

The talks James Blatherwick and the soutar had together, were now, according to Mr. Robertson, even wonderful. But it was chiefly the soutar that spoke, while James sat and listened in silence. On one occasion, however, James had spoken out freely, and indeed eloquently; and Mr. Robertson, whom the soutar accompanied to his inn that night, had said to him ere they parted -

"Do you see any good and cogent reason, Mr. MacLear, why this man should not resume his pastoral office?"

"One thing at least I am sure of," answered the soutar," - that he is far fitter for it than ever he was in his life before."

Mr. Robertson repeated this to James the next day, adding -

And I am certain every one who knows you will vote the restoration of your licence!"

"I must speak to Isy about it," answered James with simplicity.

"That is quite right, of course," rejoined Mr. Robertson: "you know I tell my wife everything that I am at liberty to tell."

"Will not some public recognition of my reinstatement be necessary?" suggested James.

"I will have a talk about it with some of the leaders of the synod, and let you know what they say," answered Mr. Robertson.

"Of course I am ready," returned Blatherwick, "to make any public confession judged necessary or desirable; but that would involve my wife; and although I know perfectly that she will be ready for anything required of her, it remains not the less my part to do my best to shield her!"

"Of one thing I think you may be sure - that, with our present moderator, your case will be handled with more than delicacy - with tenderness!"

"I must not doubt it; but for myself I would deprecate indulgence. I must have a talk with my wife about it! She is sure to know what will be best!"

"My advice is to leave it all in the hands of the moderator. We have no right to choose, appoint, or apportion our own penalties!"

George MacDonald

James went home and laid the whole matter before his wife.

Instead of looking frightened, or even anxious, Isy laid little Peter softly in his crib, threw her arms round James's neck, and cried -

"Thank God, my husband, that you have come to this! Don't think to leave me out, I beg of you. I am more than ready to accept my shame. I have always said *I* was to blame, and not you! It was me that should have known better!"

"You trusted me, and I proved quite unworthy of your confidence! - But had ever man a wife to be so proud of as I of you!"

Mr. Robertson brought the matter carefully before the synod; but neither James nor Isy ever heard anything more of it - except the announcement of the cordial renewal of James's licence. This was soon followed by the offer of a church in the poorest and most populous parish north of the Tweed.

"See the loving power at the heart of things, Isy!" said James to his wife: "out of evil He has brought good, the best good, and nothing but good! - a good ripened through my sin and selfishness and ambition, bringing upon you as well as me disgrace and suffering! The evil in me had to come out and show itself, before it could be cleared away! Some people nothing but an earthquake will rouse from their dead sleep: I was one of such. God in His mercy brought on the earthquake: it woke me and saved me from death. Ignorant creatures go about asking why God permits evil: *we* know why! It may be He could with a word cause evil to cease - but would that be to create good? The word might make us good like oxen or harmless sheep, but would that be a goodness worthy of him who was made in the image of God? If a man ceased to be *capable* of evil, he must cease to be a man! What would the goodness be that could not help being good - that had no choice in the matter, but must be such because it was so made? God chooses to be good, else he would not be God: man must choose to be good, else he cannot be the son of God! Herein we see the grand love of the Father of men - that he gives them a share, and that share as necessary as his own, in the making of themselves! Thus, and thus only, that is, by willing the good, can they become 'partakers of the divine nature!' Satan said, 'Ye shall be as gods, knowing good and evil!' God says, 'Ye shall be as gods, knowing good and evil, and choosing the good.' For the sake of this, that we may come to choose the good, all the discipline of the world exists. God is teaching us to know good and evil in some real degree *as they are*, and not as *they seem to the incomplete*; so shall we learn to choose the good and refuse the evil. He would make his children see the two things, good and evil, in some measure as they are, and then say whether they will be good children or not. If they fail, and choose the evil, he will take yet harder measures with them. If at last it should prove possible for a created being to see good and evil as they are, and choose the evil, then, and only then, there would, I presume, be nothing left for God but to set his foot upon him and crush him, as we crush a noxious insect. But God is deeper in us than our own life; yea, God's life is the very centre and creative cause of that life which we call *ours*; therefore is the Life in us stronger than the Death, in as much as the creating Good is stronger than the created Evil."

George MacDonald